NOTE TO SELF

PETER WARD

Note to Self

You can follow this author at:
Peterwardauthor.com
Blog: https://peterwardauthor.com/blog/
peterwardauthor@hotmail.co.uk

Note to Self

Richard Henley's day began with a visit from a stranger and an invitation to dinner. It ended with him receiving a note in his own handwriting warning that someone was trying to kill him—a note he had no memory of writing.

What followed would push Richard's grip on reality to the limit, forcing him to confront the inexplicable, question his past, and trust his fate to an unknown ally.

Note to Self takes Richard on a journey to places he never knew existed, explores the role of technology in the modern world, and asks whether the choices we are making are really our own.

DEDICATION

For Lucy

Acknowledgements

Special thanks to Lucy Brown, Erik Brown, Hazel Appleyard and Mark Selby.

Table of Contents

ONE

I'd always found the painting on the far wall of my office to be strangely captivating, as though it were drawing me into a different world. At first glance, it looked like a regular landscape piece—a huge mountain range captured in vibrant watercolors, the snowy peaks looming high above a forest of lush evergreen trees. But if you looked at the picture for long enough, little details would draw you in, and you'd begin to notice things that didn't make any sense. Palm trees were nestled in amongst the alpine vegetation, strange species of birds were circling around in the sky, and a shimmering white beach lay in the foreground, in total contrast to the rest of the scene. As an image, it shouldn't have worked, yet I often found myself staring vacantly through the canvas as though it were a window to another realm, a gateway to a fantasy world, far away from my office in central London.

How a painting like this ended up in my office, I had no idea. It just appeared on the wall one morning about four years ago, hanging up in place of the generic motivational poster that had been there the day before. Every office on the floor had one of these posters, presumably chosen by the accountancy firm I worked for to inspire its employees. Inject a bit of enthusiasm into their lives. Every office also had a rubber plant in one corner of the room (watered every other day by a nice lady from Brazil), a blue rug on the floor, a standing lamp by the window, and a fairly drab wall calendar. Other than that, the walls were all white, the desks were all chrome, and the air-conditioning was set at a constant seventy-five degrees. Some people tried to make their offices a little different by moving the plant, or if they were feeling really reckless, repositioning the rug, but I didn't see the point—moving the furniture around wasn't going to make me feel different to anyone else. We all did the same dull job, whether the rubber plant was next to the door or not.

"Um…Mr. Henley?" came a quiet, female voice. It had a soft warmth to it, like someone running a silk handkerchief over a velvet cushion.

I tore my gaze away from the watercolor mountains, rubbed some sleep out of the corner of my eye, and turned around in my chair. A girl was leaning in through the doorway, one high-heeled foot poised to enter, the other out of sight in the corridor. She was dressed in a smart, pin-striped trouser suit and pale green blouse, her dark brown hair neatly tied up in a ponytail. Her thin face was pale in complexion, her makeup subtle and understated, and her brown eyes had a cool elegance to them. She looked as though she was in her early twenties—about half my age—and her slender fig-ure suggested she was careful about what she ate. Judging by her immaculate appearance and the fact that I hadn't seen her around before, I figured she must have been new.

"Call me Richard," I said, taking off my reading glasses and putting them to one side. I knew some of the other accountants liked to be addressed by their surname, but this didn't sit right with me. I felt uncomfortable being called "sir"—even in a fast-food restaurant.

"May I come in?" she asked.

"Sure," I said, gesturing toward an empty chair on the other side of my desk. "Please, have a seat."

Without saying a word, she stepped inside and shut the door behind her with a click. From the way she was dressed, I was expect-ing her to slink across the room like a cat and descend into the chair gracefully, but she actually seemed a little uncomfortable in what she was wearing, walking toward me as if she had a stone in her shoe and sitting down with a sigh like she'd just carried two heavy bags of shopping in with her. There was something strangely familiar about this girl, but I couldn't quite place it.

"My name is Cassandra," she said, extending a delicate-looking hand across the desk to shake mine. It was well manicured, with faint pink varnish coating each fingernail. I returned the gesture with care as if I were about to press my hand against an antique porcelain vase, but to my surprise she had an extremely firm grip.

"Have we met before?" I asked. The fragrance of her perfume was just beginning to drift under my nose—it smelled expensive.

"No," she replied, tucking a stray hair behind her ear. "At least, not that I'm aware of…"

My eyes drifted vacantly toward the ceiling as I thought about this for a moment. She was right—as far as I could remember, we'd never met, yet somehow the sight of this girl had stirred a vague emotional reaction in the back of my mind, as if I had some sort of connection to her.

"Mr. Henley?"

I pulled my chair toward the desk and smiled, leaning forward on my elbows. Everything around me was a bit of a mess—unopened post was spilling out of my in-tray, computer printouts were scattered over my keyboard, and several handwritten reminders were stuck to the sides of my computer screen.

"Please—Richard," I corrected her. "Now, how can I help?"

"Well, this may sound a bit strange," Cassandra said, adjusting a bracelet on her wrist, "but can I ask you a favor?"

"A favor?"

"Yes."

"Well that depends," I said. "Before we go any further, do you mind telling me who you are?"

"What do you mean?" the girl said, gently creasing her brow.

"I mean what department do you work for? Are you new here? A temp? Just joined the graduate scheme?" I noticed half a mug of coffee on top of some old files and lifted it to my mouth to take a sip. It was cold.

"Oh no," she replied, wrinkling her nose. It was a small nose, about the size of a thimble. "No—I don't work here."

"You don't?" I tried not to wince as I swallowed. "So you're here with a client?"

"No, I have nothing to do with this place."

"Then, forgive my asking," I said, placing the mug down to one side, "but…what exactly are you doing here?"

More importantly, I thought to myself—how did she get in? The security guards downstairs would normally stop a bee if it flew in through the door without wearing a visitor's pass, yet somehow this girl had managed to stroll in and wander up to my office with no problem whatsoever.

"I told you," she said, relaxing in her chair as if everything was perfectly normal. "I'm here to ask you a favor."

At this point, I knew the procedure. I was supposed to call security and wait for two impossibly large men to escort this girl out onto the street, probably by her ponytail. And for a moment, I felt my hand lean instinctively toward the phone, fingers poised to dial the number. Then another part of my brain took over—for some reason, I couldn't do it. It was as if some unknown force was at play, drawing my hand away from the phone and back toward my mug. I looked Cassandra in the eyes. What was it about this girl that I found so intriguing?

"Ok," I nodded, taking another sip of my cold coffee. The taste was still particularly unpleasant, but my mouth was so dry I didn't care. "I have to say—this is a little unusual, but I'm listening. What did you want to ask me?"

The girl looked at me for a moment in silence, as if she was carefully considering the right choice of words. It could have been anywhere between ten to twenty seconds before she spoke.

"What are your plans for this evening?" she asked eventually.

"Erm…I'm not sure really," I replied, putting my glasses back on and shifting some papers around to look for my diary. Most people thought I was quite old-fashioned for not using a smartphone to organize my life, but I still insisted on using a paper diary—if I could ever find it. "Why do you ask?"

"I'd like to take you out for dinner."

I stopped searching and looked up at her over the rim of my glasses.

"Dinner?" I said. "Tonight?"

Cassandra nodded.

"That's the favor you wanted to ask me?"

"Yes."

"Ok," I sighed, tossing my glasses on the desk again. I leaned back in my chair and closed my eyes. "Who put you up to this?"

"I'm sorry?"

"This is a joke right?"

I waited for a reply, but only the dull hum of the air-conditioning filled my ears. I waited a few seconds longer and opened my eyes again. Cassandra was sitting in exactly the same position, her expression unchanged.

"You're serious?" I said.

"Yes, I'm serious," she replied.

"It's just…it's a bit odd, don't you think?" I said, getting to my feet and pacing over to the other side of the room.

"Odd?" she said, tilting her head curiously.

"Yeah—I mean, why do you want to take me out for dinner?"

"I can't tell you."

"You can't?"

"All I can tell you is that it is vitally important that you meet me tonight."

"But—we're complete strangers!" I said. "Why is it important?"

"Like I said Mr. Henley—I can't tell you. But if you meet me tonight, I'll explain everything."

I wasn't sure I liked the sound of this. Was I being propositioned? Having been single for a few years now, I'd always dreamt that a mysterious, beautiful woman would one day walk into my life, but I preferred my women to be a little…older. And not crazy. As much as Cassandra interested me in some strange way, I needed to think of a way of getting out of this.

"I'm sorry, but I'm not sure my wife would be too happy about this," I lied. "Besides, I promised her I'd be home on time tonight."

"You're not married," Cassandra said, looking down at her lap nonchalantly to inspect her nails. "You've been divorced for three years, you live alone, and you're not in a relationship at the moment."

I took a step back and leaned against the wall.

"Last night you went home at seven," she continued. "You ate some pizza, read a book until ten o'clock and fell asleep with the television on. Tonight you were planning on doing exactly the same thing." She looked up from her lap and stared right at me. "Am I right?"

I narrowed my eyes.

"How do you know so much about me?" I said.

"If you come along tonight, you'll find out," she said, standing up from her chair and reaching over my desk for a pen. I loosened my tie and watched in silence as she tore a page from my notepad and scribbled something down.

"Here's the address of the restaurant," she said, folding the paper in half and handing it to me. "My mobile number is there too in case you need it."

I took the paper from her without looking at it, my eyes fixated on hers.

"So I take it you'll be there?" she asked.

"Sounds like I don't have much of a choice," I said. This whole situation was beginning to feel a little bit sinister. What would happen to me if I didn't show up?

Cassandra appeared to sense my anxiety.

"Listen—I didn't mean to scare you," she smiled, pressing her hand gently against my arm. "It's just…I had to convince you to be there somehow. I can't tell you how important it is."

I could feel myself beginning to sweat. I wiped the back of my sleeve across my forehead and unfolded the note to see what she'd written. I'd heard of this restaurant. It was one of those fine dining affairs—small portions, stuffy, expensive—not really my sort of thing. I hadn't been there myself, but some of my colleagues often talked about it—if you wanted to impress a big client, this was apparently the place to take them.

"Be there at nine o'clock sharp," Cassandra said, walking over to the door and opening it to leave. "And please—don't be late."

"I won't," I said, looking down at the note again. I hoped she was paying for this—on my salary, there was no way I could afford to eat here.

When I looked up again, the girl was gone.

"Hey!" I called after her.

I rushed over to the door and looked up and down the corridor. The only person I could see was the nice lady from Brazil watering a rubber plant a few feet away.

"Excuse me," I said, stepping into the corridor to look around some more. "Did you see which way that girl went?"

"Girl?" the lady said.

"Yes—the girl who just left my office. Did you see which way she went?"

"No, sir," she answered, putting down her watering can. "I didn't see anybody."

"What do you mean?"

"I mean I didn't see anybody. Nobody came out of your office."

For a minute I thought perhaps the nice lady from Brazil didn't understand me properly, but her English was too good for this mystery to be explained away as a translation issue. Somehow, it seemed Cassandra had vanished without a trace.

Two

The last time I'd set foot in a restaurant was well over three years ago on Valentine's Day with my then-wife. We'd faced each other across a small table in silence for most of the evening. The table was black, square, and set with a plastic orchid stem sticking out of a little glass vase in the middle. The vase had some water in it for no reason. And that was all there was to say about our table, apart from the fact that I'd had to fold my napkin under one leg at the beginning of the meal to stop it from wobbling.

The corner of the restaurant we were sat in was dimly lit and smelled of leather, the scent overpowering the taste of every course we had eaten that night. The seats were leather, the walls were padded with leather—even the menus were bound in the stuff. The aroma made the place feel dark and claustrophobic, wrapping itself around us like a heavy, invisible fog.

Our desserts had just arrived. I carved a slice out of my tiramisu, lifted the spoon to my mouth, and looked around—couples like us were facing each other across their own small black tables: some deep in conversation, others just staring into each other's eyes, hands touching. The mood at our table was very different.

"Richard," my wife said, not touching her lemon sorbet, "do you think this is working out?"

"No," I said, still holding the spoon to my lips. "I knew we should've stayed in tonight. The service is slow, the food is expensive…"

"That's not what I meant," she replied, leaning forward into the light so I could see her properly. The sleeve of her print dress slipped down her arm to reveal a bra strap. She didn't bother pulling it up.

I placed my spoon down and stopped breathing.

"What are you talking about?" I said.

"I'm not sure. It's just—I don't think I'm very happy at the moment. And I don't think I've been very happy for a while. Sometimes I feel..." She trailed off and looked away.

"What?" I said. "What do you feel?" I heard myself ask the question, but if I were honest, I already knew what she was going to say. Something had happened to us over the last few months. Conversations had turned into nothing more than an exchange of facts about our day, we hadn't had sex for weeks, and I couldn't remember the last time we'd made each other laugh. Most importantly, I no longer felt that sense of excitement when I came home from work and saw her—these days, she was just someone I shared the flat with: someone I cared about and got on with well enough, but not someone I was in love with anymore.

"Do you think we made the right decision?" she said in a hush, looking down and kneading her napkin. "Getting married, I mean?"

I rubbed the back of my neck and took a deep breath. The couple on the table next to us exchanged an awkward glance and went quiet.

"I don't know," I whispered. "What do you think?"

My wife dabbed her eyes with the napkin. In the five years that I'd known her, I'd never seen her cry.

"I'm so sorry," she said, standing up to gather her coat and bag.

I pushed my dessert to one side and signaled for the check.

"Is your wife leaving?" the waiter asked, looking across the restaurant as she hurried outside.

"Looks that way," I replied.

THREE

Nine o'clock.

Well, ten minutes past. I knew Cassandra had told me not to be late, but it was difficult to park in this part of town. Especially if you're no good at parking. Then there was the restaurant itself, which wasn't exactly the easiest place to find. I'd actually walked past it without knowing three or four times before noticing the name embossed on a tiny brass plaque, which hung above the entrance to a tall Victorian townhouse. It was almost as if it didn't want to be found.

From the outside, the building looked no different to all the other houses in the terrace—it was four stories high with white stone clad walls and majestic bay windows, set back a few feet from the pavement and lined with an ornate iron railing. I couldn't see inside from the street—the shutters were drawn across the windows at ground level with only a slither of light escaping through the cracks. I climbed the eight or so steps to the shiny, black front door, which was polished to such a fine sheen that I could see my reflection in it as I approached. It opened of its own accord just as I reached for the handle.

I stood back. A man emerged and looked at me.

He was rather formally dressed—immaculate, as if he was about to attend a royal ceremony. The handkerchief sticking out of the breast pocket of his well-tailored morning suit looked as though it had been folded by an origami expert and placed with utmost care so it was in precise proportion with the rest of his attire. His white shirt cuffs both protruded exactly the same length from the arms of his jacket, silver cuff links square with the ends of his sleeves.

Just under six feet tall, roughly the same age as me, hair distinguished with a few flecks of gray around the temples, lips thin, eyes cold and blue. His angular face looked as though it was carved out of a block of oak. He regarded me with a stare that made me feel like I was standing on somebody's grave.

"Can I be of any assistance, sir?" he asked. The man had a deep voice, the words cracking in his mouth like chocolate.

"Yes—I'm supposed to be eating here this evening," I replied, "but I'm running a little late."

"You must be Mr. Henley," the man said, stepping to one side to let me past.

"Erm … that's right," I nodded, slightly surprised that he should know who I was.

A few moments later I found myself standing at the end of a long, brightly lit corridor. It had cream walls, dark floorboards, and a beautiful crystal chandelier hanging from a high ceiling. A gentle clatter of plates and quiet conversation echoed around me, though it was unclear where the sound was coming from. The only furniture I could see was an old hat stand, which stood empty in the corner like a bare, forgotten tree, and a handsome wooden closet. It looked antique, with a sanded white finish and curved gold handles. Everything had a feeling of being preserved in time, as if I was the first human being to set eyes on this place for many years.

"May I take your coat?" the man said, closing the front door silently behind him.

"Thanks," I said, transferring a few belongings to my trouser pockets and shrugging the coat into his hands.

"You will need a jacket before you enter the restaurant," the man informed me, folding my coat carefully over his arm.

"Why?" I said, looking at him over my shoulder. "Has the heating gone?"

"No, sir—we have a dress code," he replied, walking over to the closet and opening it. "But don't worry. I think we have one in your size."

He searched inside the closet and handed me a gray, pin-striped jacket. It slipped on perfectly, fitting me even better than the over-priced suit I once had tailor-made for myself years ago. This of course was back in the days when I cared more about my appearance in the office—nowadays I'd only spend that sort of money on the things that really mattered to me, like a long holiday far away from here.

The man hung my coat up and shut the closet doors.

"Please, follow me," he said, leading me down the corridor with one arm folded behind his back at a right angle.

The corridor ended at a set of large double doors on the left. The sound of polite restaurant chatter and the clacking of plates came from the other side, and a warm, inviting smell of food began to drift under my nose. I was hungry—the only thing that had passed my lips today was a couple of slices of toast for breakfast. And that horrible coffee.

The man pushed the doors open and conducted me through to a spacious dining room, which stretched all the way toward the front of the building again. Having seen this room from the out-side, I already knew the windows were appointed with tall wooden shutters, but it was only from in here that you could really appre-ciate the level of craftsmanship involved—each one was engraved with it own unique decoration, so elaborate that your eyes could get lost in the patterns if you stared for too long. A similar amount of care seemed to be taken over the ceiling, which was framed with delicately carved coving. Two chandeliers much like the one in the corridor hung at either end, casting a low light over the dozen or so tables, and an original Victorian fireplace was providing heat from the far wall, the sound of its glowing embers crackling in the background. The warmth from the fire gave the room a feeling of intimacy and cosiness despite how large it was.

"Have a very pleasant evening, sir," the man said, retreating back into the corridor and closing the doors behind him.

I took a few cautious steps forward and looked across the room for Cassandra, hoping it didn't matter too much that I was late for our appointment.

I couldn't see her.

The table nearest to me was occupied by a young, attractive couple. They looked as though they were halfway through their main course. The guy wore a dark suit with a white silk tie, the girl an elegant blue sequined dress. In the middle of the room, six men and women in business suits were being served a selection of cheeses from a trolley. One of the men was very overweight. And over in the far corner of the room, the sommelier was recommending some wine to an older couple, both of whom looked about retirement age. That just about covered everyone I could see—the rest of the tables were empty. No sign of Cassandra.

"Good evening, Mr. Henley," came a small voice from behind me.

I looked round. A young waitress had emerged from a narrow passageway I must have overlooked during my initial assessment of the room, which presumably led to the kitchen. She was quite pretty in an ordinary sort of way, her face free of any distinguishing makeup, her cropped blonde hair tucked behind a small pair of ears. The uniform she wore was black, blouse buttoned to the very top, apron tied neatly round her waist, shoes plain and flat. She stood a few inches shorter than me.

"Um…Hello there" was my stilted response. I felt a little unnerved that everyone knew my name, but decided not to mention it.

"Table for one, wasn't it?" she asked, smiling at me like a children's television presenter.

I shook my head. "Two, I think."

"No problem," the waitress said, tucking a couple of menus under her arm and leading me across the room. "Will your guest be arriving soon?"

"Actually, I thought she'd already be here," I said, glancing around once more for Cassandra in case I'd somehow missed her. I hoped she hadn't been and gone already. "We were supposed to meet at nine o'clock. You wouldn't happen to know if she was here earlier?"

"I'm not sure," the waitress said, stopping by a small round table next to the fireplace. "Can you describe her for me?" She pulled a chair out and gestured me to sit down.

"She's about your age," I said, sliding myself into position. "Dark hair?"

I wasn't sure how much more detail to go into, so I left it at that.

"Sorry," the waitress said, tucking the chair back underneath me as I lowered myself down. "Do you mind telling me her name in case she arrives later?"

"Cassandra," I said, resting my hands on the table and inter-locking them in front of me. The tablecloth was pure white and smooth to the touch, hanging off the table the way a master patis-serie would drape a sheet of icing over a cake.

"Cassandra?" the waitress said, handing me a menu. "But...that's the name of the lady who booked this table."

"That's right."

"I think there may have been a misunderstanding," she said. "Your friend said you would be dining alone this evening..."

"Really?" I said, placing the menu down to one side.

"I'm certain," the waitress insisted. "I took the call myself."

"There must be some mistake," I said, putting my glasses on and rummaging inside my trouser pocket for the note Cassandra had written earlier. "Would you mind giving me a couple of minutes?"

"Of course," the waitress replied, placing the other menu in front of the empty chair opposite. She left to tend to another table.

I laid the note out in front of me and began to unfold it. Why had Cassandra gone to all that trouble of inviting me out for dinner when she had no intention of showing up? I needed to give her a call.

"I've got some bad news for you," the note said.

I stopped reading and examined the piece of paper again, turn-ing it over to look at the back in case I'd missed something. I was pretty sure this was the same note Cassandra had given me ear-lier—the one with her phone number on it—yet for some reason it now said something completely different. I rubbed my eyes under my glasses and carried on reading.

"Cassandra will no longer be joining you this evening," it continued.

Great, I thought.

"I'm afraid that's not all," it read. "I've also had to relieve you of your wallet."

I laughed under my breath and checked my pockets—that couldn't be true; I remembered distinctly transferring it from my coat only a few moments ago.

But my wallet wasn't there. At least, it wasn't where I thought I had put it. I checked my pockets again, this time standing up to look more thoroughly.

Nothing. I sat down again and carried on reading the note. How could someone have taken it without me noticing?

"Don't worry," the note continued. "I'll give it back to you later. And the meal will be fully paid for, so order whatever you like. I'm told the crab terrine is particularly good here, as well as the … wait, your waitress is coming back, so I'll speak to you later." With that, the note ended.

I looked up. Just as the note had said, the waitress was making her way back over to my table. I stuffed the paper back in my pocket.

"Is everything all right, Mr. Henley?" she asked.

I explained the situation about my wallet, glancing around the restaurant to see who might have done this to me, but I would have been surprised if it was any of the other diners—wouldn't they have just made a run for it?

"Oh dear," she said, looking around at the floor. "Are you sure you didn't drop it somewhere?"

"Pretty sure."

I was just about to ask her to call the police when a thought crossed my mind.

"Tell me," I said, "am I right in thinking this meal is already paid for?"

"That's correct," the waitress confirmed.

"So I can have anything I like?"

"Anything you like."

I opened the menu and glanced at some of the prices.

"And that includes wine?"

"It does."

I smiled. Whoever had taken my wallet probably thought this was all very amusing, but they were about to get the shock of their life.

I smoothed my napkin across my lap and looked up at the waitress.

"I think I'm ready to order," I said.

Canapés with champagne, sashimi with pickled ginger, lobster bisque scented with saffron, fillet steak served with creamy dauphinoise potatoes—the twelve-course taster menu had proven to be quite a test of stamina. It must have been nearly three hours before I took a final spoonful of my Belgian chocolate tart, washing it down with the most expensive dessert wine recommended to me by the sommelier. This place was in a different gastronomic league to the last restaurant I'd eaten in, where they still thought it was pretty cool to serve lemon sorbet in a hollowed out lemon.

I folded my cutlery down on the plate, dabbed the sides of my mouth with my napkin, and slumped back in my chair, one hand resting gently over my stomach—I was full.

If my calculations were correct, that meal had just cost the best part of a week's salary once you took the alcohol into account. An obscene amount of money to spend in one evening, and not very nice for whoever was paying the check. But then perhaps they should have thought about that before they decided to steal my wallet.

I let out a slow yawn and checked my watch. Just gone midnight.

Various people had come and gone over the course of the evening, the restaurant being particularly busy around ten o'clock when most of the tables had been occupied. Now I was the only person left.

"How was that for you?" the waitress asked, brushing a few crumbs from the table and removing my plate.

"Delicious," I answered, trying not to move too much. "In fact I think that was the best meal I've ever eaten."

"I'm glad you enjoyed it," she smiled. "Now, can I get you anything else? Some coffee perhaps?"

"No thanks," I said, shifting my weight slightly. "I think that's about as much as I can manage."

"As you wish," the waitress said. "If you change your mind, just give me a shout."

I said I would and watched as she retreated back into the kitchen.

I shut my eyes and sat quietly to let my food go down. After a big meal like that, I always liked to relax for a moment, empty my mind of all thoughts and be at peace. A police siren wailed quietly in the background. Rain began to patter on the windows like a hundred impatient fingertips drumming on the glass.

Something was bothering me.

Something about that note.

I opened my eyes again and pulled it out of my pocket.

"Well that's going to be a bit more expensive than I anticipated," it read. "Thanks for that."

I dropped the note in front of me and edged back in my chair. How could it be different? I'd been sitting alone at this table for the whole evening. No one could have swapped it without me realizing.

"I think it's time for you to leave," it said, this time looking as though it was magically rewriting itself before my eyes.

I rubbed my eyes. Did that just happen? How was this possible?

"That's a good question," the note replied, this time changing as if it was able to read my mind. "But more importantly, why did Cassandra tell you to come here this evening? Have you thought about that?"

I didn't care about that anymore. All I cared about was this note, which now appeared to be engaging me in conversation. I leaned forward and examined the paper more closely. Unless I was mistaken, this was my handwriting. This note, along with the one I'd received earlier, both looked like they were written by me.

That was what had been bugging me.

"I wondered how long it would take you to notice," it said.

That dessert wine must have been stronger than I thought. I left the note on the table and stood up.

Definitely time to leave.

Four

I'd always made a conscious effort to avoid watching the weather forecast—my life was predictable enough without someone telling me the chances of rain, or how cold it was going to be on a particular day. I liked things to be spontaneous—I liked the weather to surprise me. It was the same reason I didn't have a sat-nav. For one thing, I felt the ability to read a map was becoming a lost art. These days, people just relied on a machine to tell them where to go. But not knowing which way I was supposed to be heading reminded me that I didn't live on a set path, that things outside my control could send my life off in many different directions. It was quite reassuring to see my days evolve in an unexpected ways, and I couldn't help but feel that sat-navs and knowing the weather forecast took a little bit of that freedom away from me.

At least, that was the theory.

The soft patter of rain I'd heard from inside the restaurant had now turned into quite a downpour, the sound filling my ears like the white noise from an old television set. As I stood under the porch of the building, collar of my overcoat pressed against my neck to keep out the chill, I found myself questioning my principle of not watching the weather forecast. Had I known it was going to be like this, I probably would have brought an umbrella. Or a boat.

That said, the rain looked as though it was coming down too heavily to last a long time, so I shoved my hands in my pockets and waited for it to pass, shifting my weight impatiently from one foot to the other in the hope that this would somehow make me feel warmer. It didn't. I waited a couple more minutes and lit a cigarette.

I wasn't a big smoker, but I still enjoyed one now and again—particularly after a meal.

A few minutes passed. The high Victorian gutters around me were beginning to overflow, water spilling from the seams like ribbons of flowing silk. In the street, drains were swelling up and disappearing into deepening puddles. And across the road, people had huddled together in doorways or under tarpaulin, looking up at the sky for a sign of respite. Occasionally a car would glide past at low speed, the driver leaning forward and squinting through frantic windscreen wipers at the blur of rain and headlights ahead. A few people in the apartments opposite were stood by their windows, probably looking down at me and being grateful that they were indoors. I took a final drag of my cigarette and flicked it to the edge to the curb, watching it extinguish with a satisfying hiss as it hit the floor.

Standing under the porch wasn't keeping me particularly dry. Now and then the wind would pick up and skew the rain at such an angle that it caught me right up to the neck, and after a few more minutes, I couldn't be bothered to wait any longer. I stepped down from the porch and wrapped my coat tight round my body to stop it blowing open—it was time to make a run for the car.

I shielded my face with one arm and dashed along the street. Within seconds I could feel rain seeping into my shoes, the cold water squelching through my socks as I ran. I suppose it served me right for being too lazy to get the soles fixed after they'd split a year ago. It wasn't much longer before my trousers were completely drenched below the knee, the damp fabric clinging round my ankles like two wet dogs.

I turned the corner to see my car exactly where I'd left it, parked in between two much nicer cars on a posh residential road. I drove an old Nissan Silvia: a gray coupé with pop-up lights, orange seats, and a dodgy clutch. Sometimes it refused to start, other times it refused to turn itself off. One of the doors was a slightly different color to the rest of it from when somebody sideswiped me a few years ago, and I'd had trouble finding a suitable replacement. The car was so old that it actually qualified as a classic, though I doubted it would be featuring in any motoring magazines anytime soon. I loved it. I hurried over to the driver side door and leaned against it, fumbling around in my coat pocket for the keys.

The pocket was empty.

I wiped the rain from my face and tried the opposite pocket in case I'd put them in there, but that was empty too.

So I checked and double-checked every pocket, turned my coat inside out, even feeling the lining in case the keys had slipped through a hole. I didn't care about how wet I was getting anymore—I just wanted to get in my car and go home. But the keys were nowhere to be found. I retraced my steps and studied the ground, checking to see if they'd fallen out as I'd been running. Nothing. I then thought they might have dropped out of my coat in the restaurant, but when I returned to the building the lights were off. No answer at the door.

I wandered back to the car again, footsteps slow, head hung low in quiet defeat. I was soaking wet. How could I lose my keys? I wasn't normally so careless.

I looked up at my car as I approached it and imagined myself nestling inside, turning up the heating and listening to some classical music on the radio. It was then that I noticed something flapping under the left windscreen wiper.

A note.

I lifted the wiper up and peeled the wet paper off the windshield, draping it over my hand to read. The ink was beginning to run, but I could tell that this note, like the ones I'd received in the restaurant, was written in my handwriting. It was the *y's*. I wrote them in a very distinctive way, overly curling the tail so they looked like those little paper clips that were too small to be used for paper-clipping anything.

"Sorry about this," the note read, "but I had to take your car keys as well. Can't have you driving around in the old Nissan—far too conspicuous. They'd find you in no time."

Did I just read that correctly? Was someone looking for me?

"Why else do you think Cassandra sent you to that restaurant?" the note said, rewriting itself in my hand just as the other one had done earlier. "Fine dining? Stuffy atmosphere? That's the last place they'd expect to find you."

Who was 'they'? And why did this person keep stealing my stuff?

"There's no time to explain," the note continued, "But for now, don't go anywhere you would normally go. Don't go to work tomorrow, don't visit your friends, and definitely don't go home—they've got someone waiting in the flat."

Someone was in my flat? This was too much.

"What the hell is going on?" I blurted out.

A lady across the road lifted her umbrella and looked at me as if I was crazy. I chuckled back and gave her a dismissive wave. She lowered her umbrella again and hurried on her way.

I wiped my face and looked down at the note again.

"Why is someone looking for me?" I whispered under my breath, my voice almost lost in the sound of the downpour. "And how do they know where I live?"

"Look, we need to get you off the streets," the note replied, ignoring my questions. "I've booked you a room at the Hotel Carnaby, two blocks north of here. Be there in five minutes."

The paper was beginning to disintegrate in my hands, so I brushed it off and let the wet scraps fall to the pavement. I didn't want to stay in a hotel—I needed to get home and see if somebody really was there. And what was that about not going to work tomorrow? Not seeing my friends? Was I in some sort of danger?

For the moment, those questions would have to wait—I was really starting to shiver. My clothes were now so wet I felt like I'd just been for swim whilst wearing them, and as much as I wanted to go home, with no wallet and no keys I was running out of options. What was I going to do—start the two hour walk back to my flat, or find this hotel? And which way was north?

Now I wished I had a sat-nav.

"Hello?" I called out to nobody in particular as I stood dripping in the deserted lobby of the Hotel Carnaby.

No answer.

I unbuttoned my coat and looked around. The lobby was a difficult place to describe. Neither large nor small, it felt spacious in many ways, but at the same time cramped and claustrophobic. The focal point of the room appeared to be a tall grandfather clock, which stood proudly against the far wall, pendulum tick-tocking through an otherwise silent ambience. The walls of the room were decorated in olive green wallpaper, which was peeling away from the skirting boards in several places and curling up like the ends of a tattered medieval scroll. Paint was flaking from the doorframes and picture rails, and above my head a chandelier was attempting to light the room with only a few of its bulbs working, casting certain areas in feint shadow. An old piano was slumped in the corner of the room, half covered in a dusty sheet, and the air smelled stale, thick with that strange musk you normally get when you come home after a three week holiday.

To my right stood an old mahogany check-in desk. Probably quite an impressive piece of furniture in its day, but now it was in desperate need of refurbishment, with wooden panels coming away at the base and scratches all over the surface. A sign small said 'ring bell for assistance,' but I couldn't see a bell. I leaned over the counter to glimpse into the office behind. A green banker's light was illuminating a table inside, but other than that the room appeared to be empty.

I took a few steps deeper into the hotel. Beyond the check-in desk the room opened out into a small seating area appointed with several traditional high-back wing chairs, upholstered in deep red leather. The far corner of the room housed a broad stairwell with an ornate, wrought iron banister. I laid my coat over the arm of the nearest chair and sat down, a cloud of dust wheezing out from under me as I sank into the seat. No harm in waiting a few minutes,

I supposed. A few newspapers were scattered on the coffee table in front of me. I picked one up to read, but soon discarded it again when I noticed it was from last month.

The grandfather clock chimed one in the morning.

"Is someone there?" a voice called. It had an elderly croak to it, like a rusty hinge on an old cellar door.

I stood up. The voice appeared to be coming from the top of the stairwell.

"Yes," I said, grabbing my coat and wandering over to the source of the sound. "I'd erm … I'd like to check in, please."

I reached the bottom of the stairs and looked up—an old man was peering over the banister about two flights up. It was tricky to determine his age, although I guessed he must have been over seventy. He wore thick, black-rimmed glasses, his skin had the texture of kneaded clay, and his hair curled round the top of his head like a thin wisp of white smoke evaporating into the air.

"You the gentleman who sent us the letter?" he asked.

"Letter?"

"Yes," the man said, grabbing onto the banister for support as he hobbled down the stairs one step at a time. "Mr. Henley, right?"

"Erm … That's right," I said, watching as he descended toward me. He walked like an awkwardly controlled wooden puppet, each step making the staircase creak like the deck of an old galleon.

"You're right on time," he smiled through yellowed teeth. "Smoking room wasn't it?"

"If you say so," I answered.

"Well that's what you asked for, son," the man informed me. "We got the exact room made up just like you wanted."

FIVE

The "exact room" that had apparently been reserved for me was on the fourth floor, about three quarters of the way along a dimly lit corridor. The corridor was in a similar state of disrepair to the lobby downstairs. Threadbare carpet, chipped paintwork, and cream wallpaper that turned a murky shade of yellow as you looked toward the wood panelled ceiling, probably stained by years of cigarette smoke. Despite its condition, I found the hotel to have a certain charm to it. It felt dignified, like an aging film star choosing to forgo cosmetic surgery and grow old gracefully.

There didn't seem to be anything special about my room from the outside, and it made me wonder why I'd been booked into this room in particular—the tall wooden door looked identical to all the other doors I could see. Dull brass handle, slightly crooked room number, dark wood. Getting it to open proved to be a little difficult as I inserted the key and twisted it in the lock, but after two or three attempts the latch finally clicked.

I was just about to go inside when I heard the lift at the other end of the hall—it was one of these old-fashioned designs with a metal concertina door you had to manually pull to one side, and the screeching noise it made as it opened was hard to ignore. I looked round to see a chambermaid emerge with a trolley full of towels and cleaning products, closing the door behind her with the same deafening screech. I frowned to myself as I watched her make her way toward me—it was a little late for housekeeping, wasn't it?

The girl didn't look at me. She stopped at the first room and pulled out a set of keys from her apron, eyes fixed on the floor the whole time. I couldn't tell much about her from this distance—it wasn't very well lit where she was standing, and her long brown hair was draped around her head like a shawl, obscuring any view I had of her face. All I could see as she fumbled with the keys was her hands. Well-manicured hands. Delicate looking hands. I didn't think much of this until a familiar scent of perfume filled the air.

"Cassandra?" I called out, allowing the door to my room to click shut.

The girl didn't react, although she now seemed to be searching through her keys in a hurry.

"Hey!" I said, taking a few steps toward her.

Still the girl didn't respond.

I watched as she quickly selected a key and inserted it into the lock.

"Wait!" I said, walking a little bit faster.

The girl opened the door to the room and stepped inside, leaving her trolley behind.

I tried to catch the chambermaid before she disappeared, but the door shut just as I got there. I stood alone in the corridor for a moment and stared at where she had been standing. I was sure it was Cassandra—although she now wore her hair differently, she had the same build, wore the same perfume, and had the same delicate-looking hands. It couldn't have been a coincidence.

I pressed my ear to the door and listened.

"Hello?" I called out.

No reply.

"Hello?" I repeated.

Again there was no reply.

I took a deep breath.

"Listen, Cassandra," I said, standing back. "I know it's you. Do you want to tell me what's going on here?"

It was no use. She seemed to be ignoring me.

I tried the handle. To my surprise, it turned.

"I'm coming in," I said, wedging my foot under the door as I opened it to stop her shutting it on me. "I just want to talk."

My attempts at conversation were met with silence, the only sound coming from the creak of my footsteps as I edged inside. It was dark, although a little bit of light was glowing from the streetlamps outside through a large sash window. I reached around for the light switch and turned it on.

The room was bigger than I expected, with a king-sized four-poster bed, a high ceiling, and lots of floor space. It felt surprisingly luxurious. Pale green wallpaper, oatmeal carpet, dark wooden furniture, lots of little ornaments scattered around to catch the eye—this was exactly the sort of look I would have gone for had I lived in a period property rather than the identikit, new-build flat my salary afforded me.

I moved further inside. The room felt as though it was currently unoccupied—every cushion on the sofa was perfectly straight, every complimentary magazine on the coffee table untouched. Even the bed was made to mathematical precision, pillows plump and duvet crease free as if it were about to have its photograph taken for a brochure.

No sign of Cassandra.

I checked the bathroom—empty. I opened the wardrobe—empty. I even got down on my hands and knees and checked under the bed—nothing. Had she left through the window? I ran over and opened it, but there was no way she could have escaped this way—there was no balcony, nothing to climb onto, and a fifty foot drop to the street below. Still raining outside.

Now, it wasn't unusual for women to find ingenious ways of avoiding me, but this was getting ridiculous. Where the hell did she go this time?

A girl that kept vanishing. Stolen belongings. Notes rewriting themselves before my eyes. Was this really happening to me, or was I going mad? I could feel myself beginning to panic, my heart beating erratically. I wandered back to my room in a daze and shut the door, tossing my wet coat over a tatty leather sofa.

I needed to think.

Looking around, my hotel room felt like a poor relation to the one Cassandra had just disappeared from. It was the same size, with the same four-poster bed and same free magazines on the coffee table, but for some reason it was in far worse condition, like the malnourished brother to a fit and healthy twin. The oatmeal carpet was worn away in patches, thick cobwebs clung to the corners of the grimy ceiling, and the far wall had a large pale square on it, presumably where a picture once hung.

I took a deep breath. The air was quite stuffy, so I lifted the sash window open as far as it would go and allowed the smell of old newspapers and stale cigarette smoke to drift out. Still the rain showed no sign of letting up. I leaned out over the ledge and looked down at the narrow alleyway below. A cat was sitting on top of a dustbin looking back up at me, eyes shining in the dark. It didn't look very happy at being wet and quickly jumped down to crawl under a van. I knew how it felt—I wished I could run away and hide.

I ducked back into the room and rubbed the back of my neck— I needed something to take my mind off things; I needed to calm down. I flicked the television on and decided to investigate the minibar.

The television was one of those old black-and-white ones. Dusty gray screen, wooden finish, dial on the side for changing channels. The picture was so blurry that I couldn't really make out what I was watching, but I managed to find something resembling the news and shakily poured myself a glass of whisky.

The top stories were fairly depressing, but somehow I found their predictability to be strangely reassuring after everything I'd been through today: Food shortages around the world were resulting in an unprecedented increase in price. Fuel costs were rocketing. And a big study was being done about how our modern lifestyles were causing a breakdown in the family unit. However, to lighten the mood, a viewer had sent in some footage of their dog on a skateboard. Maxwell, his name was. Apparently he was an

Internet star. Then there was the weather forecast, in which a nice female presenter reminded everyone that it was going to be a wet evening. No shit, I thought to myself as I looked out of the window, savoring the whisky at it warmed the sides of my throat. Sport next. Team A had beaten team B in some sort of never-ending championship league, which apparently was all very exciting.

I didn't do sport.

Finally, the anchorman said that they would love to hear the viewer's opinions about anything and everything they'd covered on tonight's show. You could text them, log onto their homepage, e-mail, write in, use one of many different gizmos on your phone, whatever. In any event, they wanted to know what *you* thought. I couldn't understand this. Why give airtime to the millions of different uninformed opinions about the events of the day? I didn't want to know what Bill from Dagenham thought about the state of the economy—I wanted to hear more from an experienced journalist on the matter. Different people perceived things in different ways, and most of us were in no position to have our views broadcast to the world. But it was happening. As the sea of opinion got deeper and deeper, it was almost impossible for someone to anchor themselves in reality, to distinguish the truth from the ebb and flow of interpretations that surrounded it.

Then again, by my own argument, that was only my opinion.

I turned the dial to look through a few more channels, but nothing else of interest seemed to be on. At one point, I noticed the same actor appearing on two different stations at the same time and amused myself by flicking back and forth between them quickly, transporting the character from a Western movie to a hospital drama and back again and imagining his surprise at suddenly being thrown into a new environment.

Once I got bored of my little game, I switched the television off, took another sip of whisky and lit a cigarette. Cigarettes always helped me relax. Of course there was the downside of a slow and painful death, as the packet kindly reminded me in its friendly, lowercase lettering, but I wasn't bothered by that. Watching soap operas for too long caused a slow and painful death, but you didn't see a warning on those.

I sat down on the bed and kicked off my shoes, peeling my wet socks from my feet and laying them on the floor. My hair still felt damp from the rain, so I extinguished my cigarette halfway through and wandered into the bathroom, pulling the cord for the light and grabbing a towel from the side to pat myself dry. An old fluorescent bulb reluctantly flickered to life above the mirror, casting the room in a pale orange glow.

The bathroom was small, cold, and in a similar state of disrepair to the bedroom. Tiles on the walls were either cracked or missing altogether, the claw-foot bathtub had an inch of brown water resting in the bottom, and the air smelled damp, like an entire rugby team had just cleaned themselves up in here after a long game.

I leaned over the limescale-encrusted sink and yawned at my reflection, feeling the day's worth of stubble on my chin. The mirror was dirty, so I wiped a streak across it with my sleeve. My eyes looked a little heavy, the left one bloodshot. Pale skin. Chapped lips. I wasn't looking my best.

I felt exhausted, but my mind was too active for me to go to sleep, my thoughts bursting with all kind of emotions. Confusion, apprehension, nervousness, anger, defiance; I could feel each sensation bubbling to the surface with a different intensity as I flitted between them like the slides of a photo reel. I switched off the bathroom light and staggered over to the bed, sprawling myself over the cold sheets, arms outstretched. I needed to close my eyes for a second and try to get my thoughts in order.

I couldn't say how much time passed before I heard a knock at the door. Three slow knocks, resonating off of every surface in the room like a gentle rumble of thunder. I propped myself up in the bed and tried to ask who it was, but for some reason I couldn't speak—when I opened my mouth the words refused to come out, trapped inside my throat in a pocket of air. I wasn't concerned about this, and sat there in silence for a while.

The knocks came again. This time louder.

I got to my feet and walked sluggishly toward the door, each footstep carrying me slowly across the room as if I was wading through a pool of water. I felt weak. When I finally got to the door, I noticed the handle was missing. Confused, I pressed my hands against the surface and pushed, but it wouldn't budge.

Three more knocks. Again I tried to speak to whoever was outside, but it was no use. My voice remained mute.

All of a sudden, I felt the texture of the door change as I pressed my hands against it, the hard wooden surface melting into a malleable material that bulged between my fingers like putty. I tried to pull away, but my hands were now submerged in the wood—I was being sucked in.

I opened my mouth and let out a silent scream as my wrists disappeared into the door like quicksand, feet kicking against the worn carpet as I tried to slow myself down. It was hopeless. Within moments, I was submerged up to my elbows.

I shut my eyes as my face made contact, the soft wood wrapping itself around my body like a thick tar. I couldn't breathe. I continued to struggle, but after a few seconds I had been completely absorbed.

Cold.

I opened my eyes to see that I had emerged in the far corner of a room similar to my own, only this one was falling apart. Above my head, the ceiling had worn away to reveal a row of charred wooden beams, some of them buckling in the middle. The walls were crumbling away into dust, the exposed brickwork gaping with jagged holes like pieces missing from a jigsaw. The four-poster bed had collapsed, the wooden frame rotting away into the ether like a mouldy plate of food. Color had been drained from everything, leaving the room looking like a faded photograph. The only thing that seemed to be unaffected by all this decay was the door, which stood on the other side of the room in pristine condition.

The three knocks came again.

I took a few steps forward, the floorboards creaking under my feet as if they were going to give way at any second. The air was heavy in my lungs, thick with a taste of ash.

I approached the door cautiously. This time it opened by itself. A bright light shone from the other side, flooding the room in its warm glow. I raised my hand to shield my eyes. A silhouette was standing in the doorway, beckoning me closer.

I hesitated.

As my eyes adjusted to the light I lowered my hand. The silhouette in the doorway was Cassandra, her arms outstretched. She was dressed in the clothes she had worn to my office earlier—pinstriped trouser suit, green blouse, high-heeled shoes. I reached out to grab her hand, and she pulled me through the door.

Again I found myself standing in a room almost identical to my own, although this one was like the room Cassandra had disappeared from when she was dressed like a chambermaid—furniture immaculate, decoration to the highest standard.

She led me into the middle before turning to face me, hands resting on my shoulders. She looked as though she was moving in slow motion. I looked into her eyes. She was crying. I placed a hand over the back of her head and stroked her hair. She moved toward me and nestled against my chest. I could feel her weeping.

After a few moments she stepped back and opened her mouth to speak, but all I could hear was a muffled noise. I knew she was trying to tell me something, something important, but her words were indistinguishable.

Then her expression changed—eyes wide, mouth hanging open, bottom lip trembling. She was focussing on something behind me. I felt something sharp hit the back of my neck and looked round. It was a paper airplane, which fell to the floor by my feet. I picked it up to examine—the craftsmanship was extremely precise, wings folded in perfect symmetry, nose ending in a perfect tip. Unfolding it, the paper looked as though it was from my notebook.

Something was written inside but I couldn't read it—the black ink was blurry on the page, the symbols meaningless. I dropped it to the floor and looked back at Cassandra—she had taken a few steps back, arm raised, finger pointing to something behind me again. I tried to move toward her but she crouched on the ground, arms wrapped over her head, knees tucked in as if to protect herself.

I turned to see what was scaring her and immediately lurched my arm up to shield my face—hundreds of paper airplanes were now flying toward me at speed. And just as they were about to strike, I woke up on the bed bolt upright, my heart pounding so hard it was almost as if I could hear it.

I'd been dreaming. I must have fallen asleep. I rubbed my eyes and looked at my watch. It was half past three in the morning. Still dark outside.

I lay down and took a few deep breaths, closing my eyes again and folding my hands over my chest. It was then that I felt something resting on top of me. Something light. I lifted my head and looked down my body. It was a paper airplane—expertly crafted, just like the ones in my dream. But that wasn't all—either side of me, the sheets were completely covered in more paper planes, with several others lying on the floor.

I leapt to my feet and pressed myself flat against the wall as if a snake had just slithered into the room—where the hell had all these come from?

My question was soon answered as another plane glided in through the window I'd left open and landed softly at my feet. I stood frozen to the spot and stared down at it, arms limp at my side. I was afraid to touch it.

It took me a few moments to crouch down and pick the plane up, unfolding the paper nervously in my hands. A message was written inside. I immediately recognized the handwriting, but this time it looked as though it had been written in a hurry.

"They've found you!" it read. "You have to leave now! RUN!"

SIX

I dropped the note to the floor and pressed the palms of my hands into my eyes. This couldn't be real. I must have still been dreaming.

I made my way shakily into the bathroom, one hand leaning against the wall for support. My legs felt numb. I pulled the light switch on and hung my head over the sink, waiting for the bulb to flicker to life. Turning on the tap, I splashed some cold water on my face and massaged my eyes gently through my eyelids. I could hear the florescent strip buzzing intermittently above my head as it struggled to switch itself on, but the noise soon settled down as the bathroom was finally cast in its dull, orange light. I patted my face with a towel and looked up at the mirror to check my reflection, but what I saw made me leap back in shock.

The entire mirror was covered in Post-it notes from top to bottom, each one overlapping another haphazardly as if they'd been stuck there with haste.

I peeled one off and examined it.

"RUN!" it said, in thick capital letters.

"GET OUT!" said another.

Each note was written in thick, red ink.

I stumbled backward against the opposite wall and slumped down on the cold, tiled floor, knees hugged to my chest, body shivering. I couldn't take this anymore. The tap was still running. I sat quietly and listened to it for a few minutes, body rigid, eyes wide open. I could feel my eyes beginning to well up, but it wasn't because I was upset—I just couldn't bring myself to blink.

Then came a knock at the door.

Three knocks, just like my dream.

I hunched my knees closer to my chest and remained quiet.

After a few seconds came another three knocks, this time louder. What was I going to do? I couldn't just sit here.

"H-Hello?" I stammered.

No response.

"Who's there?" I asked, speaking up a little.

"Mr. Henley?" came a male voice. Cigarette-hoarse. East London accent.

"Erm … Yes?" I said.

"We got an urgent call for you in reception," the man gruffed. "You mind opening the door?"

I didn't know what to do. Even though the notes appeared to be warning me about whoever was outside, I found it strangely reassuring to hear someone else speak. It was as though the sound of another person was bringing me back to reality, away from the madness of Post-it notes and paper planes. And why should I believe the notes anyway? All they'd done this evening was scare me to death.

Maybe I should speak to this guy, I thought. Perhaps he could explain what was going on.

"Give me a minute," I said, standing up and straightening my shirt. "Just putting some clothes on …"

I sat on the bed and pulled my clinging wet socks back over my feet, slipping my shoes on and grabbing my damp coat from the sofa.

Time for some answers.

But just as I reached for the door handle, another paper plane fell at my feet. I bent down and unfolded it quietly.

"If you open that door," it said, "you're a dead man."

"Mr. Henley?" the voice asked from outside. "Everything okay?"

"Yes, yes," I said, ignoring the note and grabbing the door handle. "Just coming …"

"This is taking too long!" another voice blurted in the background. "Shoot the lock!"

"Quiet!" the other voice whispered. "Let him come to us!"

I leapt back from the door and dropped my coat. The notes were right! These people *were* after me!

"What do I do?" I thought, looking down at the note in desperation.

"You need to jump out of the window," it replied.

"What?" I whispered, glancing over at it. I shook my head. There was no way I could jump from this height—falling four stories would kill me.

"Jump out of the window!" the note said, the words scribbling themselves out frantically before my eyes.

I ran over to the window and looked down. It was a long way to the alleyway below, and there was nothing to break my fall. Was I really going to do this?

"Do it!" the note said. "You're out of time!"

I clambered over the window ledge, legs dangling against the side of the building. I couldn't do it.

"Jump!" the note said, fluttering in my hand.

"I can't!" I said.

For a moment the note remained unchanged. Then, in very calm, slow handwriting, it simply said, "Trust me."

I closed my eyes and shuffled a little further forward, but I still couldn't do it. What if the note wasn't right about this?

"He isn't coming!" the second voice shouted from behind the door. "Get out of the way!"

"Wait!" the other voice said.

All of a sudden my ears were filled with an eruption of gunfire, bullets ripping though the door and ricocheting around the room like the insides of a pinball machine. Behind me, the furniture exploded into splinters; the bed coughing up a thick cloud of dust as the mattress took two or three shots; the television shattering across the floor in tiny pieces. One shot even whistled straight past my left ear, the bullet coming so close I could have sworn the casing had brushed the side of my face. It was unlike anything I had felt before, and the sensation was so intense I completely lost my balance.

The next thing I knew, I was falling toward the cold, hard pavement below, arms flailing, mouth wide open, and muscles tensed for a very unpleasant landing.

SEVEN

People often say that at the moment of death, your life flashes before your eyes. I was never sure how anyone could know this for certain, but it was a nice idea.

Turns out it's true.

As I fell from the hotel window, I could feel my mind regressing back through the years, replaying moments from my past.

My first memory dated back to when I was four years old. I was in kindergarten, and I was trying to build a train set so it led out of our classroom and into the classroom next door. I remember being bored with making my train go round in circles—I wanted it to go somewhere, to have a destination. So whilst the teacher had her back turned, I scurried outside with a bundle of track in my arms, laid them down on the floor, and began to move my train into the unknown, along the corridor of brightly colored crayon drawings and oversized letters of the alphabet. What a great idea I thought—to have a train that could run between two different rooms!

I think I made it about halfway before the teacher noticed I was missing and rushed outside, picking me up off my hands and knees and putting me back with the other children. I got quite a telling off. We weren't allowed to leave the classroom, I was told. It was dangerous outside. We had to stay where people could see us at all times. I still remembered the scene vividly—the look of concern in the teacher's eyes as she lectured me. The artificial scent of the orange plastic chair I was sitting in. The texture of the denim dungarees I was wearing. The faces of the other children as they watched from the reading corner. It was the only distinct memory I had from my early years, isolated in my consciousness like the sole photograph at an otherwise empty exhibition.

My teenage years had been a fairly pleasant experience. I had good parents. My friends were well-adjusted. I studied hard at school. I went on holiday with my family every year. There were no emotional traumas to speak of, no shock bereavements. I dated a couple of girls. All very average.

Then I met Alice.

Alice Everett, her name was. I met her in the first year of university under quite painful circumstances by cycling into her on the way to a business studies lecture. Not the most romantic of first encounters, particularly when you throw in the fact that I was hungover from the previous evening and cycling on the pavement. Poor Alice was just minding her own business. Any normal person would have been furious at being knocked to the ground, books and papers scattered everywhere, but Alice found the whole incident to be quite intriguing. As I stopped to apologize, she was already thinking about the significance of what had happened.

Wasn't it funny, she'd said, holding on to my arm as I helped her to her feet, how a series of random events, capable of branching off in many different directions, had culminated in this collision? A second later, a second before, and we would have passed each other by without incident. But now our separate journeys—the paths of two previously independent people—had become momentarily intertwined. Were we somehow gravitated toward each other without realizing it, or could the collision have been avoided? Wasn't that fascinating?

I started to worry about how hard I'd hit her, or worse, that I'd bumped into a girl who read too many romance novels and would start gushing about fate. But as I bent down to help her collect the things she'd dropped, I found myself picking up books on particle physics. Quantum decoherence. Entanglement theory. Something told me she was already preoccupied with this before I'd hit her.

I asked if she was studying science.

Quantum physics, she told me, removing her round, wire frame glasses and letting her hair down so she could tie it back up again neatly.

Oh good, I'd replied. For a minute I thought I might have given her brain damage.

I remembered the way Alice had laughed when I said this. She giggled quietly, bringing a hand up to her mouth as if she was embarrassed to be finding something funny. I thought it was cute habit.

This chance encounter ended up with us swapping numbers, which in turn led to us having a few drinks later that evening. Next thing I knew, we were in a relationship. Over the two years that we were together, she would often describe the story of our meeting as a prime example of cause and effect. I just thought it was a lucky coincidence.

With a slim figure and standing only an inch shorter than me, Alice was an attractive girl. I wouldn't have described her as having classically beautiful features, but there was an innocence to her eyes that made her seem easily approachable. Never that concerned with her physical appearance, she often tied her long blonde hair in a bun, held in place with a pencil. She rarely wore makeup, or any accessories for that matter. Her nose was undersized for her face, and one of her cutest habits was the way she used to adjust the bridge of her glasses every time they slid out of place. She had a small jaw, full lips, creamy skin, and her pale green eyes were constantly filled with a sense of wonder and curiosity, as if everything she could see was teaching her something new. Always enthusiastic, her smile radiated a warmth that seemed to lift everyone around her.

Physical appearances were one thing, but what attracted me the most about Alice was the way she was never at a loss for anything to do. A wonderfully creative person, she would often spend her spare time either playing the piano, reading her textbooks, or painting, which she had a real gift for—landscape paintings in particular. And her intelligence was off the chart—particularly when it came to science. Most people might have felt intimidated by her encyclopedic knowledge, but I liked it. She would often talk about the experiments she was working on in the physics lab or some theory she was studying. Half the time I wouldn't have clue what she was talking about, but I always found it deeply encouraging that someone could be so passionate about what they were doing.

But in the second year of our relationship, something changed. She stopped talking to me about her theories, wouldn't share a thing about what she was working on, and began to appear a little distant, as if something was preoccupying her. At first I thought it was me. Had I done something wrong? Had she gone off me? Was she upset? Whenever I tried to talk to her about it, she told me not to worry, that everything was fine between us. It was just stress. Problems with her experiments. I wanted to believe her, but somehow I got the feeling she wasn't telling me everything, that she was holding something back.

I never found out if I was right. A few weeks later, an experiment she was working on went catastrophically wrong. There was an explosion at her lab, and she was killed. I didn't find out until much later in the day—she had wanted to meet up that evening for a meal to talk to me about something, and I remembered just standing outside the restaurant in the rain, waiting. After twenty minutes I started to worry. She was usually so punctual, arriving at precisely the arranged time. Mobile phones weren't really around back then so I had no way of contacting her; all I could do was stand outside and wait. After an hour, I gave up and went to her flat, but when I got there, the only people waiting for me were a group of solemn-looking police officers. I could never bring myself to go to the scene of the accident to see the extent of the damage to her lab, but I remember reading in the paper that the entire ground floor of the physics block had been vaporized, leaving literally nothing behind. It was a miracle no one else was hurt, but apparently the explosion happened in the early evening, after many people had gone home. It must have been something she was working on alone.

They never found a body, and the university never revealed what experiment could have caused such a devastating explosion. I was a mess for about a year and nearly failed my degree because of the grief. I managed to scrape through my exams and get a reasonably decent grade, though I suspect my tutors were lenient on my marks because of what I went through.

Although I'd never reached a resolution with what happened to Alice—I never did find out what had been bothering her in the weeks leading up to her death or what she wanted to talk to me about the night she died—it was strange for me to think of her more than twenty years later as I fell out of a fourth floor hotel window. I suppose it was one of the most upsetting times in my life and I'd never been as close to anyone since, but Alice's death was a long time ago and I'd tried to move on. So why was I thinking about her? Why wasn't I thinking about my ex-wife? Or any other girl I'd been out with since for that matter? Perhaps it was something to do with Cassandra. The more I thought about it, the more I thought she had the same sort of funny nose.

And that was the last thing I thought about before I hit the ground.

Cassandra's nose.

At least, I thought it was the ground. Whatever I'd hit was pretty hard and hurt a lot, but it couldn't have been the ground, because I was still alive. For a few moments I lay on my back in shock and stared vacantly up at my hotel window, eyes open, breath still, thoughts oblivious to anything else around me. I didn't notice the freezing wind biting at my neck, the dull ache spreading across my back, or the rain pattering softly against my face—I felt numb, as if all my senses had shut down momentarily.

As my connection with the real world gradually returned, I sat up and looked around. I was lying on a pile of cardboard boxes, the layers splayed beneath me like a crumpled deck of cards. Where had these come from? I was certain there had been nothing beneath the window to break my fall, yet these boxes seemed to have appeared out of nowhere.

I clambered to my feet and took a few steps back, my body twitching with pain as I limped over to the other side of the alleyway and steadied myself against a wall. Two voices were shouting from above.

"You bloody idiot!" one of the men barked. "Couldn't you wait two more fucking seconds? He was about to come out!"

"Ah, shut up!" the other man replied. "We're in, aren't we?"

"Yeah, but he's no use to us dead is he? If he dies, we die! Remember?"

"Quit moaning. Let's just find him and get out of here…"

I backed out of the alleyway as quietly as I could—footsteps slow, eyes fixed on my hotel window the way an antelope might watch a sleeping predator. Two shadows were darting frantically around inside, the commotion of furniture being overturned breaking through the sound of heavy rainfall.

They must not have seen me fall.

"Where the fuck is he?" one of the voices soon said.

"I don't know," the other voice replied. "You looked outside?"

I tried to hasten my retreat, but my left leg was really beginning to hurt, a sharp pain searing through my body with every step I took.

One of the men leaned out of the window and looked down to survey the alley. His large frame barely fit through the gap, his arms bulging over the ledge like a couple of heavy sandbags. He held a gun in his right hand and wore dark clothes: overcoat collar folded up around his neck, black scarf wrapped across his mouth. His face looked like something you might see hanging up at the butcher's hall. Shaved head. Recessed eyes. Boxer's nose. Wide jawline. An inky black birthmark stretched across his right cheek.

It didn't take long for him to spot me.

"He's here!" the man shouted. Without warning, he pointed his gun directly at me and fired, the sound of the shot piercing my ears as it echoed all around.

The bullet missed by a few inches, burying itself deep into the soft, redbrick wall to my right. I stumbled back and tripped over a bag of rubbish, falling backward into a murky puddle of rainwater.

"Are you crazy?" the other man said, rushing to the window and wrestling the gun from his partner. "Didn't you hear what I said? We can't kill him!"

This man was of a similar build to the guy who had just shot at me, which was to say he looked like a tree trunk in an overcoat. He was a bit more pleasing to the eye, with short dark hair, a rounder face, and eyes with a hint of reason to them, but you still wouldn't have wanted to meet him down a dark alley, even if there were four stories separating you. By a strange coincidence, he also had a birthmark on his face, although this one was planted on his forehead, stretching from the tip of his left eyebrow and disappearing beneath his hairline. Like his partner, the mark was black like ink.

The two men looked down at the boxes beneath the window, but they didn't look like they would be able to break a second person's fall.

"Think we can make it?" the man with the scarf over his mouth said. His voice somehow managed to boom with aggression despite being muffled under the fabric.

The other man shook his head and ducked inside, followed immediately by his partner. I needed to get out of here.

I scurried back up to my feet and hobbled out of the alleyway onto the main road, my clothes completely soaked through like a damp second skin. The street was deserted. Shop windows sat dull and lifeless, newsstands had their shutters down, and not even the background hum of late-night traffic could be heard.

It was just me and the rain.

I folded my arms across my chest and shivered, trying to work out which way to go.

Then I remembered the note.

With everything that had just happened, I'd completely forgotten I was still holding it. I knew I didn't have much time, so I opened it quickly to see what I should do next.

It was blank.

This couldn't be right. I wiped the rain from my face and gave the paper a good shake.

Still, nothing appeared.

"Hello?" I tried.

It was no use.

I could feel my hands beginning to tense up with anger. How could it say nothing at a time like this? I'd fallen out a window, been shot at, and now two men were chasing after me. Now might have been a pretty good time to tell me what to do, but no—apparently I was on my own. I crumpled the note up tightly in my hands, stuffed it deep into my trouser pocket, and limped away from the hotel as fast as I could.

All of a sudden, a parked car across the road started up its engine, flicked on its headlights, and swung around to my side of the street. Unless I was mistaken, this was *my* car—my old Nissan Silvia. What was it doing here, and who was driving it?

The passenger door opened.

"Get in!" said a voice.

I walked over and bent down to see who was inside.

It was me, sitting in the driver's seat.

Or at least someone who looked very similar to me. I stood up, rubbed the rain out of my eyes, and bent down again to have another look, just in case I was mistaken.

No, the resemblance was uncanny. The man had slightly shorter hair and different clothes on, but there was no mistaking that face, staring right at me. I stared back. It wasn't quite like looking in a mirror, more like seeing a photograph of yourself where you see things at a different angle than you're used to and can't believe you look like that in real life. But he had the same eyes, the same nose—even the moles on his face were in the same place. I began to think about the notes. Since they were all written in my handwriting, did this mean I was looking at the person who had written them? And how was this possible?

"Who the hell are you?" I asked, my voice quivering. I wasn't sure if that was a stupid question or not.

"Who do I look like?" the man replied. "I'm you!"

"What?" I stammered.

I felt dizzy, pressing my shoulder against the roof of the car for support.

"I'm you!" the man repeated. "We're the same person, but…look, we can have this conversation now, or I can get you out of here and explain later. Will you just get in?"

I looked at him blankly for a second before sliding on to the passenger seat and closing the door. My "other self" slammed his foot on the accelerator and sped away through the streets as fast the Nissan could go.

"okay—what is going on?" I said, fastening my seatbelt. "Why do you look like me? And what are you doing in my car?"

"Hey, it's my car too," the man replied, jumping a red light. "Now, first things first—are you all right?"

"No, not really!" I winced, rolling up my left trouser leg to inspect the damage to my calf. There was a nasty cut down one side, but it didn't look too deep. "To be honest, I'm a little bit freaked out!"

"Look, I know this must all seem a little weird," the man said. "But you're just going to have to trust me."

"A little weird?" I said. "First I keep getting these notes—which I assume are your handiwork by the way—then someone tries to kill me, and now you show up! You call this a little weird?"

"They weren't trying to kill you," the man said.

"Then why were they shooting at me?" I said, turning the heating up and rubbing my hands against the surge of hot air.

"They shot at you?" the man frowned, taking a sharp left onto a busier main road. "But…they need you alive."

"Who needs me alive?" I asked. "Why do they need me at all?"

"Look, I can't tell you right now," the man said. "Probably better if you don't know for the time being, for your own safety."

"Right," I sighed, rolling my trouser leg back down and looking out of the window. "My own safety." It was difficult to tell where we were—the backdrop of sixties office blocks and blurry city lights merged into an indistinguishable pallet of yellows and grays in the rain.

"Can you at least tell me where we're going?" I asked.

"Somewhere safe," the man answered, not taking his eyes off the road. As he changed gear, the car lurched slightly.

"You really need to get this clutch fixed," he said.

I turned in my seat and looked closely at his face. The similarity was remarkable—his blue eyes were a slightly different shade to each other just like my own, his nose had the same small dip where it joined his forehead, and his two front teeth had the same narrow gap between them. It was crazy.

But there was one small physical difference between us.

"Hey," I said. "You don't have a scar."

"Scar?" he replied.

"Yeah. I've got a scar on my left temple from when I was sixteen. Nearly broke my neck in a go-kart race."

"Really?"

I turned my face to show him. It wasn't a noticeable scar—only about an inch long and very faded—but the fact remained that it was missing from his face. I'd got it from slamming into a tire wall at high speed during a race. My mother had refused to let me sit in a go-kart since.

"I see," the man said, still not turning his attention away from the road.

"Where's yours?"

"I don't have one."

"Why not?"

The man sighed. "How can I put this?" he said. "I'm you, but I'm also not you. I'm like … a different version of you. Does that make sense?"

"Not really."

"It's quite hard to explain," the man said, moving to overtake the car in front. "Can this wait?"

As we made our way through London's mild nighttime traffic, I noticed the scar wasn't the only difference between us—this man's taste in clothes was also quite unlike my own. His dark suit was far more expensive than anything I owned, and his shirt maintained a crisp, pressed appearance as if it had been starched. Brown leather shoes, pink silk tie, gold watch—it was all a little too refined for my liking. He also had a black mark on the back of his right hand that spilled over his knuckle like a misshapen tattoo.

"What's that mark on your hand?" I asked.

"Oh that?" he said, lifting his fingers off the steering wheel and flexing them. "It's nothing. Just a birthmark."

"That's pretty dark for a birthmark," I said, feeling inside my trouser pocket—to my relief, I'd remembered to pick up my cigarettes from the bedside table before I'd gone to answer the door. I wasn't a big smoker, but I always liked to have one if I'd just experienced something traumatic, like falling out of a window. I put one to my mouth and lit it, opening the window a slither to let the smoke out.

My other self started coughing.

"You smoke?" he spluttered.

I took another drag of my cigarette and looked at him.

"What's the problem?" I asked.

"I quit years ago," he said, waving his hand in front of his face. "Can't stand the smell now. Can you put it out?"

"But this is my car," I said, putting my lips to the crack in the window and exhaling. "I always smoke in it."

"Well I don't," the man hissed, opening the window on his side. "Can you at least smoke it quickly?"

"Fine," I said, taking one long drag and flicking the remainder out of the window. Strange to think I was arguing with myself. "You happy?"

The man said nothing. He just closed his window and continued staring at the road ahead.

It was at this point that a very small alarm bell went off in my head. If this man was the same person who had been writing the notes to me all evening, the man who had just saved my life, then he should have known that I smoked. After all, whoever had sent me to that hotel earlier had booked me into a smoking room. If this man didn't know that I smoked, then he couldn't have been who I thought he was.

But I was sure there was a reasonable explanation. I reached into my trouser pocket and pulled out the notepaper, uncrumpling it in my hands.

"So are you going to explain how you've been sending me these?" I asked, smoothing the paper over my knee. "I mean, how is it possible for them to rewrite themselves?"

"That's not important right now," he replied. "All that matters is the fact that I was able to protect you."

I looked down at the paper again.

"He's lying," the note said.

For a moment I just gazed through the words, as if I was focussing on something behind them. I stopped breathing. Did I just read that right?

"Yes, you read that right," the note continued, the words just starting to appear in front of my eyes. "In case you hadn't figured it out for yourself already, this isn't the man who has been writing to you. He's an impostor."

I turned my head slowly toward the man sitting next to me.

"An impostor?" I thought. "Are you sure?"

"Of course I'm sure!" the note said. "If he was the one writing these notes to you, why would he now be telling you this?"

"But he ..."

"Yes, he looks like you," the note continued, anticipating my thoughts. "But he's just one of many Richard Henleys, and one you really don't want to be socializing with right now. Believe me— whilst you're with him, you are in incredible danger."

"But, how do I know *you're* not the impostor? I mean, the man who wrote to me earlier said he'd taken my car keys, and now this man is driving my car. How do you explain that?"

"Take a look at the ignition. No keys."

I flicked my eyes over to the other side of the dashboard. The note was right—the keys were missing. Instead, a few wires were meshed together under the steering column. Hotwired, I guessed.

"I'm the one who took your car keys, not him. I'm holding them in my hand right now."

I could feel my mouth going dry.

"Why didn't you warn me?" I thought, suddenly twitching as though the seatbelt was restraining me like a straightjacket. "I looked at this note before, but it was blank!"

"Something came up," the note answered.

"Something came up?"

"Yes. And right now, all that matters is that you get out of there."

"And how do you suppose I do that?" I thought. "Do I jump again? Do you want me to throw myself out of a moving car?"

"No. just make some excuse—any excuse. You've just got to get out of that car. He's taking you to …"

"Nearly there," the man interrupted, looking round at me and smiling.

"Great." I sounded nervous. "Listen, can we stop a second?"

"Stop?"

"Yeah," I said, clutching my seatbelt. "I need some more cigarettes. Can you pull over if you pass a shop?" That was a lie—I still had half a pack left, but it was only thing I could think of on the spot.

"But we're less than five minutes away," my other self insisted. "I'm sure someone will have some cigarettes when we get there."

"Why?" I asked, folding the paper up slowly in my lap and sliding it back into my pocket. "Who are we meeting?"

"Just … some people," the man replied, reaching for the radio. "Do you want to listen to any music?"

EIGHT

Tchaikovsky's Piano Concerto No. 1 was just drawing to a close as we pulled into a disused wharf on the far side of town. As the music finished, the radio announcer informed us that we had just listened to the first version of the composition, which was quite unusual to hear these days—apparently the piece was revised twice by Tchaikovsky after receiving heavy criticism from Nikolai Rubinstein, one of the most famous pianists of his day.

The announcer was just about to explain the differences between the different versions when my other self turned the radio off, slowing the car to a crawl as we drove down an old industrial pier. The right hand side was lined with a row of abandoned warehouses and decommissioned factories, most of which were in an extreme state of disrepair. Rusty iron doors, faded paint, crumbling brickwork, broken windows—it was clear these buildings hadn't been used in years. To our left was the waterfront. From memory, I think local fisherman used to dock here to sell their catch at an early morning market, but that was a long time ago, before the bigger commercial ports on the coast took over and drove the area out of business. Now, only a few dilapidated boats remained, bobbing quietly in the water like relics discarded from a naval museum. A few seagulls sat asleep in the rigging.

We came to a stop outside one of the last factories at the end of the pier. The building was three stories high, with sheets of corrugated iron for walls and a large faded sign that hung over a red loading bay door. I couldn't read what the sign said—the letters had worn away. All the windows appeared to have been blacked out from the inside, although I could see cracks of light shining through a few gaps in the structure. A few oil drums and old wooden crates were stacked outside.

"Well, here we are," my other self announced, pulling the handbrake on. I noticed he didn't turn the engine off—since there were no keys in the ignition, he just took his foot off the clutch to stall the car.

"Great," I replied, trying not to sound nervous as I unbuckled my seatbelt.

My other self opened his door and got out.

It had finally stopped raining—the night sky was now totally clear and full of stars, the moon casting its soft glow across the still water.

I remained inside.

"You coming?" he asked.

"Yes, just…er…give me a second," I stuttered, trying to think of a good excuse for hesitating.

At that moment, the loading bay door began to slide open horizontally, spilling a bright light across the pier. The rusty mechanism of the door screeched like the worn out brakes of a steam train. I winced and covered my ears. The noise was loud enough to startle a few of the seagulls, many of which took to the sky and began circling above the water.

My other self turned his attention toward two people who had emerged from the building, their silhouettes barely distinguishable against the light shining behind them. He raised an arm to shield his eyes from the glare.

This was it—this was my chance to escape. I quickly arched my back over the gear stick and handbrake, sidled over to the driver's side of the car, and slumped in front of the steering wheel, slamming the driver door shut and jabbing the central locking button as fast as I could. My other self snapped his head back in my direction and frantically pulled at the door handle.

"Hey!" he said. "What are you doing?"

"I'm getting out of here," I replied, reaching for the keys that weren't there.

I'd completely forgotten they were missing.

It took my brain a couple of seconds to comprehend the problem. Without the keys, I had no idea how to start the engine. I began to sweat. What was I going to do? I fumbled with the wires underneath the dashboard in the hope I'd get lucky at hotwiring the thing, but it turned out to be much harder than they made it look in the movies.

I looked back toward the factory. The two men were much closer now, their silhouettes filling out with more detail as they approached. The man on the right was short. He was perhaps a couple of years younger than me, though he'd lost most of his hair and was a little overweight. His face lacked a certain balance that made me feel unsettled—he had quite a large forehead, with straight eyebrows and a narrow nose. His lips were thin, firmly closed as if they rarely broke into a smile, and his eyes were a little too close together. Sunken cheeks. He wore a bleached white laboratory coat buttoned to the top, shirt and tie underneath, gray trousers, and a pair of dirty white tennis shoes. He held a clipboard in his left hand.

The other man was well over six feet tall. Quite handsome, with a smart haircut and a well-trimmed beard. He looked about my age, maybe a little older. His facial features were in good proportion to each other, with a strong jawline, a solid nose, and a broad mouth. His skin was tanned, his teeth white, and he wore a gray pin-striped suit with a plain shirt undone at the collar. It looked like he kept himself in good shape, with not an ounce of unnecessary fat on his body to speak of. As I watched him approach, I found myself drawn to his intense stare, his dark blue eyes looking straight into mine. He walked with purpose, each crisp footstep following the last in a precise, decisive rhythm.

The only thing both men seemed to physically have in common was the blemish on their faces—the short man had a black blotch over his right ear, the taller guy had one on his cheek. Why did everyone have these marks?

I didn't have time to think about that now. I needed to get out of here. I turned my attention back to the wires under the steering wheel, desperately crossing them in different combinations to see if I could get the car started.

"I got him," my other self called out, walking over to greet the two men.

"So it would appear," the taller man replied, bending down to peer at me through the car window as if I were a caged animal. He was well-spoken, his voice measured and calm. "Where's Harry and Martin?"

"Should be on their way," my other self answered. "We had to split up."

"I see," the man said, looking back up at my other self. "So... tell me what happened."

"It was just like you said, Gabriel. Someone's been helping him—sending him places they didn't think we'd look. First it was that posh restaurant you told us about, then some weird hotel round the corner..."

The tall man—Gabriel—ran his fingers smoothly through the tip of his beard.

"Interesting," he said, looking round at the man in the lab coat. "Looks like you were right, doctor—it was worth observing this one first before bringing him in."

The man in the lab coat nodded. "Any idea how they might be communicating with him?" he asked, writing something down on his clipboard.

"They're sending him notes."

"Notes?"

"That's what he told me in the car. We saw him reading from a small piece of paper when he left the restaurant, and just a moment ago he asked me how they appeared to be rewriting themselves."

"Well that's certainly an interesting way of manipulating the technology," the doctor mused. "This is useful information."

I frowned to myself—what was he talking about?

Gabriel pressed his hands together, interlocking his long, thick fingers.

"Okay," he said, "talk me through the pickup."

"We came up with a plan," my other self explained, pacing slowly up and down. "Harry and Martin would try to apprehend him in the hotel, but if he managed to escape, I'd be waiting outside."

"So you posed as his friend."

"That's right. Just as we'd expected, he gave them the slip. My guess is the notes probably warned him. But I was there to pick him up once he got outside."

"And I suppose stealing the car was Harry's idea?"

"He thought it would be more convincing if I showed up in it, yes."

"Well I have to hand it to you," Gabriel said, casually pulling a gun out from inside his suit jacket. "I never knew the three of you could be so … creative."

I could feel my body beginning to tense up as I watched the man flick the chamber of his gun open and look inside, my hands still hastily crossing wires under the dashboard.

"Hey, what's with the gun?" my other self asked. "I thought you said we needed him alive?"

"We do," Gabriel replied, snapping the barrel shut and stepping forward. "Unfortunately, the same can't be said of you."

He raised the gun, pointing it at my other self.

"W-What?" my other self spluttered, eyes darting desperately between the two men as he backed away.

"Think about it," the doctor said from behind Gabriel. "Now that we've got this one, you're not terribly useful to us anymore, are you?"

My other self stared at me through the windshield of the car. Eyes red, mouth wide open, skin dripping with sweat—he looked terrified.

"But we had a deal!" he cried, holding his hands out in front of him. "You said that if I helped you find the right Richard Henley, you'd … you'd …"

"Deal's off," Gabriel said, pulling the trigger.

I lurched back in my seat as the gunshot ripped across the wharf like the shock wave from an earthquake. The seagulls took to the air again in fright, circling around in the sky the way vultures hover over a carcass.

I watched in horror as the bullet pierced the center of my other self's forehead, exploding out the other side almost instantaneously. His body slumped over the car and slid lifelessly onto the ground, a streak of blood smearing across the hood in his wake. A few specks of blood splattered across the windshield, dribbling down the glass in thin rivulets of red.

I wanted to be sick. A few hours ago, after my excessive meal, I'd felt full up. Now my stomach felt completely empty—hollow.

I'd just witnessed my own murder.

At that moment, a pair of headlights shone in the distance at the entrance to the wharf, the glare slowly getting bigger as a black Range Rover headed down the pier toward us. Gabriel looked up as the lights got closer, smiling as he shielded his eyes from the brightness. I watched as the vehicle passed by. It drove on ahead for a few meters before circling back round to face us.

The lights went out, the engine turned off, and the two men from the hotel emerged. I assumed this was Harry and Martin, though I wasn't sure who was who. They both looked even more menacing close up, eyes free of any warmth, jaws rigid, arms crossed firmly over their chests.

"I see we got him," one of them said. It was the man who'd told the other one not to shoot at me in the alleyway.

"Yes, Harry—we got him," Gabriel replied.

So that was Harry.

"What happened to the other guy?" he asked, looking down at the dead body of my other self.

"I shot him," Gabriel replied.

"Fair enough," Harry said. "No point having two of 'em around, I guess."

"Indeed," Gabriel said. "Speaking of which," he said, pointing at the body, "would you two mind getting rid of that?"

Without saying a word, the two men walked forward, picked up the body of my other self at either end, and slung it over the edge of the pier into the dark water below. I watched in disgust as they carried out the task with cold indifference—they might as well have been tossing out a bag of rubbish.

It was then that Gabriel turned his attention to me. For a moment he just stared at me in silence, as if weighing up his next move in a game of chess.

A few seconds passed like this.

Just staring.

Then he walked around the car, crouched down by the passenger door, and raised his gun to the window, tapping the barrel twice against the glass, slowly.

Tap.

Tap.

I clenched the steering wheel firmly in my hands and swallowed—neck stiff, shoulders locked, eyes facing forward.

"Hello, Richard," he said.

I felt a shiver run through my body. I could sense his face looming at the window out of the corner of my eye but couldn't bring myself to look round.

"My name is Gabriel."

Up close his voice had a velvety tone to it, the words drifting from his mouth like thick cigar smoke. He spoke efficiently and to the point, his sentences as lean as his physique.

I remained silent.

"Look at me," he said.

I turned to face him, my head rotating slowly like a tightened bolt stubbornly coming loose.

Gabriel smiled, his eyes unblinking. He had a look that seemed to cut into my soul. I found myself staring at the black mark on his cheek, smeared across the side of his face like a dried streak of crude oil. It didn't look natural, yet I couldn't think what else it could be. A tattoo maybe?

"Get out of the car."

"I'd … I mean I …" I tried to speak, but the words just came out strangled.

"That wasn't a request," he said, glancing down at his watch. "Just to avoid any confusion."

"W-What…what if I don't want to?" I said quietly, my voice taking on a strange transparency.

"I'll make it easy for you," Gabriel said, lowering the tone of his voice to a rumbling growl. "You can either come out by yourself, or I'll shoot this window and pull you out by your fucking eyelids."

Gabriel's expression didn't change as he spoke, yet his face looked different, like a blue sky suddenly clouding over before a storm. A cold sweat began to form down the center of my back.

"Up to you," he said, standing back and pointing his gun at the window. "I'll give you three seconds to decide. Three, two …"

"W-wait!" I said, flinging the door open without hesitation. "Don't shoot! I'm coming, I'm coming!"

I stepped out of the car and held my hands up.

"Thank you," Gabriel said, holstering his gun underneath his jacket. He looked over at Harry and Martin, cocking his head in my direction. "Take him inside."

The two men grabbed me firmly by both arms and marched me toward the factory. Gabriel and the doctor led the way.

"Hey!" I said.

I tried to break free from their grip, but it was no use—they were just too strong. Even when I resisted the pace they were walking at, they simply dragged me along by my arms, feet scraping along the ground.

"Let go of me!" I cried.

As we approached the loading bay door, Gabriel stood to one side as I was hauled past. He pulled a mobile phone out from inside his jacket and began dialing a number.

"Listen," I pleaded, struggling to look back as he put the phone to his ear. "I don't know what this is about, but you've got the wrong guy! You *must* have the wrong guy!"

Gabriel raised an eyebrow.

"I assure you—we haven't," he said, grabbing the edge of the loading bay door with his free hand and pulling it closed behind him.

"Please!" I said, flailing my arms and legs about in a final attempt to break free. "Just tell me what you want!"

"It's me," Gabriel said, putting a finger to his ear to block me out as he turned his attention to the phone. "We've got him."

NINE

The inside of the factory reminded me of the place my father used to work when I was growing up. Back then, he was employed as a sheet steel engineer for an automobile company, molding various body parts for the vehicles they produced. I remembered him coming home every evening in his black, slippery overalls, smudges on his skin, the smell of oil drifting through the house. I liked the smell. Even to this day, if I caught the same scent, a warm feeling of nostalgia would wash over me, and vivid images of him relaxing in his armchair with a mug of tea would project themselves against the walls of my mind.

Sheet steel engineering wasn't a career he'd landed in by choice. When he was fifteen, he was forced to leave school unexpectedly and find work when his father suffered a stroke and could no longer support the family. The factory manager allowed my dad to take his place on the production line, and that was that.

I'd always admired how selfless he had been to make that sacrifice, to abandon his own ambitions for the sake of looking after his mother and sister. He'd told me the story many times, how strange it was to see his life change so dramatically—to suddenly become burdened with such responsibility. One minute he was preparing for his exams, thinking about the subjects he might want to take as A-levels, the next he was in a factory with no qualifications, learning how to cut and mold sheet metal. It was a pity—he was a smart guy, and I'd always wondered how he might have turned out had things been different. The air in that place was always thick with soot—in another life, maybe he wouldn't have died of lung cancer before reaching sixty.

The air in this factory tasted clean, with a sterile, bleach-like edge that burned my nostrils. From the smell you would have expected everything to be spotless, but the place was absolutely filthy. And although the building looked as though it was three stories high from the outside, inside it was one big shell, housing a mothballed production line that stretched from one end to the other. The production line was recessed into the ground like a trench, about three meters wide, and had two metal rails hanging directly above. As we walked alongside it, I noticed the trench was littered with old piping, splinters of wood, and shards of scrap metal. Several gantry cranes arched overhead at regular intervals, some of which were collapsing with age. On the other side of the factory floor, a broken conveyor belt snaked across the room, joining together large pieces of rusty assembly equipment. It wasn't clear what they used to manufacture here.

The factory was unbearably bright, with floodlights beaming down on us from all directions. It almost reminded me of a film set. The light was so intense, not a single shadow was cast in any direction, and all the colors I could see appeared washed out. Above our heads, rows and rows of black rubber cables ran along the ceiling. Many of them had come loose and draped all the way down to the floor, curling round like vines hanging from the canopy of a rainforest. In one corner, a couple of shipping containers were stacked on top of each other. Doors open. Empty. A bank of old forklift trucks sat lifeless to our left, most likely unmoved for years, and I found myself stepping over murky puddles of water on the floor, probably from where rain had leaked in through the damaged ceiling.

"Please," I said, still struggling against the grip of my two burly escorts. "Can you just tell me what this is about? What have I done?"

Gabriel snapped his mobile phone shut and looked at me.

"You haven't done anything," he answered.

"Then … why are you doing this to me?"

"Patience," he said.

As we moved deeper into the building, the factory began to change. The first thing I noticed was the temperature. It was starting to feel uncomfortably warm, like a greenhouse. Then I began to detect a low level hum pressing in on me from all directions. It hadn't registered straight away, but soon the sound was burrowing into my skull like a feedback loop from a microphone.

The noise appeared to be coming from the far end of the factory, which looked as though it had been cleared away to make room for a small, open-plan office area. As we approached, it felt like we were stepping into another world. Where there were once rotting crates and aging industrial equipment, I now began to see desks covered in charts and technical diagrams. White computer terminals. Shiny databanks. Everything looked brand new. A few people in lab coats were hunched over laptops, studying tables of figures and complex graphs that glowed from their screens. A few of them looked up and followed me with their eyes, muttering quietly to each other. I couldn't make out what was being said.

Gabriel was still following closely behind, his footsteps retaining their crisp, rhythmic pattern on the factory floor.

"What is this place?" I asked over my shoulder.

"None of your concern," he replied curtly.

We soon arrived at the back of the factory, which was appointed with a set of brown rusty stairs that zigzagged high up to a narrow metal gangway. I followed the path of the gangway with my eyes—it stretched across the back wall and led to a small elevated room tucked away in the top corner. The room was windowless and no bigger than ten square feet, with brushed steel walls, a single metal door, and thick bolts pinning it to the ceiling. There were no supports underneath—it was as though the room had floated up to the roof and got stuck there ever since. As we climbed the stairs, rust began to flake off in my hands as I held on to the railing, and a few of the steps buckled slightly under my feet. This didn't feel safe.

Once we were on the gangway, I gazed across the factory floor. We must have been at least thirty feet high. It was then that something caught my attention—something I hadn't seen from down below.

Medical beds.

I didn't get a chance to look at them for very long, but I must have counted at least ten, hidden behind a row of computer terminals. Each bed was occupied by someone with more of those strange black marks, although the condition of their skin was far worse, as if an infection was spreading across their entire body. They looked in pain.

"Eyes straight, please," Gabriel ordered, stopping outside the elevated room. He produced a small key from his pocket and unlocked the door.

Harry and Martin released their grip on my arms and pushed me through the door as Gabriel opened it. I stumbled in and tripped over my own feet, my knees grazing against the metal floor. I scuttled across the room and cowered in the corner, clasping my hands around my legs.

The room was cold.

"Back in a minute," Gabriel smiled, slamming the door shut and locking it.

I sat in the corner of the room, shaking, my heart beating so hard I could feel my pulse through my fingertips.

After a few moments I rose to my feet, rubbed my knees, and looked around. The room was completely empty, with the exception of a single foldable chair in the middle and a video camera looking down on me from one corner. A single bare lightbulb hung from the ceiling. Apart from that, there wasn't much else to say. The walls were the same brushed steel I had seen from the outside, there were no windows to look out of, and the floor was made of black sheet metal, with a small crisscross pattern etched into it.

I patted my clothes down and sat in the chair. It wasn't particularly comfortable, and in a strange way it reminded me of the small plastic one I'd sat in back at kindergarten when I'd been told off for leaving the class.

With its uniform shape and featureless design, the room gave a feeling of being totally cut off from the outside world. There were no distractions in here. No external stimulation. Nothing to indicate the passage of time. In a strange way, the cool temperature and shiny metal walls made me feel as though I was frozen in a block of ice.

Then, like a blind person who learns to sharpen his other senses once deprived of sight, I began to detect things I wouldn't have picked up on normally: the subtle vibrations of Gabriel's footsteps on the gangway as they reverberated through the floor; the creaking sound of the metal staircase as he descended it; the muffled conversations of people downstairs. When I shut my eyes, I could almost visualize the scene in my mind, like a disembodied observer looking down on the world from above.

I wanted to look at the note in my pocket, but I had my own disembodied observer to worry about, looking down on from above—the video camera. So I rotated my chair to face the other direction and carefully slid the paper out of my pocket, being sure not to use any exaggerated movements. From behind, I hoped I just looked like I was itching my leg.

"What part of 'get out of the car' didn't you understand?" it said.

"There wasn't an opportunity!" I whispered under my breath.

"Quiet," the note said, rewriting itself. "There's no need to speak—I can read your thoughts, remember?"

"Please—what is happening to me?" I asked in my head. "What do these people want?"

"That might be a little too much for you to take in at the moment," the note said. "It's not an easy thing to explain ..."

"Try me," I thought.

"Look, we don't have much time, but here's a few things you need to know. Firstly—no matter how bad this all seems, you are in no danger. Secondly, these people are probably going to ask you a series of questions. Answer them truthfully. And thirdly—please be assured that we're working on getting you out of there as quickly as possible."

"Questions?" I asked. "What sort of questions? Are they going to ask me about you? About these notes? What if I don't know the answer?"

"I guarantee you will be able to answer every single question with ease. As for asking about the notes—well, you heard them. They already know how we're communicating with you, so I doubt they'll bring it up. Now put this away— somebody's coming."

The note was right—I could feel the room vibrate slightly from an approaching set of footsteps, walls pulsating like a beating heart. I folded up the paper, stuffed it in my trouser pocket and listened.

Footsteps.

Silence.

A key in the lock.

Click.

Handle turning.

I looked up at the door as it opened. Gabriel stepped inside. He had removed his suit jacket and rolled the sleeves of his shirt up. He still looked smart, and his appearance made me recall those photos you see in the paper of politicians visiting a construction site, trying to look like they could muck in with everyone else. He didn't acknowledge me as he entered.

Gabriel was followed into the room by the smaller, balding man I'd seen outside. Holding his clipboard under one arm, he was dressed exactly the same as earlier. Lab coat. Shirt and tie. Tennis shoes. In his left hand he held a black briefcase. He closed the door behind him with a click and leaned his back against it, lowering the case to the floor.

"Richard Alexander Henley," Gabriel said, pacing slowly round me like a shark circling a swimmer in the middle of the ocean. "Forty-two years old, born in London, divorced three years ago from wife Rebecca, no children, employed as an accountant for the last fifteen years at Randell Clark Fitzpatick, no criminal record."

I followed Gabriel around the room with my eyes as he spoke, saying nothing.

He stopped walking and looked at me with his intense blue eyes. "Correct?" he said.

I nodded.

"Good. Now I'd like you to meet a friend of mine. The man standing by the door is Doctor Naylor."

The doctor took a couple of steps forward, removed a pen from his breast pocket, and began making a few notes on his clipboard.

"Doctor Naylor is going to ask you a few questions," Gabriel continued. "I want you to answer them as best you can."

"Q-Questions?" I said.

"Yes."

"What sort of questions?"

"Just a few simple things about yourself," Doctor Naylor cut in, still jotting a few things down. "Memories from your childhood, things about your job, people you've known in the past, that sort of thing."

"But…why?"

"Shall we begin?" said Gabriel, inspecting the back of his right hand.

"Okay," the doctor said, "first of all—can you tell me your favorite color?"

I opened my mouth to speak, but nothing came out.

"My…favorite color?" I eventually managed.

"Yes."

"Why would you want to know that?"

"Just answer him," Gabriel said, his voice flat.

Despite feeling a little confused, I didn't really see any harm in revealing this, so I told them it was blue.

"That's correct," Doctor Naylor said, making a note on his clipboard.

"Correct?" I said. "But…how can a question like that have a wrong answer?"

Gabriel stopped inspecting his hand and looked at me.

"Richard," he said, "I'm not sure you're completely familiar with how this sort of interrogation works, so let me just clarify it for you: We ask the questions, you answer. That is it. At no point do you ask a question, and we answer. Understand?"

"Yes," I said, trying to keep my answer as short as possible.

"Continue," Gabriel said to the doctor, walking over to lean against the wall to my right. Despite the room being identically proportioned all the way round, the area he stood in seemed to have a different sense of gravity, as if light and sound wanted to behave unnaturally wherever he stood.

"Do you smoke?" the doctor asked.

"Not really. Well, sometimes. I'm not a big smoker, but…"

"'Sometimes' will do," Gabriel said.

"The scar on your face," the doctor said. "Tell me how you got it."

I told them about the time I crashed my go-kart when I was a teenager, but again, I didn't understand why that would be important.

"So you're not into racing?" the doctor said.

"Racing? What, like on television?"

"No, no. I mean, you don't race cars yourself?"

I shook my head.

"Excellent." The doctor sounded excited.

"Thoughts so far?" Gabriel said.

"He smokes, his full name is correct, and he's not a racing car driver," the doctor summarized, writing a few more notes on his clipboard. "Those three things narrow it down a lot—particularly the career."

"I don't believe it," Gabriel said, looking at me again with one of his intense stares. "So he could be the one?"

"I still need to ask him a few more questions, but the chances are very good."

Over the next half an hour or so the doctor continued to ask me a series of increasingly bizarre questions about my past: What were my grades like at school? Did I like Marmite? What year did my father die? Had I ever been skiing? What were my opinions on abortion? How many sugars did I put in my tea? The questions ranged from deeply personal to utterly inane, and I had trouble seeing what purpose my disconnected answers could serve anyone. I came to the conclusion that I was in the company of lunatics—it was the only explanation.

"I have just a few final questions," Doctor Naylor eventually said, "and it is especially critical that you answer these carefully. Are we clear?"

"We're clear," I replied. I couldn't really describe how I felt at this point. I was still nervous, but somehow the doctor's bizarre line of questioning made me feel increasingly irritable. Defiant.

"Tell me—did you ever know a girl called Alice?"

"Alice?"

"Yes. Alice Everett. And I'm talking a while back, perhaps when you were at university."

"What has this got to do with Alice?"

"Just answer the question."

The girl had been dead for years, so like everything else I'd been asked so far, I didn't see the harm in telling the truth.

"Yes, I knew a girl called Alice," I admitted. "But that was years and years ago. We were dating for a while, but she died in an accident."

"An accident?"

"Yes."

"What sort of accident?"

"The laboratory she was in exploded."

"And what was she doing in the laboratory at the time?"

"I don't know. She studied quantum physics—the stuff she did was way over my head. All I know is that something went wrong during an experiment, and she was killed."

The doctor looked at Gabriel.

"If he answers this next question correctly, we've got our man," he said.

"What's Alice got to do with all this?" I asked again.

"Did they ever find Alice's body?" the doctor said, ignoring my question.

"You didn't answer me!" I said, standing up from my chair. "What's this got to do with Alice?"

Gabriel jolted forward from the wall, lunging toward at me the way a boxer moves to tackle his opponent.

"Hey!" he spat, placing his hands on my shoulders and pushing me down into the chair again. His face was no more than an inch away from mine, mouth screwed up as if he'd just drunk a cup of vinegar, eyes like two raging black holes sapping away at my spirit. At this distance, I got a good look at the scar on his cheek—roughly star shaped, it appeared to be completely colorless, as if it were absorbing all light and reflecting nothing back.

Gabriel didn't say another word, but then he didn't need to. Lifting his hands off me, he returned to the corner of the room and gave the doctor a nod to continue.

"I'll ask you again," the doctor said. "Did they ever find Alice's body?"

I let out a defeated sigh.

"It's funny," I said, looking up at them both. "I was thinking about Alice earlier today for some reason. Haven't thought about that girl for years, but today...I don't know. Something made me think of her. And now you're asking me if I ever knew her. Strange, don't you think?"

"Wait a minute," the doctor said. "Why did you think of her today?"

I hesitated for a moment.

"No reason," I replied.

"I see..." the doctor said, giving me a suspicious look. "Back to my original question then—did they ever find Alice's body after she was killed?"

"No, they never found her body—it was vaporized or something. The whole lab was completely blown to bits—they hardly found a trace of anything."

"It's him," the doctor said, walking over to Gabriel to show him the notes he'd made. "He's our guy."

"You sure?"

"One hundred percent positive," the doctor said. "Every question he's answered matches the profile we were given."

"I still want to test him, just to be … agh!"

At that moment, Gabriel winced in pain and clutched his face, dragging the doctor down by the shoulder as he reached out for support. He looked as though he'd suddenly been struck by an intense migraine, completely out of the blue.

"Easy," the doctor said, jamming his clipboard between his knees and grabbing both of Gabriel's arms to stop him falling to the floor. "Just let it pass."

Gabriel appeared to regain his composure quite quickly, but when he removed his hand from his face, I noticed the black mark on his cheek had gotten a little bigger, like a fresh ink stain pressed onto a piece of paper.

"You okay?" the doctor asked.

"Fantastic," Gabriel winced, taking a bottle of pills out of pocket and popping a couple in his mouth. "How do I look?"

"The condition is moving into the secondary stage," the doctor said, examining Gabriel's face closely. "Your medication isn't going to keep it at bay for much longer."

"Then we've got no time to lose," he replied, swallowing hard. "Let's test him right away."

"Are you sure that's necessary?" the doctor said. "I'm not quite sure how he'd react to the normal test conditions—if we're not careful, we may lose him."

"That's a risk I'm willing to take. We've got to be sure."

"Well, okay …" the doctor said, walking over to the briefcase he'd left by the door. He crouched down beside it, popped the latches free, and opened the case flat on the floor. Inside lay an assortment of medical implements pressed into a molded felt interior. Scalpels. Scissors. Pipettes. Vials of liquid. Drill heads. I watched as he ran his stubby index finger across the tools.

"How do you want to do this?" he asked.

"The same as we did with that other candidate," Gabriel replied. "Put him on a long lead and send him somewhere for a couple of hours. But somewhere nice, okay? If he really is who you think, I wouldn't want any harm to come to him ..."

"Agreed," the doctor said, prying a small syringe free from its compartment. He removed a small vial of liquid from another groove with his free hand.

"Now hold on a second," I said, slowly rising up from my seat and backing into the far corner of the room. "What are you going to do to me?"

"Relax," the doctor said, taking a couple of steps toward me. He pierced the syringe into the top of the vial and drew out an inch of clear liquid. "This is just a little something to help you sleep ..."

Ten

Dark.

Headache.

Arm sore.

Something cold pressed against my face.

Body aching.

Mechanical sounds.

As I stirred from my drug-induced sleep, I could feel each of my senses returning one after the other, like a computer activating its different systems during a laborious start-up procedure.

"Hey, mister!" came a voice. "You all right?" It sounded distant yet close at the same time. Male. Youngish.

I opened my eyes. For a few seconds I was unable to comprehend anything. I could see and touch and smell and taste, but my body stayed frozen in position, as if I needed to wait for an internal barometer to calibrate itself before regaining control. Until then, I was just a passive observer, a semi-conscious being unable to fully react to the world around me.

Once my body had completed the necessary adjustments, the first thing I realized was that I was lying facedown on a concrete floor, my left cheek pressed against the cool stony surface. The second thing I realized was that I was not alone—someone's hand was placed on my back, rocking my body back and forth as if to wake me.

"You okay?" the voice asked.

I let out a quiet groan and sat up, rubbing the top of my arm. It hurt like hell.

A man I didn't recognize was crouched down beside me, studying my eyes as though they were a complex equation he needed to solve. As the sound of his voice had suggested, he was young—probably mid twenties, with a thin face and a small build. He had a cleft chin, a regular sized mouth, and a broad nose, though his features appeared slightly flattened, as if his face was pressed against a sheet of glass. He wore a high visibility jacket, black jeans, and held a grubby white hard hat in his hand. Judging by the pink indentation across his forehead and the flattened state of his dark hair, it looked as though he'd just taken the hat off.

"Can you talk?" he asked.

I cleared my throat before telling him that I could.

"Let's get you up," he said, helping me to my feet.

I looked around, my joints creaking like taut leather straps as I turned to take in my surroundings. It didn't take me long to recognize where I was—I was standing on the ground floor of the factory, right next to the start of the disused production line I'd seen as I was brought in.

But something was different—this production line was fully operational.

I stared in amazement as various components were automatically assembled in front of me, suspended from the two rails overhead, and fed by an array of whirring conveyor belts and robotic arms. Up above, the previously broken gantry cranes were dancing a smooth mechanical ballet, lifting sheets of metal into position, screwing bolts into place, and soldering joints, blue sparks scattering across the floor like fairies disappearing into the ether.

I closed my eyes for a moment. Last night, this factory had been falling apart. Cables had been hanging from the ceiling, machinery was lying in decay, and the whole building looked as though it had been neglected for many years. Today I couldn't see a single piece of broken equipment, not a scrap of debris. Every machine was running like clockwork, every inch of the floor spotless. It was as though I was standing in a newly commissioned facility. The contrast to the factory I'd seen before was so stark that I was almost tempted to think this was a different building, but architecturally it was identical. As impossible as it all seemed, it looked as though this place had been completely renovated within the space of a few hours.

This was of course assuming I'd only been unconscious for a few hours—I actually had no idea how long I'd been asleep.

I took a couple of slow footsteps deeper into the factory, mouth open in shock, eyes still fixed on the production line. Here and there, a few workers were operating various pieces of equipment, adjusting the settings on machines, and examining computer readouts. Glancing down to the other end of the assembly process, I could see the finished product was a forklift truck, much like the derelict ones I'd seen lined up against the wall before. There was no sign of that strange, open-plan office area to the rear of the building, no trace of that sterile odor in the air, and no Gabriel.

"How you feeling?" the man said, placing his hard hat back on his head.

"Erm…fine, I think…" I replied, twisting a few creases out of my back. "My head hurts a bit, but I think I'll be ok."

"Glad to hear it—you had me worried there for a second."

"What happened?" I said, rubbing the back of my head.

"You tell me," the man replied. "I was just carrying out my normal safety check on section two, and there you were, lying on the floor unconscious. Took a couple minutes before you woke up."

"A couple of minutes?"

"I was just about to call an ambulance. How'd you get in here anyway?"

"I'm not sure," I said, looking down at my watch. Ten in the morning. "Tell me —what day is it?"

"What day? It's Friday."

"Friday…?"

"The first of December."

That couldn't be right. If that were true, then I'd only been unconscious for about six hours. How was it possible for an entire factory to be renovated in such a short period of time?

Then I remembered the note in my pocket. I pulled it out in the hope it would provide some sort of explanation, but it was blank.

Typical.

"Where's Gabriel?" I said, folding the note up again.

"Gabriel?" the man said. "Who's Gabriel?"

"He's um … He's …" I realized as I spoke that I had no idea who he was. "Okay, let me put it another way. Have you seen a group of men around here? Wearing white coats? Black marks on their faces?"

"Can't say that I have," the man said, pushing his hat back to scratch his hairline. "Now, if you don't mind, I really need to escort you from the building."

"Oh, of course."

"Rules, you understand," he said, rolling his eyes in an almost apologetic way. "It's not safe for you here."

As we walked away from the production line, it occurred to me how terribly polite this man had been to me so far, considering the circumstances. For all he knew, I could have stumbled into this place drunk last night and fallen asleep on the floor.

He led me over to the red loading bay door I'd been dragged through only a few hours ago, tugging it open a few feet with both hands to let me out.

"Sorry to have bothered you," I said, stepping out onto the wharf, my face suddenly bathed in morning sunlight.

"No problem," the man smiled, closing the door behind me.

I stood alone for a moment to think. This was quite confusing—had I been released? And after all the effort made to catch me last night, why would this be? Was I not the person they were looking for after all? Maybe I'd failed whatever test they were going to do to me while I was unconscious. Whatever had happened, I was glad Gabriel and his strange associates had finally decided to leave me alone.

The weather outside was cool but bright, sky blue, sun shining faintly from behind a thin brushstroke of white cloud. A gentle breeze sent ripples across the bay, boats bobbing up and down, water lapping against the edge of the pier. In front of me, a row of small fishing vessels were moored along the waterfront with baskets of fresh seafood on display, and all around people were wandering between the boats, browsing the catch and helping themselves to tasting samples. It was a wonderfully rustic scene, but something was bothering me about what I saw—I thought this place had been abandoned years ago. It had certainly looked that way last night with all the dilapidated boats rotting in the water and crumbling warehouses lining the pier, but today all the buildings looked immaculate, all the boats more than seaworthy. I even spotted the odd yacht in the distance.

"Hey, you there!" a man called out. "You want to buy some fish?"

The voice sounded like the plumbing of an old house. It belonged to a man standing in front of a nearby boat, maybe in his fifties or sixties, with craggy eyes, red cheeks, and a short white beard that yellowed around the pipe sticking out of his mouth. He wore a thick, navy blue jumper, waterproof trousers, and a cap. Although I often shied away from stereotyping people based on their appearance, in this instance I guessed he was probably a fisherman.

"Who me?" I replied, pointing to myself as I walked toward him.

"Got some lovely fresh sea trout today," the man said, his pipe wedged deep into the side of his mouth as he spoke.

I stopped by the boat and cast my eyes across the baskets of fish laid out before me. The air had a salty taste to it, the smell of the sea clearing my head with every breath I took.

"I'm ok, thanks," I said. "But do you mind if I ask you a question?"

"Sure."

"How long has this market been here?"

"Well, I'm not sure," the fisherman replied, turning to serve a lady who was pointing at a rather large haddock. "It's been here as long as I have, I know that. And I've been here a while. Before then, I couldn't say."

"I could have sworn this place was closed down years ago," I said, glancing up and down the dock for any sign of my car. I couldn't see it.

"What?" the fisherman said, sliding his pipe over to the other side of his mouth as he picked up the haddock and began wrapping it in newspaper.

"Yeah, I remember hearing something about it on the news at the time. Didn't some big company shut this place down?"

"You sure you're thinking about the right place?" the fisherman said, tying the parcel together with a little string and handing it to the lady. She gave him a few coins and walked away with the fish sticking out of her handbag.

"Fairly sure," I said, fumbling around my pocket for my cigarettes. I put one between my lips and lit it.

"Well, you can ask around," the fisherman said, gesturing to the rest of the market with his pipe, "but I'm sure everyone will tell you the same thing. This place has been around for years."

My conversations with a few of the other fishermen seemed to support his version of events rather than mine. Apparently, there *had* been a time when a large corporation wanted to take over the market, but the local residents successfully petitioned the council to step in and protect it. Ever since then, the market had continued to sell fresh seafood to the hundreds of people who visited it every morning, and no company would ever be able to buy it, as it was technically owned by the general public and not available for sale at any price. I was surprised this story had escaped me—I read the newspaper every day and took a keen interest in these sorts of public victories. How had I missed it?

I spent a few minutes describing my car to passersby in case anyone had seen it around, but no one had. I was told the wharf was closed to all traffic, so it was unlikely to be nearby. I persisted a little longer in my search, walking to the entrance and glancing up and down the neighboring streets, but it was no use—the Nissan had vanished.

I decided to just get a taxi home and worry about it later. What I needed now was a long shower, a change of clothes, and a good cup of tea. Maybe then I'd be able to get my thoughts in order and decide my next course of action.

I wasn't sure where exactly in London I was, but after turning down a few side streets I stumbled upon a main road. A few minutes later I was sitting in a black cab, heading back to my flat.

"There's one thing," I said to the taxi driver, suddenly remembering about my missing wallet. "I don't have any cash on me."

"Oh really?" the taxi driver replied, looking at me in his rear-view mirror.

The driver was probably in his early forties, with medium length brown hair parted in the middle, pale skin, and a silver stud through his left earlobe. He had a stumpy nose, a weak chin, and his eyes were obscured by a pair of dark sunglasses. A touch overweight, he wore a light blue t-shirt and a gold chain round his neck.

"Yeah, my wallet got stolen last night," I explained, "but I've got some money at home I can pay you with." I hoped he didn't mind—in my experience, a lot of cabbies didn't like being kept waiting at the end of a journey.

"That's terrible," the driver said, his expression visibly changing into a look of concern. "Didn't think that sort of thing happened anymore…"

"What sort of thing is that?"

"Are you sure you didn't just lose it? I mean, no one really steals stuff these days, do they?"

"What?"

The driver took his eyes off the road a moment to look round at me. "Come on, don't you read the papers? They've just knocked down another prison because they can't fill it. Crime rates are rock bottom at the moment…"

"They are?"

"I read that there's only a couple of jails left now, and most of the inmates are really old. I think they were convicted before the government's social equality initiatives were launched or something."

"That's impossible," I said. "I thought crime was getting worse."

"Maybe where you're from," the driver said, "but here in London they're even talking about reducing the numbers of police officers on the streets. We just don't need 'em."

I slumped back in my seat and looked out of the window at the passing blur of traffic and people as I headed home. Was I having some sort of bizarre dream? First I wake up in a factory that had somehow been renovated to perfection overnight, then I find out a fishing market I'd thought had closed down was actually open for business, and now an unusually compassionate taxi driver was telling me that crime was virtually nonexistent.

What was going on here?

I lived in the East End of London, about halfway up an modern, eight-story apartment block that was not unlike many of the other modern apartment blocks that kept appearing everywhere these days. The building was probably no more than five years old, yet it was already beginning to look dated. My flat had one double bedroom (meaning it was just large enough to accommodate a double bed if you weren't that fussed about having a wardrobe), a small lounge, a kitchen and a bathroom. I think there was also a utility cupboard somewhere, but it hadn't been opened for a long time. As I understood, all the flats in the block were of a similar layout. It was cramped, with thin walls and windows that rattled every time a truck drove past, but the mortgage was affordable and the neighbors were okay most of the time.

I'd moved into my flat a few weeks after getting divorced. Having been born in East London, there was something quite comforting about returning to the familiar streets of my childhood, especially after the trauma of splitting up. And whilst the relationship with my wife had changed over time, evolving into something I no longer recognized, at least I could rely on the area I grew up in to remain the same.

"Here we are," the driver said, slowing down as we turned into my road. "Which house is it?"

I looked out of the window to show him the apartment block, but it was nowhere to be seen. Instead, the road was lined with a number of large, detached houses. Georgian in style, each house was three stories high, with a panelled front door in the center and large rectangular windows. Two smaller dormer windows were set into slanted, gray slate roofs, each of which had chimneys on either side. Despite being the same design, every house felt unique, as if the owners had taken great care to give their home a sense of identity. Walls were painted in a wide variety of faded pastel colors, gardens were presented in different ways, and the front doors ranged from glossy black to bright red.

"I think you've got the wrong street," I said, looking up at the magnificent sycamore trees on either side of the road. They must have been well over a hundred years old, the sunlight twinkling between the bare, antler-like branches as they towered into the sky.

"Well this is the address you gave me," the driver said, pulling over to the side of the road and checking his meter. "Carroll Avenue."

"But it can't be," I said, pressing my face to the glass. "There aren't two Carroll Avenues are there? You sure this is the right one?"

The driver swiveled round in his seat to look at me. "Positive."

I was just about to ask again if there was any way he could have been mistaken when I noticed something a little further down the road, parked outside one of the houses in the driveway.

It was a Nissan Silvia.

I looked at it in silence for a second. Nissan Silvas weren't exactly common these days. Was that my car, or was this an amazing coincidence?

The driver lifted his sunglasses up and rested them on the top of his head to look at me directly

"You all right?" he asked, narrowing his eyes.

"Um…yes. Yes, I'm fine," I said, rubbing the ends of my index fingers into the corners of my eyes. "Would you mind pulling up outside that house with the gray car in the drive?"

"Sure," the driver nodded, edging the taxi forward a few yards.

As we stopped in front of the Nissan, I glanced down at the number plate. No doubt about it—this was my car. Why was it parked here, outside a strange house? And what had happened to the street anyway? If this was Carroll Avenue, where was my apartment block? And the old petrol station opposite that was always closed? And the multistory parking lot that always had the same battered vehicles inside? I mean, it was certainly heartwarming to see everything around me looking so much more picturesque and homely, but at the same time I could feel the color draining out of my face as I tried to comprehend the transformation. How was it possible for an entire street to be so different?

"This you?" the driver said.

"I…don't know," I said, still staring at my car. "I think so…"

"Look," the driver said. "I've been thinking. You look like you've had a rough day. And I'm sorry to hear about your wallet, so I'm going to waive the fare. Terrible thing, to think that happened to you…"

"Are you sure?" I said. "I mean, I can always…"

"No, no," the driver smiled, holding a hand up. "I insist."

"That's extremely generous of you," I said, opening the door to the taxi and stepping onto the street. "Thanks."

"No worries," he replied, flicking his sunglasses back down over his eyes.

I stood on the pavement and watched as the driver performed a swift three-point turn and drove off into the distance, whistling a cheerful tune to himself. Over on the other side of the road, an elderly man was watering a couple of hanging baskets outside his house. He seemed to notice me looking at him and lowered the hose to give me a wave.

"Morning!" he called out, before turning his attention toward a large flowerbed in the middle of his lawn.

"G-good morning!" I responded, almost automatically.

Further up the street, a group of schoolchildren were playing soccer in the middle of the road. There wasn't any traffic to speak of, so it was quite safe, and I watched for a moment as they chased each other around, trying to take control of the ball. Two coats had been laid a few yards apart on the curb, which I assumed were acting as goalposts, and it wasn't long before somebody scored. The ball bounced off the curb, ricocheted harmlessly off a parked car, and rolled along the ground toward me. I stopped the ball with my foot, picked it up, and tossed it back toward them.

"Thanks, Mr. Henley!" one of the children shouted.

I smiled at the boy, saying nothing, hands trembling slightly. How did he know my name?

I took a deep breath and looked round at the house my car was parked outside. It certainly looked like a nice place to live. To the left of the driveway was a bright green lawn, still rich with morning dew. It was bordered by colorful flowerbeds, thick shrubs and potted plants. A small pond lay near the rear corner of the garden, with clumps of reeds growing round the edges, and a twisting stone path weaved its way around everything like an elaborate piece of calligraphy.

I followed the path up to the house, arching my head back to take in the details of the structure as I approached it. Like the other houses in the street, it was Georgian in style, with pale cream walls and large rectangular sash windows arranged symmetrically either side of a shiny teal front door. The first floor comprised of four smaller windows, again arranged in perfect symmetry, and the roof was embellished with a stone cornice, which ran around the top of the building like a decorative crown.

I looked around to get my bearings. On the Carroll Street I knew, this is where the parking lot would have been.

As I climbed the three steps to the front door, I noticed some post sticking out of the letterbox. Hands still shaking, I took my glasses out from my jacket pocket and pulled a letter free to examine it closely.

It was addressed to me.

I dropped the letter and looked at the door. A traditional brass knocker was set in the center, molded in the shape of a lion's head, polished to a shiny luster. I lifted the heavy ring hinged in the animal's mouth and knocked twice.

No answer.

I knocked again and waited a couple of minutes, but still there was no response.

After a moment's hesitation, I reached for the handle and twisted it. To my surprise, it turned freely in my hand, and I found myself holding my breath as the door creaked open before me. I was amazed that a place like this would be left unlocked, but as I stepped inside, I noticed there didn't seem to be a keyhole or even a latch on the door anywhere, as if such a thing was unnecessary.

I closed the door quietly behind me and took a few cautious steps into the hallway. The first thing that struck me was a smell of fresh flowers, which were sitting in a vase on a small table to my left. I thought they might be carnations, but I wasn't quite sure.

The hallway had a solid wooden floor, magnolia walls, a white picture rail, and a high ceiling. To my right, a number of coats were hanging from an old-fashioned hat stand, with a few pairs of shoes tucked underneath a small, narrow bench. A large ornate mirror reflected a couple of oil paintings on the opposite wall. The paintings were beautiful landscape works, one depicting an overcast, highland vista, the other a busy village scene. A carpeted staircase led up to the first floor landing, which was appointed with delicately carved banisters.

I walked down to the end of the hallway, which split off in two different directions. The door to my left led into a spacious living room. Inside, a row of bookshelves ran along the back wall, brimming with a vast selection of leather-bound volumes, modern fiction, and tatty encyclopedias. In the center of the room, two antique leather sofas were arranged around a square coffee table, facing a handsome marble fireplace, and over by the window a round dining table was set with a gold candelabra and red placemats. A black, stand-up piano graced the far corner of the room, and a thick Turkish rug was spread across most of the floor, giving the room a cozy feel. There didn't seem to be a television or any other electrical equipment—in here, it seemed the entertainment came from books and music only.

The opposite door led to a kitchen, which was equipped with wooden cabinets, marble work surfaces, and a large iron stove. A central island was surrounded by four or five wooden stools, and few pots and pans dangled from a piece of apparatus that hung from the ceiling. Various jars of colourful ingredients were scattered in different places, and the whole room smelled of freshly baked bread. The sun broke in through a tall set of windows on the rear wall, which looked out onto the expansive greenery of the back garden. I felt as though I was looking at a photograph in one of those "these homes are way better than yours" magazines.

I wandered back along the hallway and began climbing the stairs. To my left, I noticed several framed photos hanging on the wall. I stopped and unhooked one to look at in more detail. It was a photo of me. They were all photos of me. Some showed me standing on podiums holding trophies; others were shots of me sitting in different cars, a triumphant fist in the air as if I'd just won a race. Replacing the photo carefully back on the wall, I could feel my legs weakening under me, and I found myself clinging on to the banister for support as I climbed the rest of the way to the landing.

My exploration of the first floor revealed a white-tiled bathroom, two small guest bedrooms decorated in neutral colors, and a large master bedroom. I walked into the master bedroom to investigate further. Roughly the same size as the living room downstairs, it contained three freestanding wooden wardrobes, a solid oak ottoman, and an elegant cream dressing table with three beveled mirrors and an upholstered stool.

The centerpiece of the room, however, was a luxurious four-poster bed. Made from dark wood and draped with pale green bed linen, it stood against the far wall, curtains half drawn around each side. Imposing in size and delicately carved, the bed reminded me of those elaborate ceremonial carriages used to transport royalty.

All of a sudden, something moved under the covers. Though my view was obscured, I could just about make out a woman lying asleep on the left side of the bed, her body curled under the green duvet like the gentle verge on the bend to a country lane.

"Erm … hello?" I said, taking a few steps forward.

The woman stirred slightly, straightened her legs, but didn't wake up.

I moved closer again.

"Hello?" I repeated softly.

"Mmmm …." The woman moaned. She raised her head from the pillow and looked at me over the edge of the duvet.

I stumbled back, nearly falling over my own feet in shock. I knew those eyes instantly. They were twenty years older than I remembered, but I knew them. They belonged to Alice—the girl I'd lost all those years ago.

For a moment I couldn't think. All I could do was stare at her in astonishment, eyes wide open, body frozen to the spot. Somehow, this was an older Alice, an Alice that looked the same age as me, as if she'd never been killed in that accident.

"Oh, hello," she yawned, pressing her pillow upright against the headboard and sitting up to look at me. "I didn't hear you come in. Was the race canceled?"

She still wore her blonde hair long, although now there were a few silvery streaks running through it. Her skin looked soft, with just a few extra wrinkles across her forehead and round her mouth, and her small nose hadn't changed one bit. The look in her eyes was exactly the same as I remembered it, as if a hundred different thoughts were buzzing around her mind at once.

I was so overcome with emotion I didn't stop to wonder how any of this was possible. I ran over to her side of the bed, dropped to my knees, and placed both hands on her shoulders, my eyes fixated on hers. Her skin felt smooth, her body warm.

"You okay?" she said, wiping a tear from my cheek.

It was at this moment that I realized I'd never quite accepted the fact that Alice was dead. Maybe it was because they'd never found her body, but part of me had always prayed she would some-how return. I'd often wondered what I would say to her if I ever saw her again, and there had been many times when I'd secretly played out the conversation in my mind, hoping one day that I'd be able to talk to her for real. Now was my chance.

"I'm having a very strange day," I said.

"Really?" she laughed. "And why is that?"

But I never got the chance to tell her because a split second later, she was gone forever.

ELEVEN

It happened without warning.

All around me, everything changed. Alice vanished before my eyes, the bedroom evaporated away, and the floor beneath my feet disappeared.

The next thing I knew, I was standing inside a multistory parking lot. The change was instantaneous, soundless, and for a moment I recalled the actor I'd flung between different television channels back at the hotel, altering his environment effortlessly with the flick of a switch.

I turned a few degrees to take in my surroundings, my eyes unable to move in their sockets. Cold, gray tarmac stretched in every direction, stained with black tire marks and motor oil. The low ceiling above my head was supported by several chipped concrete pillars, many of which had worn away to reveal a mesh of wire frame steel. A yellow door to a stairwell stood to my right, orange bulb flickering overhead, and a couple of old cars lay dormant in a few parking spaces, most likely unmoved for weeks. Everywhere was dimly lit, and the whole place smelled of exhaust fumes and petrol.

It took me a second to realize it, but I knew where I was. This was the parking lot on Carroll Avenue—at least, the Carroll Avenue I was familiar with.

"Welcome back," a voice breathed in my ear.

I recognized its velvety tone immediately, the hairs on my neck standing on end as the words drifted through me. But before I had a chance to react, something struck the side of my head, and everything went black.

TWELVE

“**I**s he awake yet?”

Gabriel’s voice reached out through the darkness and pulled me from my sleep as though it were uprooting a tree from the middle of a field. As always, he was softly spoken, with a relaxed tone and a gentle rhythm to his words, yet somehow his voice carried with it an underlying tension, piercing the recesses of my mind and arresting me with a deep feeling of anxiety.

“He is now,” Dr. Naylor replied, looking down at me as I opened my eyes.

It didn’t take long for me to realize where I was. I was lying face up on a medical bed; nostrils saturated with a familiar, sterile odor; eyes staring high up at a corroded metal ceiling. Unless I was mistaken, I was back at the factory, although for some reason it had returned to the condition it was in when I was first brought here. Run-down. Neglected. Falling apart.

I tried to move but my arms and legs were held securely in place by thick leather straps, my wrists and ankles locked inside cold steel shackles, fixed to the frame of the bed.

“Keep still,” the doctor said, scanning his eyes over a few computer printouts in his hand. “We’ve still got you hooked up.” He took a pen from his jacket pocket and began chewing on the end.

It was at this point that something dawned on me—something I’d sensed from the moment I’d regained consciousness but was unable to process until now.

I was completely naked.

I raised my head a couple of inches and looked down at my exposed body, my neck straining as it pressed against the thick leather strap wrapped around it. Various colored wires were clipped to my arms, feet, knees, elbows—even the tips of my fingers. The wires draped over the side of the bed and merged together into one thick cable, which in turn snaked across the floor and eventually connected up to a large databank towering against the far wall. From the corner of my eye, I could make out a number of other beds in the vicinity. Some were empty; others were occupied by unmoving, weak figures. Occasionally someone would let out a quite moan as if they were in pain, their hollow voice hanging in the air like a ghostly vapor.

I lowered my head again, took a deep breath, and thought about my surroundings. This place was familiar. I'd seen it before from above, back when I was being led into that metal room in the top corner of the building. This was the area hidden from the rest of the factory floor, buried behind a row of computer terminals and machinery.

I felt Gabriel's shadow pass over me as he approached the edge of the bed, his large hands tightening the strap around my neck. I couldn't see his face.

"He said don't move."

"This is encouraging," the doctor said, attaching the computer printouts to a clipboard at the end of the bed and placing his pen behind his ear. "No physical displacement, brain activity and genetic sequencing normal—looks like he's clean."

"Any idea where you sent him?" Gabriel asked.

"Yes—he's just spent the last few hours in a world of low crime, with a well-balanced population and good environmental ethics—it's actually somewhere we've been studying for a while to see if we can implement some of their social measures ourselves, as it happens. One of the more pleasant dimensions."

"Good," Gabriel said.

Pleasant dimensions? What were they talking about?

Amidst all the confusion, I found myself closing my eyes and thinking of Alice. The look in her eyes. The warmth of her body.

The softness of her skin. She had been right in front of me. She had touched my cheek. Was she real, or had it all been a dream?

"Hey!" Gabriel shook me by the shoulder. "Wake up. We've got some questions for you."

I opened my eyes. Doctor Naylor was standing at the other end of the bed, scanning through his notes again.

"Where's…Alice?" I wheezed. The leather strap pressing against my neck made it difficult to talk, but I had to know. It was all I cared about. It was everything. "What…what have you done with her?"

Suddenly a hand reached over my head and pulled my eyes back. Gabriel looked down at me, eyes narrow, lips open a crack to reveal his gritted, white teeth. The black mark on his face was a lot bigger than before, spreading right across his cheek and down the side of his neck.

"Now Richard, we've spoken about this," he said, his long fingers digging into the ridges of my eye sockets. "You don't get to ask the questions, remember?"

I wasn't frightened. The thought of Alice being alive had ignited a passion deep inside me, something I hadn't felt for a long time. And the thought that these people might have done something to her only turned that passion into an insatiable anger. I wanted answers.

"Fuck…you," I croaked.

Gabriel released his grip on my face, his lips curling into a thin smile.

"Fuck me?" he said, walking round the side of the bed. "Fuck me?"

"Gabriel…" the doctor said, throwing the clipboard down and rushing toward him. "Don't do anything stupid here now…"

Gabriel wasn't listening. He lunged over my chest and slammed his elbow deep into my ribs. A sharp pain shot through my body like a bullet, but for some reason it barely registered in my mind. I didn't flinch, I didn't cry out, and I didn't care whether he was going to do it again. All I cared about was knowing what had happened to Alice. All other concerns were secondary, including myself.

Gabriel lifted his elbow and leaned toward my face.

"Are we ready to talk yet?" he said.

"I'm … not telling you … shit," I gasped, "until you tell me what happened to her …"

"Wrong answer!" he said, readying himself to deliver another blow. His usually calm voice started to quiver with emotion. "Do you think you're the only one who's lost someone in all of this? Someone you cared about? Now, you're gonna tell us what we need to know, or I'll …"

"Wait!" the doctor said, pulling Gabriel away. "We can't afford to injure him!"

"Get off me!" Gabriel said, wrestling himself free from the doctor's grip.

"Listen," Doctor Naylor said, grabbing Gabriel by the shoulders. "Listen. I understand what you're going through, believe me, I do. Everyone here does. We all volunteered for this project in the hope it would bring someone back, didn't we? Now please, try to calm down …"

Gabriel shut his eyes and took a deep breath.

"I'm sorry," he said. "It's just that sometimes, when I think how we might be able to get everyone back, and then see this guy getting in the way … it just … becomes too much …"

"I know, Gabriel, I know. But this might go a lot quicker if we just tell him what he wants to know …"

Gabriel stared at the doctor.

"You're serious?"

"Sure. I mean—what harm can it do? He's not going anywhere. If he wants to know what happened to Alice, why don't we just tell him?"

Gabriel looked at me in silence for a moment. His eyes still had a burning intensity to them, but I didn't find them threatening anymore.

"Fine," he said, taking a couple of steps back. "But make it quick."

"Okay," the doctor sighed, collecting his clipboard from the end of the bed and smoothing his jacket down. "Now Richard—you wanted to know about Alice?"

"Where … is she?" I asked again.

"She's exactly where you left her—at home, in bed."

"But she…she disappeared!"

"No, *you're* the one who disappeared. At least, from her point of view."

"What?"

"You've just come back from another dimension," Gabriel said, his voice creeping into the conversation from somewhere outside my field of vision. "We sent you there this morning, and now we've brought you back."

"Another dimension?"

"Think of it as a parallel world," the doctor explained. "An alternate reality. That's where you've just been. The Alice you just met was the Alice from that dimension—a different version of the woman you once knew."

I thought about this for a moment. It sounded impossible, but after everything I'd seen over the last couple of days, could this be true?

A small noise came from the back of my throat as I struggled to speak.

"Is she okay?" I said eventually.

"She's fine," the doctor reassured me. "After you left, she went back to sleep. And when she woke up again, she thought seeing you was just a dream."

I frowned to myself. How did they know all this?

"We have the ability to monitor other dimensions directly from here," the doctor said, as if anticipating my next question. "Like a fly on the wall. But we can also interpret people's thoughts to tell us what they're thinking."

"That's nonsense," I said. "You mean to tell me you read her mind?"

The doctor nodded.

"That's right."

I laughed.

"Something funny?" Gabriel said, emerging from the shadows. "How else do you explain the notes you've been receiving? The ones that are somehow able to read your mind? Respond to everything that's happening around you? Do think that's magic, or could something else be at work there?"

I stopped laughing and looked at both of them.

"I don't know…" I admitted.

"It's the same technology," the doctor said.

"Any other questions?" Gabriel said impatiently. "Or are we done?"

"Just one," I said. "Why am I…naked?"

"We needed to check your body for any signs of this," Gabriel said, pointing to the black mark on his face.

"It's a condition that affects everyone who's ever traveled to another dimension," the doctor added, scratching the top of his balding head. "We call it Quantum Displacement Disorder. It's like an infection. And we're trying to find the cure."

"But…what's this got to do with me?

"Well, if our theory is correct, you should be immune."

"Immune? Why…would I be immune?"

"That's what we're trying to figure out," Gabriel said. "Now, I think it's our turn for some questions, don't you think?"

"Fine," I conceded.

"First of all," the doctor began, leaning over my face and shining a light in my eyes, "how do you feel?"

"How do I feel?"

"Yes. Do you have a headache? Ringing in the ears?"

"No. I feel okay."

"Are you absolutely sure?" the doctor said. "Nothing unusual at all? Pins and needles? Heavy breathing? Anything?"

I told him I felt normal.

"Okay. Next I want you to cast your mind back to the moment you returned to this dimension. Was the transition instantaneous, or did anything else happen?"

"Like what?"

"I can't really describe it. But you'd know it if you saw it."

"I didn't see anything. One minute I was with Alice; the next minute, I was standing in the parking lot."

"So what's the verdict?" Gabriel asked, taking a mobile phone out from his jacket pocket. "I need to give an update."

"Well, as you can see, there are no visual signs of any tissue degradation," the doctor said, grabbing a transparent chart from a table to his side and holding it up to the light, "and all genetic material remains a complete match to the samples we took before he left. He's in good health, all displacement tests are coming back negative, and it seems he didn't experience any interference during his trip."

"So he really is the right guy?" Gabriel said, raising his eyebrows.

"No doubt about it."

Gabriel put his hand to his mouth and coughed loudly for a few seconds—he didn't sound good.

"Ok," he said, wiping his mouth on the back of his hand. "Let him get dressed and take him back upstairs. I need to make a phone call."

Gabriel walked over to the far corner of the warehouse and punched a few numbers into his phone. At the same time, Doctor Naylor removed the wires attached to my body and unfastened the restraining straps. Up close, I could see the black mark on his face looked bigger too.

"Here," the doctor said, pulling my clothes out from under the medical table and handing them to me. "You can put these back on."

I snatched my shirt and trousers from the doctor and watched Gabriel from the corner of my eye as I got dressed. Although he had been the one to make the phone call, he appeared to be doing most of the listening now. It was frustrating—I was deliberately taking as long as possible putting my clothes on to eavesdrop, but he hardly spoke. All I could hear as I buttoned my shirt was the occasional "yes, sir," or "agreed"—whoever was on the other end of that phone must have been in charge. At one point I thought I heard the name "Russell," but I might have been mistaken.

"Come on," the doctor said, giving me a suspicious look.

I finished tying my shoelaces and got to my feet. For a split second I thought about making a run for the exit while Gabriel was distracted, but in my heart I knew I didn't have the strength. Someone would have caught up with me in no time.

Now that I was free to look around, I took the opportunity to inspect my surroundings. The medical bed I was lying on was one of about ten others, all of which were occupied by people in a far more advanced stage of this "infection" than anything I'd seen so far. The patient in the bed next to mine was hunched on his side, hands clutching his stomach, face and arms completely covered in the strange black marks. It looked as though he had been dipped in a vat of ink. The bed next to his was draped with a blue plastic sheet. I shuddered to think what was underneath it.

The doctor motioned me to follow him.

"You ready?" he said, collecting a stack of papers from a nearby workstation and flicking through them.

"I guess," I replied, taking a few steps toward him. In my peripheral vision I noticed Harry and Martin appear out of nowhere, following me at a discreet distance. A small pistol poked out of the rim of Harry's trousers, and I presumed Martin had a weapon to hand as well. Like everyone else, the marks on their faces appeared to be getting worse.

"Why is this happening to everyone?" I asked as we walked past a man barely distinguishable from his own shadow.

"That's what we're hoping to find out," the doctor said, shuffling the papers in his hands into a different order.

"So can you tell me more about what you're doing here?" I asked, walking a little faster to catch up with him. "I mean, traveling to other dimensions? Alternate realities? How the hell is all this possible?"

"I think we've told you enough," the doctor said.

I took one final drag of my second-to-last cigarette and dropped the butt to my feet, twisting it under my shoe and smearing a crescent of dark ash across the floor. I'd been locked away in the elevated room for almost two hours now. There wasn't much to do except smoke and think, but I barely noticed the time pass—the number of unanswered questions running through my mind was more than enough to keep me preoccupied.

Foremost of these questions was how I was going to get out of here. In a strange way, I felt a bit conflicted about wanting to escape—after all, they needed me to understand more about the mysterious condition affecting them. But I only had to think about how these people behaved toward me—how they'd murdered my other self—to realize I needed to get as far away from them as possible.

But how? The room only had one door, bolted from the outside, and the walls, although pretty thin, weren't exactly the sort you could break though. I looked up at the ceiling for a possible exit, but there were no signs of any conveniently placed trapdoors or ventilation ducts, and the floor was one large expanse of black metal, with no obvious means of dropping down to the factory floor below. And even if there had been—it would be a long fall.

I decided to go through my pockets to see if I had anything that could help me escape. In my jacket I found my packet of Marlboro Lights with one cigarette remaining, a cheap lighter, and my wallet. I placed them neatly on the chair in front of me as a soldier would arrange his kit for inspection, each item lined up perfectly with the one next to it.

Then something struck me—hadn't I lost my wallet in the restaurant last night? How had it ended up back in my jacket? I picked it up from the chair and turned it over in my hands, opening it to have a look inside—all of my bank cards were still present along with the token amount of loose change I always seemed to carry with me. It was as though it had never been taken.

Puzzled at its sudden reappearance, I placed the wallet back down on the chair and checked my trouser pockets. Inside, I found the notepaper I'd stashed away earlier. I unfolded it to see if anything helpful was written inside.

"Help is on the way," it said.

I could just about hear a distant murmur of voices but couldn't make out who was talking or what they were saying. I returned the note and all my other items to my pockets, walked over to the far wall, and pressed my ear to its cold surface to listen. One of the voices sounded like Gabriel, but his words were too muffled to pull out anything discernable. I strained my ears to see if I could hear anything at all, but it was useless. Just as I was about to give up, I felt someone suddenly touch me on the shoulder.

"Hey, Richard…" a female voice whispered from behind me. It had the same soft warmth as the last time I'd heard it, gently melting the silence in the room like the sun thawing a frozen lake.

Any other voice would have made me spin around on the spot immediately to identify the person, but I already knew who this was and found myself filled with a deep sense of calm. I stopped listening to the faint murmurs coming from outside, moved away from the wall, and turned slowly to face the girl who had just breathed my name.

Cassandra was here.

THIRTEEN

Her appearance was different to the last time I had seen her, but then this was someone who didn't exactly have a track record of dressing the same way—when I'd seen her in my office she'd worn a smart, pin-striped trouser suit, then later at the hotel she'd been dressed in a frilly chambermaid's uniform. Now, she was wearing dark jeans and trainers, with a tight, black leather jacket done up to her neck, fingerless woollen gloves, and a black scarf. Her face looked free of any makeup, there was no sign of any jewelry or accessories on her, and she wore her long brown hair down around her shoulders. Her stance had a real sense of purpose—shoulders back, legs straight, hands on hips, and her eyes had a bright alertness to them, darting from side to side as if she was trying to absorb everything as fast as possible.

"Cassandra?" I whispered, tilting my head quizzically. "What the hell are you doing here?"

"I've come to rescue you," she replied, taking a few quick steps back into the middle of the room and looking up at the video camera.

"Get away from there!" I said, pressing myself against the wall. "They'll see you!"

Cassandra lifted her arms and started waving.

"That's the idea," she replied, jumping up and down as she flung her arms about. "I need to get their attention."

"What!? You don't understand—these people are dangerous!"

She stopped jumping and looked at me.

"I know they are. But I need someone to unlock the door."

"You mean it's still locked?"

"Uh-huh."

I shimmied over to it along the wall and tried the handle. She was right—it wouldn't budge.

"I'm confused," I said. "How exactly did you get in?"

"I materialized in the middle of the room." The words sounded so blasé she might as well have told me she'd come here by bus.

"You what?"

"I said I materialized in the middle of the room," she repeated.

"Oh," I said, not really processing her answer. "You can do that, can you?"

"In a manner of speaking—yes," she replied, still waving her hands. "Listen—how much do you know about what's going on here?"

"I'm not sure," I said, stroking my fingers through my hair and rubbing the back of my neck. "I mean, they told me something about alternate realities and travelling to other dimensions, but I'm not sure I believed them. It's nonsense, right?"

Cassandra shook her head.

"I'm afraid it's the truth. In fact that's exactly where I've just some from."

"You've ... come from another dimension?"

"That's right."

I raised my eyebrows skeptically.

"I'm still not sure I believe all this."

"How else could I have appeared in the middle of a locked room?" she said, gesturing at the floor. "Or vanished from outside your office?"

"I don't know. Wait—is that how you disappeared from that hotel room too?"

"Yes—I was only supposed to be keeping an eye on you, but it turns out I'm not very good at doing it discretely. When you caught me, I had to get out of there."

I paused for a moment to think about what Cassandra had said. If I'd thought she was strange when I'd met her in my office, this was something else altogether. Still, as crazy as it all sounded, something in the back of my mind urged me to trust her. Something instinctive.

"Okay," I said, looking at her straight in the eyes. "Let's say I believe you for a second. If you've really just come here from another dimension, where are your black marks?"

"Black marks?"

"Yeah. Apparently I'm the only one who can travel between worlds without suffering from this…weird disease thing."

"You mean Quantum Displacement Disorder?"

"That's right. They said that everyone who goes to another dimension gets sick. Starts turning black. Everyone apart from me, that is."

"Well, that's not strictly true," Cassandra said.

"It's not?"

"I'm also unaffected."

"And why's that?"

Cassandra sighed.

"I'll explain when we get out of here," she said, waving her arms at the camera again. "That is, *if* we get out of here…"

"Can't you just click your fingers and take us someplace else?" I asked. "Like you did in the hotel room?"

"Unfortunately not. These guys have got some serious technology preventing any inter-dimensional manipulation around you, and we're only just figuring out how it works. That's why it's taken me so long to get here. If we want to get out of here, we're going to have to do it the old-fashioned way."

"What's the 'old-fashioned way'?"

"Out the front door."

"The front door…on the other side of the warehouse?"

"Yes."

"Past all the men?"

"Yes."

"Past all the men with guns?"

"If I can get someone's bloody attention, yes."

"And that's your plan?"

"Yes."

"And then what?"

"Your car," she said. "It's still parked outside."

"No good," I said, shaking my head. "I don't have the keys."

"Don't worry about that," Cassandra smiled. She stopped waving at the camera, pulled my car keys out from her pocket, and dangled them in front of me.

"Where did you get those?" I said.

"We took them from you earlier," she replied, putting them away again. "Remember?"

"But how did you get hold of them?"

"People aren't the only things we can move through different dimensions," she replied, waving at the camera once more. "We can localize the effect to specific objects as well."

"Like my wallet?"

"And notepaper," she added.

"Well, at least I got my wallet back," I said.

"Actually…we took that away again," Cassandra winced.

"You did what?" I said, checking my pockets. She was right—my wallet was gone. "You gave my wallet back and then took it away again?"

"Yes—it was a test. Before I came here, we needed to see if…"

Suddenly, a loud commotion came from outside.

"Gabriel!" a voice echoed from downstairs. It sounded like the doctor. "Get over here now!"

"There—that did it," Cassandra said, lowering her arms. "You ready to get out of here?"

"Yes, but—how exactly do you intend on getting to the car?"

"Leave that to me," she said, adjusting the collar of her leather jacket. "But when I say 'now', brace yourself. And get ready to run."

I could hear Gabriel shouting something from downstairs, but there was too much other background noise to hear what he was saying. The room began to vibrate as several footsteps clanged up the metal stairs outside.

"What are you going to do?" I said.

"You'll see," she replied.

I quickly pulled the notepaper out of my pocket and looked at it. "Trust her," it read.

I barely had a chance to stuff the note away again before the door to the room swung open and Doctor Naylor burst in, closely followed by Gabriel. They both looked out of breath, sweat pouring down their faces, hair damp as though they'd just come in from the rain. Their condition looked even worse then before. Gabriel's eyes now looked out at me from two inky black recesses in his face, and the doctor's marks had now spread halfway over the top of his balding head. They both looked completely exhausted. The disease must have been starting to affect them beyond their physical appearance.

Behind them, a number of guards were standing on the gangway, blocking our exit. Harry and Martin were amongst them, their guns at the ready.

"I'm impressed," the doctor huffed, looking at Cassandra. "I thought it would take you much longer to bypass my shield…"

"You two know each other?" I asked, looking between them.

"It was only going to be a matter of time before we figured it out how to get here," Cassandra replied, ignoring my question.

"True," Gabriel said, stepping forward, "but I bet you haven't figured out how to get back out again—I'm told that part is a lot trickier."

She looked at Gabriel in silence.

"Am I right?" he continued, taking another step forward. A few of the men on the gangway began to file into the room behind him. "Have your team had any success with manipulating matter inside the quantum shield other than those stupid notes you've been sending him?"

"Actually, we've just managed to send his wallet through and bring it back again," Cassandra said.

Doctor Naylor laughed.

"Bravo!" he said, clapping his hands sarcastically. "So you've managed to work out how to move small objects in and out of this dimension too! Tell me—how does this 'breakthrough' help you escape exactly?"

"Well, it means this shield of yours is actually more of a net."

"Excellent observation," the doctor said. "But that doesn't mean you can remove yourselves from this dimension."

"No," Cassandra agreed. "But it does mean we can remove the bolts holding up this room."

"W-what?" the doctor gasped, his expression drooping as though someone had just let all the air out of his face.

"Now!" she said, wrapping her arms around my waist.

As if on command, the whole room suddenly went into freefall, crashing down to the floor below in an explosion of sound, the force of the impact throwing up a thick cloud of dust. Walls buckled outwards and split apart, the ceiling cracked straight down the middle like a broken eggshell, and the door sheared itself free from its hinges, narrowly missing Doctor Naylor and Gabriel as it flew through the air. It was as though an earthquake had just struck. Outside, the gangway began to collapse, and I watched as several men desperately clung to the railings as the rickety metal structure toppled forward and crashed through a row of computer equipment below.

Then silence.

For a brief moment I lay on the rubble disorientated, staring at the thick particles of dirt hanging in the air, listening to the sounds around me.

Someone coughing.

A man crying out in pain.

Something metal clanging against the floor.

A crackle of electrical static.

Now I realized why Cassandra wanted to get everyone's attention—once they were in that room, she'd been able to knock everybody out in one go, including Gabriel and the doctor. I looked around to see if I could see them anywhere, but the dust in the air was too thick.

Suddenly I felt someone grab my hand, and the next thing I knew I was being pulled to my feet.

"Come on!" Cassandra shouted, kicking a piece of dislodged flooring to one side and leading me out of the room through the buckled doorway. She was extremely agile, vaulting over two unconscious guards and ducking through the doorway in one swift movement.

We sprinted across the factory, sidestepping the loose piping hanging from the ceiling and jumping over debris as fast as we could. Cassandra appeared to be a lot fitter than me and ran ahead, flinging the loading bay door open with both hands and dashing toward my car. I wasn't sure how long it had been since I'd been brought here again, but outside it was nighttime again.

"Get after them!" Gabriel yelled from behind me as I approached the exit. I took a moment to look back—he was trapped under a piece of metal, staring at me through a gash in the wall.

Harry and Martin leapt to their feet, climbing out of the rubble and giving chase.

"And don't let them out of your sight!" the doctor shouted, stumbling out from under the collapsed gangway. "We'll monitor you from here!"

"Will you hurry up?" Cassandra shouted back to me, opening the driver side door of the car and getting in.

I ran around to the passenger side door, which Cassandra had already kicked open for me from the inside. Realizing they weren't going to catch us in time, Harry and Martin sprinted directly toward their Range Rover, which was still parked a few meters in front of the Nissan, blocking the way forward.

"Wait a minute," I said, hesitating as I placed one foot in the car. The last time I'd got in here with someone I thought I knew, they ended up betraying me. "How do know I can trust you?"

"Are you serious?" Cassandra screamed, starting the engine and looking round as the Range Rover flicked its headlights on. "I just saved your arse!"

"I know, but—can you at least tell me who you are?"

"I'm your daughter," Cassandra snapped. "Now will you get in the fucking car?"

Fourteen

"**M**y daughter?!" I said, sliding into the passenger seat and slamming the car door. "What the hell are you talking about?"

"Can this wait?" Cassandra snapped, wrestling the car into reverse and stamping on the accelerator.

My body lurched forward as we began to reverse along the cobbled wharf, and I soon found myself scrambling for the seatbelt as we bumped along at high speed away from the factory. Cassandra stretched her arm across the back of my seat and looked over her shoulder at the road behind, skilfully nudging the steering wheel left and right to compensate for the uneven surface. In front of us, Harry and Martin had already caught up, the bumper of their Range Rover scraping hard against front of the car like one bull locking its horns with another.

"Hold on!" she said, reaching down for the gear stick. She slipped the car into neutral, yanked the steering wheel hard to the right and pulled on the handbrake, letting the rear wheels lock in a cloud of smoke. The car immediately spun round with a deafening screech, and once we were facing the right direction, she dropped the handbrake, threw the car into second gear and hit the gas. Next thing I knew, we were speeding away from the Range Rover, mounting a pedestrian walkway to the side of the wharf and leaping down a row of steps to the street below. The chassis crunched underneath us as we bounced onto the tarmac and skidded past an oncoming truck to get on the right side of the road.

"Are you crazy?" I screamed over the sound of angry car horns, desperately fumbling with my seatbelt until it clicked into the lock. "Be careful!"

"We need to lose them!" Cassandra said, looking in her rear-view mirror. "As long as they know where we are, they can keep that shield around us!"

"English?" I said

"I can't get us out of this dimension until those two are off our back!"

I swiveled round in my seat to see the Range Rover jump down onto the road behind us and maintain pursuit. They weren't far behind.

"Are you really my daughter?" I said, turning to face Cassandra. Cassandra nodded.

"Who's your mother then?"

"The woman you went out with at university," she replied, screeching the car around a corner at high speed. "Alice Everett."

"But I thought Alice was … I mean … she was killed in a …"

"The experiment she was working on went wrong, but it didn't kill her," Cassandra said, glancing away from the road to look me in the eyes. "It sent her through to another world. The world I'm from."

"You mean she's alive?"

"She's alive."

For a moment I couldn't think. I couldn't speak. All sound stopped. The roar of the engine, the squeal of tires—everything dissolved away into silence. My arms fell by my side, my legs went numb, and my head fell into the back of the seat. It was as if all the muscles in my body had suddenly turned to syrup. I let out a deep breath, shut my eyes, and waited for my senses to return.

"You all right?" Cassandra said.

"Yes … Yes." I placed a hand on the dashboard to steady myself as we shot through the traffic ahead. "I'm … I mean … can I see her?"

"That all depends on whether I can get us out of here," she replied, swerving to avoid a coach in the middle of the road.

"Right," I said, shuddering as we flew through a set of red lights, barely avoiding a passing motorbike. "Just…tell me one more thing—how old are you?"

"Twenty-one."

I did the math in my head. If that was true, it meant Alice had been pregnant with our child just before the accident. Which was possible. But why didn't she tell me? And if she'd survived, why didn't she make any effort to contact me?

"By the way," Cassandra said, slowing the car down to take a tight corner. "I know it probably hasn't seemed like it, but I just want you to know—I'm really excited to finally meet you, Dad."

The words made my skin tingle. Despite the impossibility of it all, I didn't doubt that Alice was this girl's mother—her skin was pale and soft like Alice's, her eyes were brimming with that unmistakeable curiosity, and she'd definitely inherited the same small nose. I'd known there was something special about Cassandra the moment I'd laid eyes on her. But could I really be her father?

All of a sudden, Cassandra steered the car to the left, mounting the pavement to avoid a bus blocking the way ahead and smashing through a row of empty tables outside a café.

"Look out!" I said, digging my fingers into the bottom of my seat as we narrowly missed a group of screaming pedestrians.

Cassandra said nothing, swerving the car back onto the road and checking her rearview mirror. I looked over my shoulder again. The Range Rover was still right on our tail.

"Jesus," I said, grabbing on to my seatbelt to make sure it was still there. "Why can't they just leave us alone?"

Cassandra didn't answer. She appeared to be having trouble changing into fifth gear, and the car was beginning to slow down as she struggled with the gear stick.

"Fuck!" she said, looking under the dashboard at her feet. "The clutch is stuck!"

"Shit—sorry!" I said. "When it does that, you need to…"

"Too late!" Cassandra cried, flicking her eyes up to the rearview mirror and clenching her teeth.

I looked round. The Range Rover was right alongside us—Harry behind the steering wheel, Martin leaning out of the passenger window holding a gun. He steadied his aim and fired two shots—the first bullet shattering the rear window and showering the backseat with glass, the second ricocheting off the roof.

"Step on it!" I said, cowering lower into the seat.

"I got it, I got it…" Cassandra replied, finally slotting the car into fifth gear and pressing her foot on the accelerator.

But as we started to pull away, the Range Rover swerved straight into the side of us, slamming its front wing into the rear passenger door and scraping along the side of the car. I wrapped my arms around my head as both vehicles spun out of control, the sound of crunching bodywork and screeching tires erupting in my ears.

"Come on, come on!" Cassandra yelled, her arms tangling in front of her as she struggled to keep hold of the steering wheel. Amazingly, she managed to wrestle the car back under control, straightening it up in a matter of seconds and accelerating away.

"Holy shit!" I said, looking back as the Range Rover's momentum sent it veering across the road and sideswiping a row of parked cars before getting back on our tail. That maneuver had just given us significant breathing space. "Who taught you to drive like that?"

"You did," Cassandra smiled. "At least, another Richard Henley did…"

"Uh huh," I said, taking the notepaper from out of my pocket. "And I assume he's the one who's been sending me these?"

"No, he's a different one. I've met quite a number of versions of you over the years, you know."

"What?"

"I'll explain later," Cassandra said.

I was just about to ask another question, but just as I opened my mouth to speak, an articulated truck suddenly materialized a few meters in front of us, its trailer stretching from one side of the road to the other. There was no way we could stop before hitting it.

"Duck!" Cassandra yelled, steering the car toward the gap between the front and rear wheels of the trailer. She grabbed the back of my head with her free hand and pushed it under the dashboard, sliding down in her own seat and covering her face.

My ears were filled with the deafening sound of shearing metal as the car passed beneath the truck, the underside of the trailer slicing the entire top half of the car away as though it was opening a can of sardines. I sat up and looked around as we emerged on the other side—we were still moving, but the car had completely lost its roof and windshield.

"What the hell was that?" I said, brushing some broken glass off my lap.

"The note!" Cassandra shouted over the sound of the wind in our ears. "Does it say anything?"

I unfolded the paper in my hands. Something was written down.

"It says they think we're being moved between dimensions to try to slow us down!" I read aloud.

"Perfect…" Cassandra scowled, tucking her hair into the collar of her jacket to stop it blowing in her face.

I checked behind us again. Just as suddenly as it had appeared, the truck vanished into thin air again, allowing the Range Rover to pass through unscathed.

"How many of these bloody dimensions are there?" I asked.

"An almost infinite amount," Cassandra replied.

Suddenly the road ahead changed once again, this time transforming into a busy, pedestrianized market.

"Look out!" I yelled as the empty road populated itself with food stands, clothing stalls, and hundreds of people happily wandering around in front of us, going about their business.

Cassandra reacted quickly, slamming her foot on the brakes to avoid a terrified mother frozen to the spot with her two children. She lurched the car to the left, frantically jabbing the horn repeatedly to warn everyone to get out of the way, then to the right to escape hitting a group of teenagers huddled round a busker. All around, people began screaming as we plowed through a row of market stalls, missing pedestrians by a whisker, and I shut my eyes as we swerved to avoid a couple desperately yanking their stroller out of our path.

Then the sound of panic stopped.

I opened my eyes. The road had returned to normal, but behind us the Range Rover had gained on us.

"Can't you do something!?" I said.

"Not while they've got that shield around us!" she replied, pressing her foot down on the accelerator again. "But don't worry—those guys shouldn't be able to take too many more changes before they…"

Cassandra tailed off as the environment around us changed once again. This time, everything was covered in a thick layer of snow—trees suddenly looked as though they'd been dusted with icing sugar, rooftops turned a brilliant shade of white, and the road ahead shimmered with a glossy sheen of ice. On either side of the street, parked cars were half-submerged in snow, kids were running around in hats and scarves, and street lights glistened softly through a gentle sprinkle of snowflakes from above. It was all very picturesque, but with no roof to protect us from the elements we soon began to feel to the cold. I huddled my arms around my chest, teeth chattering as the temperature plummeted instantaneously.

Cassandra gripped the wheel and slowed down to avoid skidding out of control, but she was struggling to keep hold of the vehicle—the roads were just too slippery. I looked behind us again. The Range Rover was getting closer.

"Come on, give me a break…" she said as the car began to glide toward a mound of snow piled up against the edge of the road. She tried pumping her foot on the accelerator to gain some traction, but it was no use. We plowed into the snow like a train hitting the buffers at the end of the line and came to an abrupt stop.

"No, no no!" Cassandra cursed, slipping the car into reverse and hitting the gas. But the wheels just spun around on the spot, the engine over-revving as clumps of snow and ice were thrown up in the air.

"Can you see them?" she said, spinning around in her seat.

"There they are!" I said, pointing back at the Range Rover. Harry and Martin were approaching fast, but they appeared to be having a little trouble of their own on the ice, the back end of their vehicle fishtailing uncontrollably.

"They're gonna overshoot!" Cassandra said, watching as they skidded past.

Suddenly the road turned back to normal. The mound of snow in front of us disappeared, the ice beneath us transformed back to solid tarmac, and the temperature turned mild again. With Cassandra's foot still pressed firmly on the accelerator and the car in reverse, the wheels instantly made contact with the road and sent us flying backward like a coiled spring being released.

"Whoa!" she said, braking just in time to avoid hitting a lamp-post and throwing the car into first gear. To our right, the Range Rover also had regained control of itself, recovering quickly from its overshoot and skidding round to face us in a screech of tires.

"Go go go go go go go!" I said, my body shaking as if it had just had an electric current passed through it.

Cassandra stepped on the gas and sped back the way we came. She looked pissed off.

"I think it's time we lost these guys," she said, veering down a slip lane onto a freeway.

"What are you doing?" I said as we joined three lanes of traffic. We were now surrounded by swarms of vehicles—trucks in convoy; buses packed full of commuters; cars changing lanes; caravans trundling along in the slow lane; motorbikes weaving in between everyone—it was busy enough to be rush hour. And driving as we were in a car with no roof, it wasn't long before people began looking at us in bewilderment, hands pressed against windows.

"Don't worry," Cassandra said, looking at the Range Rover in her mirror. "Your other self taught me a thing or two about…how…to…" She tailed off and stared ahead, her face paralyzed.

As she'd been speaking the dimension had changed again, and in this world the traffic was heading straight toward us.

Headlights began flashing. Horns beeped in panic. Tires squealed. I was so terrified I froze to my seat, arms and legs rigid as I tensed every muscle in my body. For a moment, everything seemed to happen in a haze of slow motion, as if my brain needed to slow down my perception of events in order for it to comprehend what was going on.

"Shit!" Cassandra screamed, clinging to the steering wheel tightly as if to wring it dry. "Hang on!"

We began to speed up.

"What the hell are you doing?" I cried. "You're not actually going to drive into that, are you?"

Her lips broke into a broad smile.

"They'd be crazy to follow us, right?"

The first few cars ahead of us were already screeching to a halt, the people inside flinging their arms about, screaming wildly. But the vehicles behind failed to react quickly enough, and I watched in horror as they piled straight into the backs of the cars in front, many of them riding right up in the air and flipping over in the road. Vehicles began crashing down on their roofs in front of us, passengers hanging lifelessly inside by their seatbelts, and Cassandra found herself desperately swerving left and right to avoid the crumpled wreckages falling onto the road from above.

Still accelerating, we began to weave our way through the traffic ahead, switching lanes every few seconds to avoid the onslaught of trucks, vans, buses and motorbikes heading our way.

"Maybe this wasn't the best idea after all!" Cassandra yelled, yanking the steering wheel to the right to avoid a jeep pirouetting through the air toward us, the unconscious driver pressed against the windshield. Within seconds, she quickly had to steer in the opposite direction to nudge past a car balanced precariously on its side, onlookers rushing into the road to pull people out of the wreck. I turned round in my seat to look back—the Range Rover was still on our tail, following the path we were clearing through the traffic with relative ease.

"This isn't working!" I said.

"Wait a minute," Cassandra said, looked further down the road ahead. "I think I have an idea!"

"Whatever you're going to do, do it quick!" I said.

Saying nothing, she swerved into the fast lane, pressing her foot hard on the accelerator. In front of us, a large petrol tanker was jackknifing across the road, the back end of its trailer heading straight toward us.

"What are you doing?!" I screamed, trying to grab the wheel.

"Trust me!" Cassandra cried, holding the wheel firmly in place. It was only going to be a matter of seconds before we would crash into the tanker, which was now toppling on its side, carving its way through the tarmac toward us on a bed of sparks. The approaching bright red warning: "DANGER—Highly Flammable" burned onto my retinas as I shut my eyes and wrapped my arms around my head.

A few seconds passed.

Nothing happened.

I gently lowered my arms and opened my eyes. The road ahead was back to normal. There was no sign of the petrol tanker, the overturned cars, or any of the horrific wreckage we had just been through. The traffic was busy, but we were driving on the right side of the road again. I glanced behind us—the Range Rover was still on our tail, but beyond that the road was clear, as if nothing had happened.

I gave Cassandra a confused look.

"Did I miss something?"

"They need you alive," she replied. "Once we were about to crash into that tanker, they had no choice but to get us out of there."

I slumped back in my seat and let out a deep breath.

"At least—that's what I figured," she added.

"Can I make a suggestion?" I said.

"What's that?"

"Let's get off this road as quickly as possible."

"Agreed," she nodded.

✤   ✤   ✤

The clear night sky began to turn overcast as we took the next exit off the freeway, a blanket of thick gray clouds drifting in front of the moon like a theater curtain drawing a performance to a close.

"Take a left at this roundabout," I told Cassandra, feeling a few spots of rain pinprick against my skin.

She looked at the Range Rover again in her mirrors.

"You know where we are?"

"We're coming up to Canary Wharf," I said, pointing toward the glittering array of skyscrapers that marked one of London's major financial districts. "Don't you recognize it?"

She shook her head.

"There's nothing like this where I'm from," she replied, craning her head back to look up at the towering architecture as we sped through the streets below, her eyes filled with an almost childlike wonderment. "Incredible…"

The rain started to come down harder. Looking back, I could see the Range Rover was still getting closer.

"Keep going straight," I said as we sped past a number of late-night bars and restaurants. A few of my clients were based around here, so I knew the area pretty well. People were crowded outside on either side of the road drinking and smoking, tourists were taking photographs from open top buses, and the streets were buzzing with sounds of lively conversation, laughter, and gossip.

Then all of a sudden we changed dimensions again.

The rain stopped.

The air turned thick with ash, the sky transformed into a billowing swirl of black cloud, and an eerie silence descended upon us. In a split second, Canary Wharf lay in ruin—a postapocalpytic wasteland of decaying buildings. Empty streets. A ghost town. The only movement came from the odd piece of litter drifting in the air like tumbleweed. Roads had crumbled away into dust. Skyscrapers lay across the ground like fallen dominos, decimating everything in their path.

Something must have happened here. Something horrible.

"Jesus fucking…fuck!" Cassandra screamed, hitting the brakes to avoid crashing into a collapsed office block ahead of us, which lay across the road in a crumpled pile of glass and steel creating a dead end. I barely reacted as we came to a halt, my body numb, eyes still. I couldn't believe what I was seeing.

A few seconds passed before I finally managed to speak.

"W-what is this place?" I stammered. My eyes were beginning to sting from all the grit in the atmosphere, my throat clogging up as if I'd just smoked twenty cigarettes in a row.

Arms shaking, I lifted myself up in my seat to look around. Dead bodies were everywhere—some curled up on the ground, others slumped in doorways, many just lying flat on the pavement as if they'd fallen out of the sky. Over to my left, a few cars were disintegrating into rusty metal carcasses. On the other side of the road, a few vehicles lay on their sides. Buildings were overgrown with thick vegetation, the fascias of shops and bars barely recognizable behind the dense foliage. A row of mannequins smiled at me through the broken window of a department store, draped in the remnants of clothing they once modelled. And everything was covered in a thin membrane of ash, as if a volcanic eruption had occurred nearby. I inhaled sharply and began coughing, my lungs aching from the dust in the air.

"Sit down!" Cassandra said, pulling me back into my seat and shifting the car into reverse.

But as we backed away from the collapsed office block and swung around to make an escape, the Range Rover didn't move to intercept us. In fact it looked as though it was slowing down.

Cassandra narrowed her eyes and watched as the vehicle trundled toward us before coming to a gentle stop in the middle of the road a few meters away. We couldn't quite see inside it through the smog, but the engine was still running. Headlights on. A few flakes of ash drifted peacefully in the bright yellow beams. Other than that, the car just sat there, as if Harry and Martin had given up on the chase.

Cassandra switched our engine off and opened the door to get out.

"What are you doing?" I whispered.

"Just checking something," she said, taking a few steps toward the Range Rover. I listened as her footsteps crunched through the ash on the ground. The sound reminded me of someone walking through freshly laid snow.

"Careful!" I called out, watching from my seat as she approached the driver side door. "Those guys are dangerous!"

"Not anymore," she replied, peering through the window.

"What?"

"Come and have a look for yourself…"

I got out of the car, trudged my way over to the Range Rover and looked through the window.

Harry and Martin were gone.

"Where are they?" I said, making my way round to the passenger door and opening it to take a closer look. The car was empty.

"I thought this might happen," Cassandra replied, reaching through the window to turn off the engine. Suddenly everything went completely quiet, as if the world had been plunged into a vacuum. Without a single sound to latch onto, my ears felt strange, like a fish flapping around on a dry river bank, desperate to be returned to the water.

"You thought what might happen?" I said, the sound of my voice providing a welcome relief from the silence.

"The final phase of Quantum Displacement Disorder," Cassandra said. "Moving between all these different dimensions must have accelerated their condition faster than they anticipated."

"What's the final phase?"

"Once the black marks totally envelop the body, the subject just…disappears."

"What do you mean?"

"I mean they vanish. Into thin air."

I looked inside the Range Rover again as if to reconfirm what I'd just been told. She was right—Harry and Martin were definitely gone.

"But…where do these people go?"

"Nobody knows," Cassandra said, fanning the air in front of her to clear the dust from her eyes. "But the presiding theory is that the condition eventually moves people out of synchronization with reality, forcing them into a limbo state between worlds. A plane of existence beyond our comprehension. And that's it. The subject is lost—forever."

"That's awful…"

"Yes. Which is exactly why Gabriel and his team are trying to find a cure."

"No wonder they need us!" I said, slamming the car door shut. "I'm mean, if we hold the key to stopping all this, why aren't we helping these people? Why are we running away?"

Cassandra sighed.

"You've seen what these people are like, Richard. They are psychopaths. Murderers. And if they're ever able to move between alternate worlds as they please, the consequences would be disastrous…"

"I know, but…"

"Look around you," Cassandra interrupted me, crouching down to pick up a handful of ash from the floor and let it sift through her fingers. "Do you know what you see?"

I scanned my eyes again over the decaying surroundings. Dead bodies as far as the eye could see. Collapsed buildings turning to dust. A black sky pressing down on us from above. This was a nightmare.

"I see the end of the world," I said.

"No," Cassandra said. "You see what is at stake here. You see what Gabriel and his team are capable of. This is the reason we cannot allow you to fall into their hands again. And why they have to be stopped."

I stumbled back against the hood of the Range Rover, my knees weak.

"You mean…Gabriel did this?" I whispered, my voice barely able to make a sound. "You…You know this place?"

"Oh yes," Cassandra replied. "I know it very well…"

FIFTEEN

I staggered over to a small bench at the side of the road and brushed a thick layer of ash away with my sleeve, lowering myself down onto it slowly like someone learning of a family bereavement. In front of me stood One Canada Square—the pyramid-topped skyscraper that used to stand proudly above all other buildings in Canary Wharf—a landmark visible for miles around. Unlike most of the surrounding structures it was still upright, although most of the external windows and cladding had fallen away, leaving its steel frame exposed to the elements like a withered rib cage. For a moment I just sat there looking up at it, listening to the floors creak quietly as the wind rattled through the building's decaying architecture.

An old newspaper was snagged in the blackened branches of a nearby bush. I tore it free and examined the front page. The headlines made no reference to an impending disaster, although I did notice the date—this paper was over twenty years old.

"You won't find anything about this in the papers," Cassandra said, sitting down beside me. She placed a hand on my shoulder. "Nobody saw this coming. One minute everything was normal; the next minute, everyone was dead. Nothing on Earth survived."

"Please Cassandra—you've got to tell me. What happened here?" I released the paper into a passing gust of wind and rubbed my eyes.

"The simple answer is that this world was struck by a massive hail of asteroids," Cassandra said.

"Asteroids?"

"Thousands of them," Cassandra continued. "Some were the size of cars, others the size of small countries, and in the course of one day, this world was completely annihilated by them. The impact was devastating—the equivalent of a nuclear bomb going off on every square meter of the Earth's surface. Oceans were vaporized, mountains were leveled, and a cloud of dust was thrown up into the sky, which still blocks out most of the sun's rays to this day. It was the end of all life on the planet."

"So how can we still breathe?" I asked.

"This asteroid was much like the one that wiped out the dinosaurs," Cassandra replied. "All life was extinguished, but the devastation wasn't enough to destroy the planet's atmosphere."

"I don't understand," I said. "I thought you said Gabriel had something to do with this? What possible influence could he have had over a bunch of asteroids hitting the Earth?"

Cassandra stood up and looked at the sky. The clouds looked unnatural, like swirls of wet tarmac being churned together.

"Like I said, that was the simple answer. But it starts to get more complicated when you look at where those asteroids came from."

"What do you mean?"

"They didn't strike this planet by accident. Somebody sent them here."

"Somebody…sent them here?" I could feel my hands shaking.

"I told you it gets complicated," Cassandra said. "This is where Gabriel comes in, and the organization he works for. Believe it or not, they are responsible for everything you see before you."

I looked around in disbelief at the deserted streets once again, my eyes wandering over blackened vegetation, crumbling buildings, and dead bodies scattered everywhere. Surely nobody was capable of causing such destruction?

"This is impossible," I said.

"Not when you start to consider the technology they have at their disposal and how they choose to use it. That wave of asteroids was never supposed to hit this planet. It was supposed to hit theirs."

"What?"

"They are the reason Gabriel's world stumbled across the technology to create portals to other realities. In their dimension, those asteroids were spotted ten years before they were due to hit the planet. The governments of the world knew they were big enough to destroy every living thing on Earth, so they immediately pooled their military and scientific resources to come up with a way of stopping them."

Cassandra paused and took a deep breath.

"You okay?" I said, standing up and walking over to her.

"Yes," she said, exhaling slowly. "Just having a bit of trouble breathing in this smog. Where was I?"

"You were saying that the governments in Gabriel's world started working together to try to save their planet."

"That's right. First, they tried the military option, sending thousands of nuclear missiles on a long-range collision course. But many of the asteroids were simply too big to be destroyed, and the ones that were damaged only broke into smaller pieces. Next, they turned to the scientists, who tried to alter the speed of the Earth's orbit by changing the gravitational perturbation of the planet."

"The gravitational what?"

"It doesn't matter. Needless to say, that didn't work either. Years went by without a solution, and people began to get very nervous. The progress of the asteroids was tracked on the news every day, and in the final few months before impact, society began to break down. Martial law was declared. As things got increasingly desperate, any project that might offer a solution received government funding—more powerful weapons, more radical scientific experiments, anything. Then one day, about a week before the asteroids were due to hit and hope was almost lost, a team of scientists made an amazing discovery—they had created a portal to an alternate reality. A gateway. They could project it anywhere. Make it any size. And it led to the world you see yourself in now."

"Here?"

"That's right. Only when they discovered this world, it didn't look how it does today. This dimension used to be beautiful: a thriving example of the human race at its very best."

"You mean, like that world they sent me to earlier? The one where Alice—I mean, a different Alice—was still alive?"

"Yes—it was a lot like that dimension, only much more utopian, if you can believe it. In this world, society had developed to the stage where everyone truly understood what it meant to belong to the same species regardless of race, social class, or wealth. People were far less tribal in the attitude toward others, and the differences between somebody's religious beliefs or the color of their skin soon became celebrated rather than feared. And once the human race started working together instead of trying to blow each other up, war, disease and famine became obsolete. In this world, you could say the human race passed through a stage of enlightenment, where people lived in harmony with each other and the world around them. It was as perfect a place as you could imagine."

"So what happened?" I said, looking around some more. A few blocks away, I could see the wreckage of a large jumbo jet strewn across a huge radius, the debris of its engines, wings and fuselage scattered in an avalanche of twisted metal. To my right, a railway bridge had buckled under the weight of a small commuter train, its cars spilling over the edge and down onto the street below. Everywhere I looked I saw nothing but destruction. Death.

"Once they discovered the ability to move things between parallel worlds, the first question was clear—how could this technology be used to save the planet? And it wasn't long before someone suggested the obvious idea—why not project a giant portal into the path of the asteroids and send them through to this other world instead?"

"But they must have known they were condemning billions of people to death?" I said. "I mean, surely people objected?"

"The general public didn't get a chance to object—they were never consulted. Behind closed doors it was a hugely debated subject, but in the end, the world leaders jointly agreed to save themselves. The decision was unanimous. Make the asteroids someone else's problem."

"I feel sick," I said, shakily perching myself on the end of the bench again.

"So, on the day of the impact," Cassandra continued, "a massive portal was opened up in the path of the oncoming asteroids, sending every single one through to the dimension you see yourself in now. With only hours to react, this world never stood a chance, and in less than a day the greatest known example of the human race was made extinct, killed by an onslaught of space rock that was never even meant for them."

I could feel my stomach churning painfully, as though I'd just swallowed a bottle of paint stripper. Cassandra's story was so repulsive it was physically affecting me. I closed my eyes. Parts of me wanted her to go on, but at the same time I was desperate for her to stop.

Cassandra continued.

"Meanwhile, on the other Earth, huge worldwide celebrations were held. The public were fed a cover story about the asteroid being sent through to an *uninhabited* version their world, and everyone was happy. But no one ever got to hear the truth. No one knew that while they were partying in the streets in their world, another had been sacrificed to save them. A world that was heavily populated."

"I don't believe this," I said, resting my head in my hands. "I … I refuse to believe this. How could anyone be capable of … of …"

Cassandra hesitated.

"It gets worse," she said.

"What?" I cried. "How could it possibly get worse?"

"Following the success of the experiment, an organization was set up to identify what other dimensions existed and to develop further uses of the technology. Government leaders called the organization IDEA—the Inter-Dimensional Exploration Agency."

"So those people that are after me—they work for IDEA?"

Cassandra nodded.

"That's right. Gabriel, Martin, Harry—all those other people you saw back at the warehouse—they all work for IDEA. Anyway, not long after its inception, IDEA began to come up with a few initiatives of its own—ways of commercializing the technology to create portals between worlds. Don't want to test a nuclear weapon on your own planet? Why not do it on someone else's? Fed up of trying to find a home for toxic waste? Leave it in another dimension for someone else to deal with! Need more fossil fuels? Take them from another world! The list got longer and longer. For years now, IDEA has exploited their ability to travel between parallel worlds to propel their society forward in ways you wouldn't believe. They've copied technological capabilities from more advanced worlds, developed their cities into futuristic metropolises, and integrated technology into people's lives in ways you would have never thought possible. But there has always been one thing that has held them back: Human beings still cannot move between different worlds safely. Despite everything IDEA has been able to achieve, sending a person through to another dimension still results in some quite nasty side effects..."

"You mean the black marks."

"That's right. Quantum Displacement Disorder."

"Which is why these people are after me..."

"Yes. IDEA have lost some good people to the disease over the years: scientists trying to cure the condition. In fact, if our intelligence is correct, Gabriel's wife was one such person—a leading researcher who disappeared a few years ago whilst testing a failed vaccine."

"My God," I said. "No wonder he was getting so emotional back there. At one point, I thought he was going to kill me if I didn't tell him what he wanted to know. I guess only the loss of someone very special can bring out that kind of... anger."

"Apparently he volunteered for all of this in the hope he'd find a way of bringing her back. But so far, he's had no luck, and day by day, his condition gets worse."

"It's hard isn't it?" I said. "As ridiculous as it seems, it's difficult not to feel sorry for him."

"I know," Cassandra replied. "As for IDEA itself—their motivations are a little less personal and a little less easy to sympathize with. You see, despite starting life as an offshoot of a collection of world governments, it's now run like a regular business, with annual revenue figures, profit margins to report to the city, and so on. For the past few years it has done extremely well, but to its shareholders, the successes of the past are irrelevant. All they are interested in is what comes next. What is the next innovation? How will they annualize the previous year's growth? All that business stuff. Many believe IDEA are running out of steam, but one man in the organization believes the way forward is to start sending people to other worlds. Colonizing other realities. Problem is—they can't do it until they find a cure for Quantum Displacement Disorder, since no one wants to be sent on a suicide mission…"

"Who is this man?" I asked.

"His name is Russell Hardwick," Cassandra replied. "He's some sort of big-time director of something or other at IDEA. One of the bosses."

"Russell…Russell…Russell…" I said to myself. "You, know I think I might have heard Gabriel mention that name when he was on the phone earlier…"

"It was probably him," Cassandra said. "Gabriel is his right-hand man. Does all of Russell's dirty work."

The wind was beginning to pick up a little, whipping a layer of ash up from the floor and swirling it around us aggressively like a sandstorm. My eyes were starting to sting from all the grit in the air, my skin sore.

"Let's find some shelter," Cassandra said, shielding her face with her arm.

I stood up and followed her across the road into a small shoe shop. The sliding doors were wedged open slightly but the windows were still intact, and once inside I was surprised at how well preserved everything was. A few dusty high heels were on display in a plastic cabinet. Promotional posters hung from the ceiling—25% off this week only. A wall of tennis shoes, each pair arranged neatly in its own individual compartment. Two tills sat unopened at the front of the store. A small amount of vegetation was beginning to creep through a crack in the floor toward the far end of the room, scaling up the walls like the tentacles of an underground beast, but otherwise it felt like we were walking into a museum exhibit.

"I don't understand," I said, sitting down on a deflated padded seat in the middle of the shop floor. "You say that I'm unique in some way—that this Russell guy needs me to help them find a cure to this disorder. But what about you? And Alice? Aren't you both able to travel between dimensions as well?"

"That's correct."

"So why isn't he after you too?"

Cassandra looked at the ground, twirling the heel of her foot into the dust.

"Because he already captured both of us," she said quietly. "Six months ago."

"What?" I said, jumping to my feet. "You were captured? What happened?"

"Earlier this year, after coming under a lot pressure from its shareholders to deliver results, IDEA began to monitor other dimensions remotely to see if anyone else had the technological capability to move between dimensions. Russell Hardwick wanted to see if he could learn anything from these other worlds—to see if anyone had managed to overcome the limitations he was experiencing. He didn't have much luck—every other world that was aware of the multidimensional universe was suffering from the same problem. However, he did find out about someone who had traveled between dimensions unharmed..."

"Alice."

"That's rightMum. And it was at this point that IDEA took a serious interest in our world. They investigated everything—how the government covered up the circumstances of her arrival, how she'd helped their scientists develop their own version of the technology, and how..."

Cassandra stopped talking and took a deep breath.

"How...what?" I asked, gesturing her to continue.

"How she'd spent ten years of her life traveling between different dimensions trying to find…you," she said quietly.

"Alice was looking for me?" I said. "For ten years?"

Cassandra nodded.

"When her first experiment went wrong and sent her through to another world, she said it was like jumping from one word in an encyclopedia to another with no page reference—she didn't know how to get back. The only way for her to go back and find you was through trial and error. So once she'd helped to build the technology again and make it stable enough to use without getting lost between different worlds, we began searching for you together. Took us ten years before we finally found you."

"When was this?" I said.

"Four years ago," Cassandra said. "But you were married back then, and you seemed happy. Mum thought about approaching you and telling you everything, but in the end she didn't think it was the right thing to do. Figured it would be too traumatic seeing your old girlfriend come back from the dead. So she tried to forget about ever getting back with you. Put you out of her mind. But then IDEA arrived on the scene."

"What happened?"

"It turned out they were very interested in why the two of us had been able to travel between dimensions without suffering from Quantum Displacement Disorder. You see, in our world, we are the only two people who are able to do so."

"I don't understand," I said, rubbing a bit of grit out of my eye. "What's so special about the three of us? Why aren't we affected?"

"We have no idea," Cassandra replied. "That's what everyone has been trying to figure out, including Mum. But once IDEA caught wind that there was something special about us, they took matters into their own hands and dispatched a team to bring us back to their own world for examination."

"You mean they kidnapped you? Like they did with me?"

Cassandra shut her eyes and nodded.

"It was horrible," she said, rubbing the back of her neck. "They came in the night. While we were asleep. Wore masks." She paused for a few seconds, staring vacantly through me as though I were a mirage. "I'd rather not talk about it if that's okay. The things they did to us in that building of theirs…Well, I won't forget it."

I didn't know what to say.

"Anyway," she continued, regaining her composure, "two of the people sent to capture us were Gabriel and Doctor Naylor, both of whom volunteered for the mission. They knew traveling to our world would give them Quantum Displacement Disorder, but they didn't care. Both of them had lost someone in the past to the disease, and both were willing to sacrifice everything if it meant there was a chance of finding a cure."

"But they didn't succeed."

"No. They must have carried out hundreds of different tests on us. Taken all kinds of samples. But nothing seemed to indicate why we were immune. However, they were eventually able to determine something that connected us, something that seemed to be responsible for keeping us safe. And it was something to do with you."

"Me?"

"That's right."

"I don't understand—how could this possibly have anything to do with me?"

"We're not sure. All we know is that one day they started asking Mum lot of questions about who my father was. Which dimension he came from. Whether he was still alive. Apparently there was something about our quantum signatures that pointed toward you as the reason for our immunity to the disease."

"Let me just stop you there," I said. "Quantum signatures?"

"Think of a quantum signature as your fingerprint in the quantum plane. It identifies you from all other matter, including all other versions of yourself. Every single thing has one, from a drop of water to an entire planet, and each one grows in complexity as it encompasses the signatures of its smaller components."

"Still not sure I get it," I said. "But carry on."

"Let me put it this way: You know how you can read the rings of a tree trunk to tell you a bit about their history? How old they are, what the climate was like during different stages of its life, etcetera?"

"Yes…"

"Well IDEA has the technology to read our quantum signatures in exactly the same way. What they discovered was nothing short of a breakthrough in their eyes. My own quantum signature had remained unchanged since the day I was conceived, but it turned out Mum's was different."

"Different in what way?"

"They could only trace it back the same length of time as mine—twenty-one years. Before that, it was missing. Displaced, you could say. In other words, Mum only became immune to Quantum Displacement Disorder the day I was conceived in her womb. She only became immune because of you."

I stood up and walked toward the front doors of the shoe shop. Outside, the storm was quietening down again, the dust settling back onto the streets like the ripples in a pond going still.

"I don't believe this," I whispered.

"So IDEA set about trying to work out who you were," Cassandra continued, "but it turned out to be harder than they thought. In the end, they had no choice but to ask Mum how to find you, and it was at that point she struck a deal. Mum would agree to give them as much information as possible about you to single you out from the millions of different Richard Henleys out there, but in return we would be let go. IDEA agreed, so she told them your name, your occupation, how you got the scar on your face, every little detail that would help them find you—right down to your favorite color. The only thing she didn't tell them was the fact that she already knew where you were."

"No wonder they were asking me all those stupid questions," I said. "So you mean to tell me Alice was happy to sell me out to these guys?"

"Funny—I asked Mum the same thing. But all she said was not to worry. Told me she had a plan to keep us all safe."

"And did that plan involve writing me notes and sending me to a posh restaurant?" I said, sliding the door to the shoe shop open and stepping outside again. "Didn't work very well, did it?"

"I think they narrowed down which dimension you were from faster than she anticipated," Cassandra said, following me closely behind. "And when they finally found you, all we knew was that we had to keep you away from them. If they can somehow use you to work out how to send people between dimensions unharmed, thousands of innocent worlds will suffer. That's why we sent you to that posh restaurant and the run-down hotel. Thought it would be the last place they would look. But I guess we were too late."

My feet crunched in the dirt as I walked across the road and looked up at the sky once again—occasionally, the clouds would briefly drift apart to show a glimpse of the stars up above before merging back together again and enclosing the world in a sea of gray. If this was what IDEA were capable of, somebody had to stop them.

"So what happens now?" I asked. "Is there any way we can fight these guys?"

"Before we do anything else, we need to get back to my world," Cassandra replied. "Get back to my world and meet up with Mum."

"Right."

"Do you still have the note?"

"Yes," I said, pulling it out of my pocket and unfolding it.

"What does it say?"

"It says 'Ready when you are,'" I said.

"Good. But let's find somewhere secluded before we leave. Wouldn't want to materialize in the middle of the street in front of hundreds of people, would we?"

"Good point," I said.

It took us a few minutes to find a narrow alleyway on the outskirts of Canary Wharf, nestled to the side of a half-collapsed block of apartments. I crouched behind a bin with Cassandra and took one last look at the London skyline in tatters. I never wanted to see this sight again.

"Right—let's get out of here," she said, holding my hand.

But as I watched the surrounding landscape evaporate into the ether, my skin began to tingle.

Something didn't feel right.

Sixteen

I say this because up until this point, the sensation of traveling between dimensions had been more or less instantaneous, like someone flicking from one holiday slide to another. I thought I was going to suddenly see London restore itself before my eyes—witness the dilapidated skyscrapers instantly return to their former glory, see the dead bodies vanish and be replaced by people going about their business, and marvel at the sky clearing itself of the oppressive gray smog and turning back to a clear, starry night. This time, however, the feeling of traveling between dimensions was very different. One minute I was crouched in the alleyway with Cassandra, waiting to be transported to another world, the next minute I found myself gently floating in a strange mist. My head felt detached from my body and weightless, my thoughts drifting vacantly around in my mind without any clear meaning or purpose.

As I floated through the mist, I could feel my senses becoming more and more vague. My ears were filled with a strange muffled sound, I couldn't feel my body, and my vision was getting a little hazy. I tried to focus, but all I could only make out were a few pale colors spilling into each other in a vista of pinks and yellows. Whatever place this was, it lacked any real shape or definition. I couldn't see Cassandra.

I wasn't sure how long I remained in this state. As I continued to float gently through the air, I had no real concept of time. It could have been hours, it could have been seconds; I really didn't know. After a while, however, I began to notice a change in my surroundings. At first it was quite subtle—beneath me, the pinks and yellows were beginning to darken, and the fog around me started to thicken. I didn't think much of it at first, but as the colors beneath me got darker and darker, I found myself slowly rolling my body over to investigate, like a swimmer turning over in the sea to look at the ocean floor. As I did, the mist changed into a thick swell of black all around.

I should have been scared, but in this place my thoughts remained calm and vacant, my mind drifting in and out of consciousness with no real care about what was happening to me. I could see dark spindly shapes stretching toward me out of the black mist, almost as though they were reaching out to touch me, but I wasn't concerned—my body felt as light as a feather, my mind empty.

Then one started tightening itself around my wrist.

Suddenly, my senses returned, and I found myself entering a moment of horrific clarity—the muffled sounds in my ears became a deep, mournful wail, and the dark spindly shapes reaching out for me turned into arms, stretching toward me from the darkness, fingers clawing through the air as if they were desperate to grab hold of me. I began to panic, my body flailing about like an animal caught in a net. I tried to wriggle free from the hand that had grabbed my wrist, but it was clasped so tightly around my arm I couldn't get it off. In the end, I had no choice but to grab it with my free hand and prize the fingers open, throwing the arm back toward the rest of the approaching limbs.

The next thing I knew, I was crouching in the alleyway, dripping with sweat. Our journey to Cassandra's world appeared to have been successful; the buildings either side of us looked undamaged and the night sky was clear, but for some reason I felt different. I stood up, wiped the sweat from my forehead and looked around—Cassandra was standing next to me, her body trembling.

"What just happened?" I said.

"I … I'm not sure," she stammered. Her face looked pale. "Did you see it too? Did something … touch you?"

"Yes, right here," I said, holding up my wrist.

My bottom lip began to quiver as I stared at it for a few seconds. To my horror, it was stained with a jet black mark, precisely where I'd been grabbed in that strange mist.

"Oh my God!" I said, steadying myself against the wall of the alleyway. "Is this … is this what I think it is?"

Cassandra held out her left hand. It was black too.

"T-This is where it got me," she said, flexing her inky fingers.

"But … this can't be happening, right?" I said, rubbing the mark with my other hand to see if it would come off. It was no use. "I mean, aren't we supposed to be immune?" As I scrubbed furiously at my skin, I noticed my other hand had a black mark on it as well, right where I'd used it to prize the fingers from my wrist.

"I mean, aren't we supposed to be immune?"

"What does the note say?" Cassandra said, turning her hand over to examine the other side. The black marks curled over her knuckle like streaks of tar.

I took the paper out and unfolded it. My hands felt strange, as if they were coated in a thin layer of grease.

"It says 'Get to the lab as quickly as you can,'" I read aloud.

"That's probably a good idea," Cassandra said, taking a moment to exhale quietly and look up at the clear night sky. "We need to get to Mum. She'll know what to do …"

Seventeen

I wondered if this was how my father had felt when he discovered he had lung cancer. Found out he had something eating away at him. One minute you think you're fit and healthy, not a care in the world, the next you're thinking about how much time you have left. What to tell your family. When will it start to hurt? Am I ready for death? Have I done everything I wanted to do with my life? Do I have any regrets?

All these questions were buzzing around in my mind as I followed Cassandra out of the alleyway. But above all, I wanted to know why. Why was this happening to us? What had we done wrong? Weren't we supposed to be immune to all this? Why had the black marks appeared?

My father must have felt the same way. He'd never touched a cigarette. Led a healthy life. Exercised. Watched his weight. Yet at the age of fifty-five, he started to notice a pain in his chest. A gentle irritation, nothing too concerning. He ignored it at first. Thought it would just go away. But it persisted. He began to feel a little worse week by week. Then he started finding himself short of breath. Felt the odd twinge of pain for no reason. Something wasn't right.

When he eventually went to the doctor, he couldn't believe what they told him. Lung cancer. Advanced stage. Only a few months to live. Nothing he could do. At first he didn't believe them. This was impossible, he'd protested. He had a healthy lifestyle. Took care of himself. So how could he have lung cancer? What had he done wrong? In the end, it turned out the cause of his illness was something outside his control—it was his job; the path his life was forced to take when his own father had suffered a stroke, and he had to step in to support his family. The air in the factory was dirty, full of particulates, and something he'd been breathing in for many years. It had slowly rotted him away from the inside, and he hadn't even realized it.

He died just before I turned twenty-five at home, in bed. Didn't want to spend his last few days in hospital. Wanted to be amongst family. A few of his old friends came over to say farewell. People from work. I remember them telling me how sorry they were for me and my mother. Asking if there was anything they could do. Some people tried to offer a few words of comfort, others said nothing at all. They would just look at me with glassy eyes and closed lips, as if to acknowledge the futility of language in this situation.

I preferred those that didn't speak.

Suddenly aware of how consumed I was becoming with thoughts of my father's death, I shook my head and tried to put it out of my mind. What was needed now was a positive mental attitude—a belief that we would somehow get out of this alive. We weren't dead yet, and if Alice was still as smart as I remembered, there was a good chance she would be able to help us. I couldn't wait to see her again.

I was just about to ask Cassandra how far away the lab was when I found myself slowing down, my gaze drifting toward the night sky in wonderment like a fascinated child. This was the clearest night sky I had ever seen, a sparkling blanket of stars stretching as far as the eye could see. In my world, the light pollution from the city streets meant you could only make out the odd glimmer of light or two, and half the time it turned out you were actually looking at an airplane. But in this world, the visibility was awe-inspiring, the stars as plentiful as grains of sand on a beach, sprinkled across a patchwork quilt of dark purples, blacks and blues.

"You okay?" Cassandra said, stopping a few feet ahead of me and looking up at the sky as well. "You seen something?"

"No … it's just—I've never … seen a sky like this before," I replied vacantly, my thoughts almost lulled into a trance by the hypnotic celestial patterns swirling overhead. "It's beautiful."

"One of the few advantages of not having any street lighting," she smiled, folding her arms. "You get to see the night sky in all its glory."

"No street lighting?" I said, returning my gaze to ground level and looking around. She was right—it hadn't really registered until now, but the streets were much darker than I was used to. And it didn't take long for me to understand why—I couldn't see a single artificial light whatsoever. There were no lamp posts. No neon signs. No illuminated shop windows. Not even the brightly lit skyscrapers that normally dominated the London skyline could be seen. The only source of light came from the moon, which cast its soft glow down on us like someone shining a torch from behind a sheet of tracing paper.

But a lack of artificial light wasn't the only thing unusual about this dimension. In my world, every square foot of Canary Wharf had been developed into high-rise apartments, towering corporate headquarters, and flashy department stores. In this world, however, there were no office blocks. No high-rise apartments. In fact, much of the land remained completely untouched, with fields of grass stretching out into the darkness, hedgerows lining the roads, and bushy trees reaching up into the sky. This didn't feel like London—it felt more like a village in the countryside. The only buildings I could see were a few small rows of terraced houses, some wooden structures that looked like barns, and a couple of shops. And not a single window had a light on inside.

No sign of any traffic either—that was the next thing that struck me. No matter how late it was, the streets of London were usually jam-packed with cars and busses, the air filled with the hum of engines, the hiss of hydraulic brakes, and a distant medley of car horns and police sirens blaring out intermittently. In this world, however, the roads were so quiet you could hear people's conversations from quite a distance as they passed by. The sound of their footsteps on the pavement. The quiet rustle of leaves fluttering in the cool night breeze.

"Now I know why you didn't recognize Canary Wharf earlier," I said, making my way over to Cassandra. "This place is nothing like where I'm from…"

"Yes, it's quite different, isn't it?" she said, taking one last look around before motioning me to follow her. "More…peaceful."

"Yes, but…no street lights?" I said. "And what happened to all the skyscrapers?" I looked down at my hands again. To my alarm, the marks had already started to spread down past my wrists. I tried not to react, shoving them quickly back in my pockets. It was then that I felt the packet of cigarettes pressing against my leg. I removed the pack, took out my last Marlboro and placed it between my lips. But just as I moved to light it, I realized I didn't want to smoke anymore. For years, I had been blackening my insides with this habit, and not seeing the damage it was doing to me made it easy: You could trick yourself into thinking the vice had no consequences. But seeing the black marks spread over my skin suddenly put everything in perspective, made me think about the hidden cost of what I was doing. I removed the cigarette, put it back in the packet, and tossed the box in the nearest bin.

"So what's the deal is with this place?" I asked, hoping the question would help take my mind off things. "Why is it so different?"

"Fossil fuels," Cassandra replied. "In this dimension, the reserves of oil, gas and coal are about a fiftieth of what they are in your world."

"Why's that?" I said, glancing up at another darkened building. Without any lights it looked faceless, like an incomplete portrait waiting for its features to be drawn in. "Did they all get used up or something?"

"No, not at all—they're just naturally scarcer here. Because of that, this world evolved in a very different way to yours. The population is smaller, urban development is less advanced, and energy is conserved as much as possible."

"Which is why there are no street lights…"

"Exactly. And no traffic. Everything basically shuts down at night."

"I see. Does this mean we're *walking* to the lab?"

"Yes," Cassandra nodded. "But don't worry—it's only a few miles away."

"Did you say *miles*?" I said.

Walking through the London of Cassandra's world proved to be a strange emotional experience, and I found myself overcome with a deep feeling of uncanny as we headed further into town. At times I thought something looked familiar—a landmark, a street name, something in the distance, a brand on a billboard—in fact there were many things that registered in my mind as though I'd seen them before. At the same time, however, there were many things that seemed different. Roads were a little bit narrower. Pavements were a little bit wider. Fewer cars were parked in the street. Buildings were shorter. Traffic lights were switched off. People's clothes were unusual colors or styles. All little things here and there, but they added up to make me feel as though I was a stranger in a foreign land, a tourist trying to acquaint myself with a different culture.

Our journey took us down several quiet roads, across some empty grassland, and along a pretty footpath, which was lined on either side with colorful flowers and thick shrubs. The path threaded its way through some dense forest for a few hundred meters before opening out to run alongside a narrow river. By this point I'd completely lost my bearings, and I was amazed when I eventually saw a sign that read "River Fleet." In my world, the Fleet was a subterranean river, artificially channeled into a sewer to allow the city of London to expand over it. In this world, it weaved peacefully through the countryside, reflecting the night sky above in a mirror of ripples and currents.

As we walked, Cassandra explained more to me about the history of her world. What she liked about it. How people behaved. She spoke quickly, rarely stopping for breath, sometimes tripping over her own words as if her mind was thinking faster than could speak.

She sounded as though she had wanted to tell me about the place she had been brought up in for a long time.

One thing I was particularly interested to learn about was the way in which this world dealt with its lack of natural resources. For a start, the government was able to veto any technology that it deemed unnecessary or used up too much energy. Batteries, for instance, did not exist here. That meant there were no personal music players, no laptops—no portable technology whatsoever. They didn't even have mobile phones. I asked Cassandra if was a pain not being contactable wherever she went, but she seemed to like it, saying she couldn't understand why people in my world needed something like that on them at all times. "Isn't it a pain to *always* be contactable?" she'd replied. "I mean, if someone can always get hold of you, how can you ever be free?"

But the thing that surprised me the most was the fact that this world didn't have the Internet, apparently rejected on the grounds of it being unnecessary. Mobile phones I could understand—as useful as they were, they were nothing more than a convenience, and we'd happily got along just fine before they became a part of our everyday lives. But the Internet was another matter. I explained to Cassandra that in my world, it was almost seen as a basic human right to have access to the World Wide Web. The Internet empowered people. Educated them. Entertained them. Allowed unprecedented levels of communication across the planet. It was a revolution, and in some countries, it had the power to *start* revolutions. How could something so important be deemed unnecessary?

Cassandra appeared to be conflicted on this point. She agreed that the Internet was an amazing tool, but at the same time, she argued it was still nothing more than a convenience, almost to the point of being dangerous. "It encourages laziness," she argued. "Especially when people have it on their phones."

I asked her what she meant.

"In your world," she said, "you don't need to remember those directions to meet your friends, or the name of that actor in the film you saw yesterday, or the formula to that equation you're trying to solve. It's all there on your phone. People don't need to retain knowledge anymore because they can access it at the tap of a button, wherever they are. Phones can tell you anything you want to know. Answer any question. It's getting to the point where the phone is holding people's hand through life. That's the reason you see the Internet as a basic human right—because your world has become totally dependent on it."

I wasn't sure how far we had walked, but it was well over two hours before we arrived at the lab, the Sun just beginning to peek over the horizon in a haze of red and yellow. During this time the marks on our skin had spread at an alarming rate, to the extent that our arms were now completely black. I opened my shirt and examined my chest—the marks were now spreading across my torso, like two dark claws slowly interlocking around my body.

"There it is," Cassandra said, pointing toward a small concrete structure nestled in the middle of an overgrown field. "We'd better hurry."

The building was no bigger than twenty feet square, with gray walls, no windows, and a single metal door on one side. One side was overgrown with thick ivy, and part of the roof was beginning to crumble away. From the outside, it looked like some sort of abandoned outpost.

"This is it?" I said, looking the place up and down as we approached. I didn't know what I was expecting Alice's lab to look like, but this certainly wasn't it.

"Oh don't worry," Cassandra said, reaching for the door. "This is just the entrance. The main lab is actually deep, deep underground in a massive, disused mine." She twisted the handle and opened the door with a loud screech.

"A mine?" I said, following her inside.

The building was cold, unlit, and the air smelled stale, like pressing your face into a dusty old mattress. It took a few seconds of

Cassandra fumbling around in the dark before a single bulb illuminated our surroundings in a dim white light. The place was empty, save for a few steel barrels stacked in one corner and a large freight elevator at the far end of the room. The elevator was housed in a tall metal cage that stretched from floor to ceiling, with a rusty, horizontally sliding door over the entrance. It didn't look entirely safe.

"Mum said they used to mine for coal here," Cassandra explained, yanking the door open with both hands and stepping onto the elevator platform. "But that was years ago, when people were desperate to find every last scrap of fossil fuel they could get their hands on."

"You mean they're not like that anymore?" I asked, taking a few cautious steps into the lift and sliding the door shut behind me.

"Not really," Cassandra replied, typing a long combination of numbers into a keypad to her left. "Over time, everyone began to accept the fact that they needed to live within their means, and the demand for coal and gas shrank down to a fraction of what it was."

Suddenly, a generator over our heads rumbled to life, and the elevator began to descend with a loud judder. It was strange—this was the first mechanical sound I'd heard for a few hours, and somehow it felt alien.

"So how did Alice end up working here?" I shouted over the sound of the lift mechanism, watching with fascination as we passed through various layers of brown and gray rock. It felt as though we were being injected into the earth. "I mean, it seems like an usual place for her to set up her lab..."

"It was the government's idea," Cassandra answered.

"Right," I said. "Does this have something to do with that cover-up you mentioned earlier?"

Cassandra nodded.

"When Mum first appeared in this world out nowhere with half a laboratory building and some pretty sophisticated scientific equipment scattered around her, it didn't exactly go unnoticed. The military immediately confiscated everything, and she was taken in for questioning."

"The military?" I said.

"That's right. Believe it or not, at first they thought she was a terrorist. Thought the equipment she had with her was some sort of secret weapon. Of course, she tried to explain that she was actually a scientist from another dimension, but as you can probably imagine, it wasn't easy to convince them that she was telling the truth."

"So what did she do?" I asked, inhaling deeply. The lower we went, the harder it was to breathe.

"She told them she could prove it, that if they let her fix her equipment, she would demonstrate the technology that brought her here. The military agreed, and within a few weeks this whole place was converted into a laboratory for her to use."

"But why an abandoned mine?" I asked, tugging at my collar. It was beginning to feel a little hot.

"Two reasons, mainly," Cassandra said. She paused for minute, taking a hairband out of her pocket to tie her hair back in a ponytail. "The first was simple—the government were keen to keep everything a secret from the general public, so an underground laboratory was as inconspicuous a place as you could wish for."

"And the other reason?"

"Energy. The kind of power Mum needed to sustain her equipment was unlike anything this world was used to generating. But if her lab was based deep enough underground, geothermal energy could be harnessed. It was perfect."

The elevator continued its slow descent.

"So how far down are we going?" I asked.

"Just over two and a half miles."

"Two and a half miles!" I said. "You must be joking!"

"Not at all. And it shows you just how desperate this world used to be for fossil fuels, that they would dig so far…"

"Amazing," I said.

"It took Mum just over seven months to repair everything and get the lab working again," Cassandra continued. "In fact, by the time she was carrying out the first demonstrations, she was heavily pregnant with me."

"God—she must have been under so much pressure," I said. "I wish I could have been there for her..."

"Yeah, apparently it wasn't easy at first," Cassandra replied. "When she started showing people portals to other dimensions, the government began to ask questions about how the technology could be used—particularly how they might be able to harvest raw materials from other worlds. But when Mum showed them the potential side effects of what they were after—worlds suffering from years of overconsumption and environmental decay—they began to change their minds. And besides, once she discovered that no living being apart from the two of us could travel between worlds without suffering from Quantum Displacement Disorder, the decision was made to abandon the project."

"So that was it?"

"Not quite. The military remained concerned that if another world was able to develop its own version of this technology, they could pose a threat. So Mum was asked to stay on board to supervise any significant developments made in other realities. Report back anything important. For her this was ideal because it meant she could start cataloging all the different worlds out there and begin searching for home. More importantly, she could begin searching for you..."

Just as Cassandra finished speaking, she appeared to notice something on the side of my neck and moved a little closer to examine it.

"What is it?" I said.

"The marks," she said, pressing her hand against my skin. "I don't understand—I've never known them to spread this quickly."

Cassandra's neck had started to turn black a few minutes ago, but I'd decided not to say anything. I didn't want to worry her.

It took a long time to descend to the bottom of the mine, but eventually the elevator shaft opened out onto a huge cavern, with hundreds of glistening stalactites hanging from a domelike roof of rock.

Down below, the surface was quite uneven, although several metal platforms, stairways and narrow bridges had been constructed to make it easy to get from one area to another. Some platforms were empty; others were packed with various pieces of scientific equipment. Computer servers. Filing cabinets. At first glance, the place looked like a labyrinth: a maze of technology with no discernable pattern. But as the lift reached its destination and Cassandra slid the door open, I could see that everything appeared to lead toward a larger, raised platform at the back of the cave. It was too high up from here to see what was on it, but I assumed that was the main part of the lab.

"Where is Alice?" I said, quickly shifting my gaze from one area to another in the hope of catching a glimpse of her.

"I don't know…" Cassandra muttered. "Mum?" She called out, her voice echoing off into the distance.

No reply.

At that moment, I detected a faint smell—was that…burning?

"Do you smell that?" I said.

Cassandra nodded.

"I don't like this," she said, grabbing my hand and leading me over the nearest gangway onto a rickety metal platform.

With Cassandra in front of me, I hopped from one platform to another, stepping over various cables and negotiating my way past countless databanks, generators and terminals. We seemed to be heading toward the larger platform at the back of the cave, but as we got closer, the burning smell only got stronger. Something wasn't right.

"Come on!" Cassandra said, grabbing the handrail to the final stairway and leaping up it two steps at a time.

I followed behind as quickly as I could, but when Cassandra reached the top, she just stopped, standing on the stairs in front of me, paralyzed. Silent.

"What is it?" I said, craning my neck to look over her shoulder.

Then I saw what had startled her. In front of us, it looked as though there had been a terrible accident—a massive explosion of some kind. The place was littered with scorched metal, broken circuit boards and fragments of machinery. Rows of monitors were shattered either side of us, the insides crackling with electricity, and at the far end of the platform, a huge machine was billowing with smoke. The machine was enormous: about the size of a shipping container. It had a glass panel at the front, through which I could see a faint ball of red light. Just in front of it, a man was lying face up on a large rectangular table, lifeless, his head covered in blood. All around him, hundreds of handwritten notes were scattered around, like rose petals sprinkled on a coffin. No sign of Alice.

It took a moment for me to recognize the man from his injuries.

It was me.

It was Richard Henley.

He was dressed in a dark gray, all-in-one overall, the top half of which was unzipped down the middle to reveal an off-white t-shirt underneath. The overall was frayed in several places, arms ripped, legs covered in burn marks. On his feet he wore a pair of black leather boots, although for some reason his shoelaces were undone.

"So predictable," a velvety voice purred from a dark corner to our right. "Didn't it cross your minds that if you ever managed to escape from us, this would be the first place we'd look?"

Eighteen

"What have you done!?" Cassandra screamed, rushing over to the body of my other self and cradling his limp head in her hands. As she lifted the head up from the table and pressed it against her chest, I noticed that the surface of the table had a faint glow to it, as though it was actually some sort of computer display. Curiously, a few of the notes in contact with the screen appeared to be flickering slightly, as if they were disappearing in and out of existence. Was this the device my other self had been using to communicate with me all this time?

"Hey—I didn't touch him," the voice said, emerging from the darkness.

It was Gabriel. His face was now almost completely black, his features barely distinguishable from the shadows surrounding him, but there was no mistaking that voice, drifting through the air like a thick, ominous fog. He looked as though he was in a serious amount of pain, staggering toward us awkwardly, his gun almost slipping out of his hand. Behind him, two men I didn't recognize remained in the background, sifting through some of the damaged equipment. They didn't appear to have any black marks I could see from where I was standing, although I guessed their infection might have been in an earlier stage of development.

"Liar!!" Cassandra cried, stroking my other self's hair. "You killed him! You killed Richard!"

Gabriel let out a loud cough. He sounded terrible, as though something was scraping out the insides of his lungs with a trowel.

"As much as I hate to disappoint you," he said eventually, wiping his mouth clean on the back of his sleeve, "your friend was like that when we…" He tailed off and looked at both of us for a moment. Although the extent of the black marks on his face made it almost impossible to read his expression, it was clear that something had distracted him.

"Let me see your hands," he whispered under his breath, motioning me toward him.

I took a few steps forward, holding my palms out for him to examine.

"No…" Gabriel gasped, grabbing me by the wrist and looking down at my blackened skin. "This can't be. You're supposed to be…"

"D-Dad?" Cassandra interrupted, stepping away from my other self's body and turning to look at me. Like Gabriel, her face was now completely black, her white eyes peering toward me in desperation like two lonely stars hanging in the night sky. She clutched her stomach and fell to her knees. "I don't… feel so good…"

I rushed toward Cassandra, trying to catch her as she fell. But before I could reach my daughter, her body began to twist and distort in front of us, as if a trapped beast was trying to escape from within. Then, in an instant, the space around her seemed to fold in on itself, and she evaporated away into thin air.

"Cassandra?!" I shouted, skidding to the ground where she had just stood. "Cassandra?!"

I could feel myself shaking. I'd lost her. This couldn't be happening. What was I going to do?

Gabriel limped toward me, his gun raised.

"Now you listen to me," he said, his voice wavering. "I can't die without finding out what happened to my wife, you hear? I'm not going to vanish in a puff of smoke! Where's Alice? Did she die here too? Tell me what happened!"

I could feel a pain welling up inside me. It was like nothing I'd experienced before, as if every cell in my body was being electrocuted simultaneously.

"I-I don't know…" I winced, keeling over on the floor. "We…we thought she'd be here…"

"No you don't!" Gabriel cried. He dropped his gun, grabbed me by the collar and dragged me back up to my feet. "You're not going anywhere until you give me some answers! Now tell me—where's Alice?"

I tried to open my mouth to speak, but the pain was too intense. The blood coursing through my veins felt like it had been turned to lava, my skin like it had been set on fire.

And then, nothing—the world fell silent, my body went numb, and my vision faded to black.

Nineteen

The sound of the ocean.

That was the first thing I remember as I came to my senses.

Waves lapping against the seashore in a slow, peaceful rhythm.

The faint cawing of seagulls overhead.

And a faraway voice.

"Dad!" it shouted. "Is that you!?"

My vision slowly began to return.

It was bright.

As my eyes adjusted to the light, I found myself standing on a beautiful, deserted beach, the coastline curving off into the distance as far as the eye could see. Fine white sand lay beneath my feet, luscious palm trees swayed in a caressing warm breeze, and the pale blue ocean lay calm, rising and falling gently like the belly of a sleeping giant. The sky was blue, the sun was shining, and for the first time today, my mind was totally at ease.

"Dad!" the voice cried again. It sounded closer. "You're here!"

I looked round. Cassandra was running along the beach toward me, waving her arms frantically. As she approached, I noticed that her skin was back to normal. She was smiling as she ran, her long dark ponytail fluttering behind her in the warm coastal air.

"You're okay!" she said, wrapping her arms tightly around me.

I opened my mouth to say something, but no sound came out. I was still in a state of shock.

"This is incredible," she said, taking a step back and looking me up and down. "The marks have completely disappeared from both of us!"

"I don't understand," I finally managed, casting my eyes down the beach. It really was completely unspoiled, as if no human being had ever set foot here. "What just happened to us? How did we get here? And where are we, anyway?"

"I have no idea," Cassandra replied, unzipping her leather jacket and folding it over her arm. I tugged on my collar. It was pretty hot here.

"Maybe this is heaven," I suggested. "Maybe we're dead."

"You're not dead," a female voice said from behind us.

The voice made me freeze to the spot. The hair on my arms stood up on end, my throat went dry, and my hands began to shake. I knew immediately who it belonged to.

"Alice?" I said, turning to face her.

"Hello, Richard," she replied.

TWENTY

She looked exactly the same as I remembered her.

Long blonde hair.

Creamy skin.

Pale green eyes.

And of course, that little nose. It was still struggling to hold up the bridge of her glasses.

For a moment, it seemed as though she hadn't aged a day, but as she stepped out from the shadows of the palm trees behind us, I started to see the signs that she was now a much older woman. Little wrinkles nestled in the corners of her eyes. Lips a little thinner. Hair streaked with a few flecks of gray. She wore a long summer dress printed with blue flowers, a thin white shawl over her shoulders, and a pair of open-toed sandals.

We stared at each other in silence. She looked beautiful.

"Mum?" Cassandra said, narrowing her eyes. "Is that you?"

Alice nodded. "It's me, Cassy," she replied, not taking her eyes off mine.

"But…how…?" Cassandra asked. "What happened?"

Alice took a deep breath and sighed. A small tear ran down her cheek.

"I've missed you so much, Richard," she said, wiping her eyes. "I can't tell you how much I…I…"

This was no time for words. I moved forward, ran my fingers through her soft hair, and pressed her head gently against my chest. She put her arms around me and began to cry. And for a few minutes we just stood there. Not talking. Not thinking.

Just being together again, at last.

A family reunited.

Cassandra removed her trainers and sat down on the beach, leaning back on her hands and digging her feet into the warm sand.

"I don't understand...," she said, looking back at her mother. "Is this a dream?"

"No," Alice said, emerging from our embrace and taking a few steps toward her daughter. "This is no dream. Remember what I told you? About having a plan to keep us safe? Well this is it." She looked back at me and smiled.

"You mean to tell us...you knew we'd be sent here?" I said. "You knew that's what the black marks would do?"

Alice nodded.

"But how?" Cassandra asked. "Nobody knows a thing about Quantum Displacement Disorder! How did you know it would send us here? Or anywhere for that matter?"

"Because I'm the one who created the condition in the first place," Alice replied.

"Hold on a minute," Cassandra stammered. She stood up and looked her mother in the eyes. "*You* created Quantum Displacement Disorder?"

Alice sighed.

"Perhaps I should start at the beginning," she said.

We found a shady spot under a large palm tree on the edge of the beach and sat down while Alice explained everything. Hearing her voice again after all these years filled me with a deep feeling of nostalgia, and I was reminded of the times she used to talk excitedly to me about her scientific theories all those years ago.

"While I was studying quantum physics back at university," she began, "I wrote a paper on many-worlds theory, outlining the possible existence of multiple dimensions. My basic argument was that if a quantum system was able to exist as a multiple superposition of states until it was observed, this was equally possible on a much larger scale, to the point where reality as we knew it could exist in different forms. However, quantum systems could not be viewed in an indeterminate state. They always collapsed into one disparate reality before they were measurable, so even if parallel worlds truly existed, it would never be possible for us to perceive them. My paper outlined a theoretical way of circumventing this problem. If I was right, it would allow someone to suspend quantum decoherence and observe these multiple states, which, on a larger scale, meant it might even be possible to observe and interact with parallel worlds."

"A few weeks later, I got a phone call from the vice chancellor of the university. He told me that my paper had been studied by a certain group of benefactors, and that they were so impressed with my theory, they wanted to fund any research into proving it, no matter what the cost. My task was to find out if parallel worlds really existed, and if they did, to develop a means of moving between them. At first I thought he was joking, but when I was given my own laboratory and all the resources I needed to conduct my experiments, I realized he was serious. It was an amazing opportunity, but something didn't feel right—I was never told who I was conducting this research for, or how the technology would be used if I was successful."

"Within the first year of tests, I had made a number of significant breakthroughs, and it wasn't long before I'd built a prototype device capable of sustaining a portal between parallel realities. This portal could be projected anywhere and was able to suspend quantum decoherence, splitting out the multiple superposition of states to an almost infinite scale, then collapsing them back down again in a different formation once anything or anyone passed though it. In other words, I had confirmed the existence of parallel worlds and developed a means of traveling between them."

"I still can't believe this," I said. "All that time, I never would have thought you were working on something so ... so ... extraordinary ..."

"I know," Alice said. "And trust me—it was hard keeping my discovery a secret, especially from you. But I made a decision—before

I was going to announce anything to anyone, I wanted to be sure of my benefactor's intentions. I wanted to know who had funded my research and how they planned on using it. So I started my own little investigation. Looked through the university's records. Found a few letters to the Vice Chancellor. What I discovered frightened the life out of me—my funding was coming from the military."

"The military?" I said.

"That was my reaction as well," Alice replied. "I couldn't believe it. Why would they be interested in funding this sort of research?"

"I dread to think," I said.

"So I started digging a little deeper. Remotely accessed a few government mainframes. It was then that I found out why the military were so interested in my experiments, why the technology I had developed was so valuable to them: They wanted to use it to try out different military scenarios in other worlds. Test the outcome of bombing other countries without fear of political fallout or retaliation. Phase soldiers in and out of parallel worlds to gain tactical advantages during invasions. At that moment, I knew I couldn't let this technology fall into their hands. It needed to be destroyed, and I needed to make sure no one else could replicate it."

I placed a hand on Alice's shoulder and looked her in the eyes.

"My God," I said. "Is that what was bothering you before the accident?"

Alice nodded.

"You have no idea how close I was to telling you everything, Richard. But I was worried it would only put you in danger. And in any case, I wasn't sure you'd even believe me. Parallel worlds? Military conspiracies? You'd think I was crazy."

I wanted to say that I would have been supportive, but she was probably right—no matter how much I loved her, I would have thought she was mad.

"I spent weeks trying to think of a solution. What was I going to do? I couldn't simply blow up the lab or pretend my experiment was a dead end—I wasn't the only quantum physics expert around, and with the extensive notes I had made over the last year, somebody might have been able to recreate the technology. Then it struck me—with my knowledge of quantum decoherence, I could create an artificial field of interference between worlds: a membrane that would erode the quantum signature of anyone that passed through it. And so Quantum Displacement Disorder was born—the perfect way to deter people from moving between different realities."

"But that only solved part of the problem," Alice continued. "There still remained a laboratory full of equipment, the prototype portal, the notes on my work, and…well…me. The foremost expert on multidimensional physics. If I really wanted to stop this technology from ever being misused, I needed to dispose of everything and disappear. But where would I go? Once I'd destroyed the lab, the military would surely suspect me of sabotage, and I didn't really want to be in hiding for the rest of my life."

"Then I had an idea—I could kill two birds with one stone. If I overloaded the portal, I could transport the entire lab to another world, along with myself. All the equipment related to my work would disappear, and the military would think the whole thing was some sort of terrible accident. Best of all, I would never have to worry about my employer coming after me. After all—they'd think I was dead."

"Wait a second," Cassandra said. "You always told me that was an accident! Do you mean to tell me…you did all that deliberately?"

"Not entirely," Alice replied. "With my plan in place, I began to work on creating the interference field, which I designed to let no organic quantum signature pass through to another world without decaying upon arrival. The only person it would let through intact…would be me. Within a few days everything was set, but then something unexpected happened. A variable I hadn't considered entered the equation."

"What was that?" I said.

"I discovered I was pregnant."

Alice looked at her daughter and smiled.

"It was at that point I knew I had to talk to you, Richard. I had to let you know what was happening, and most importantly of all, that

I was carrying your child. I wanted you to come with me; I wanted us to start a family in another world. That was what I was going to talk to you about that night, in the restaurant. I was going to tell you everything."

"But you never got the chance," I said.

"No. That night, I decided to make the necessary adjustments so that you, me, and our unborn baby could travel between worlds unharmed. Now that I was pregnant with your child, your quantum signature turned out to be the perfect common denominator for all three of us, so I activated the portal and updated the interference field. But as I was making the adjustment, the portal destabilized, and the entire lab was swallowed up and sent through to another world before I had a chance to react. The next thing I knew, I was alone in a strange world. Stranded, with no means of getting back."

"This 'interference field,'" I said, rubbing my hand where the black marks had once been. "Would it by any chance have the appearance of a thick, pale mist?"

"I believe that's how it's perceived when someone comes into contact with it, yes," Alice replied. "But I've never experienced it for myself."

Cassandra stood up and looked out across the ocean, her arms crossed firmly over her chest.

"Well, we've seen it," she said, picking her trainers up and tucking her jacket under her arm. "And while we there, something weird happened. There were these … things. Reaching out for us. Black arms flailing about. And we could hear screaming. Hundreds of voices crying out in agony. It was … it was horrible."

Alice looked down at her feet. "I know," she said. "Not exactly my finest hour, creating something that would trap all those people there …"

"Wait a minute," I said. "You mean to tell us those screams were coming from the people who disappeared?"

Alice nodded. "That's what happens when somebody succumbs to Quantum Displacement Disorder," she said. "The body and mind enters into a limbo state between worlds … forever."

I took a step back, my face paralyzed with shock.

"I know what you're thinking," Alice said, looking up at the sky. "How could I condemn so many people to such a fate? How could I be so coldhearted?"

"Jesus, Mum!" Cassandra cried. "Are you insane?"

"It wasn't an easy decision," Alice replied. "But don't forget—I'm a scientist. And in science, you sometimes have to strip away any emotional or moral considerations for the greater good. In this case, I made a choice. I decided it was necessary for a few people to be sacrificed to protect the integrity of all parallel worlds."

"What about your own integrity?" Cassandra said. "Did you ever stop to think about that?"

"I'm not proud of what I did, but I stand by it as the right thing to do."

"I don't believe this," I said. "If you'd have heard those people … the pain in their voices …"

"They're not in any pain," Alice said. "It may sound as though they are, but believe me—they have no perception of where they are, no understanding of time passing by. That's the nature of being in a limbo state. They feel nothing."

Cassandra shook her head.

"I don't know what to say," she whispered under her breath.

"I know it's bad," Alice said, standing up and walking toward her daughter. "But you must understand—I did it all to protect you. To protect *us*. And the only reason I haven't told you all this until now isn't because I was scared of how you would react—it's because we're up against an organization that can read minds through the multidimensional realm just as well as we can. If you knew I was behind all this, they would have found out by now, just by looking into your thoughts."

"So why haven't they already discovered this from you?" I said. "I mean, if you're the one behind all this, why haven't they been able to uncover this from reading *your* thoughts?"

"Because my mind cannot be read that way," Alice replied. "When part of my quantum signature was erased on that first journey to another world, the ability to read my mind disappeared with it. It's a phenomenon I've been trying to recreate in others for some time but with no success, unfortunately."

"Well, you could have at least told us what you were planning just now," Cassandra said. "Do you have any idea how scared we both were when those black marks appeared on our skin?"

"I know," Alice replied, pushing the bridge of her glasses back up her nose. "And I'm sorry. But don't you see? If we ever wanted these people to stop looking for you both, we needed to convince them that you weren't immune to Quantum Displacement Disorder after all. Part of that deception was around sending you to the lab. We knew Gabriel would be looking for you there, and that it would be a perfect place to stage your disappearance. But the other part of the deception was in your minds. Because you were both terrified, not knowing anything about the true nature of your condition, IDEA would have seen that as a genuine reaction. With any luck, they now think you're both dead—lost, like so many others, to the darkness."

Cassandra began walking slowly down the beach toward the ocean.

"Honey?" Alice said, calling after her daughter.

Cassandra didn't look back.

"You understand, right? Why I did it?"

Cassandra kept walking. Looked like she needed a moment alone.

"You understand, don't you?" Alice said, turning to me.

"I don't know," I replied, watching Cassandra as she took a couple of steps into the sea and stood there, the waves gently licking around her feet. "I can see why you chose to do what you did, but my mind doesn't work like yours. I wouldn't have been able to make the choice you did, condemning all those people to exist in limbo."

"They don't *exist* in limbo," Alice replied. "That's the point. They are in a place *outside* of existence … They really can't feel a thing."

"Like I said, my mind doesn't work like yours," I said.

"Well, for what it's worth, I'm sorry," Alice said. "But it really was the only way."

I shut my eyes and tried to change the subject.

"So what is this place?" I said, standing up and taking a few steps back to get a better look inland. The plant life here was really quite beautiful, with multicolored flowers sprouting through thick grassland, tall trees of all varieties towering overhead, and large, healthy bushes all around, ripe with delicious looking berries and fruit.

For the first time in a while, Alice smiled.

"Believe it or not," she said, moving closer to me, "this is London."

"What?" I said.

"Amazing, isn't it? You're actually standing in pretty much the same spot as you were in the underground lab."

"But…I thought I was just standing two and a half miles underground?"

"You were," Alice said.

"So how can I be standing in exactly the same place?"

"Are you saying you don't believe me?"

"At this point, I'm pretty much willing to accept anything. But I'd still like to know how it's possible…"

"You just need to open your mind to how varied some of these worlds can be," Alice explained. "In this dimension for instance, it just so happens that the landscape is very different. Coastlines are a different shape, land is a different height, and sea levels are lower. Even the planet's overall diameter is slightly narrower, hence why the sea level is so much lower."

"So does a portal always take you to the exact same spot in another world?" I asked.

"Yes," Alice replied, "with the exception of the very small ones we were using to send you the notes, which work a little differently. Other than that, a portal will take you to precisely the same longitude, latitude, and altitude, just in a different world."

"So where is everyone?" I said, looking around. "Is this world deserted or something?"

"No, no," Alice replied. "Human civilization still exists here, and in many ways, it's very similar to your dimension. There are big cities. People drive cars. But certain parts of the world are completely protected. Designated areas of outstanding natural beauty, like where we are now. And you still get visitors, but it's much more strictly controlled, to protect the environment…"

"Unbelievable," I said, "I've never seen anything like this…"

"Are you sure about that?" she replied, pointing toward the horizon.

I turned my head in the direction she was indicating. In the distance, I could see a vast mountain range, the snowy peaks looming high above a lush forest of evergreen trees. I blinked a couple of times and looked closer. A few palm trees were nestled in amongst the alpine vegetation, and in the sky, some strange birds were circling around. Alice was right—I'd seen this before.

"The painting!" I said. "The painting in my office!"

Alice nodded.

"Once I got my equipment up and running again after the accident, I spent the next ten years trying to find you," she said, sliding her fingers in between mine. "And while I was searching, I discovered this place. I thought it was the most beautiful world I'd ever seen—completely unlike any other dimension I'd visited. I always dreamed that if I ever found you, I would bring you here. Show you this fantastic place. Perhaps even spend the rest of our lives here together. But when I finally tracked you down…"

"I was married." I said, looking down at the sand.

"Yes. I always knew it was possible, and when I saw you had moved on and found another woman, I didn't want to spoil that for you. You looked so happy back then, it didn't seem right to turn up out of the blue and tell you I was still alive. As much as it pained me to do so, I decided it was probably best to leave you alone."

"Sad to think that if you'd found me a year later, I would have been divorced," I said. "You might have decided to show yourself. Tell me everything. Things would have been very different."

"I know. But at the time it didn't look like it was going to be. So I tried to forget about you. Abandon my dreams of bringing you here. It was hard—I'd clung onto a vision of us both standing on this beach for so long, and now it was never going to happen. So I decided to paint a picture of it for you instead. It wasn't the same as being here with you for real, but to me it meant that in some small way, I'd still been able to show you this other world. Leaving that picture for you in your office gave me a sense of closure, and I took comfort in knowing there would always be that small connection between us, even if you didn't know it."

"Alice," I said, clutching her hand tightly, "it's a beautiful picture. You have no idea how often I used to get lost in it. Knowing now that you painted it…well, it all makes sense. Thank you."

I turned away from the view I knew so well and cast my eyes along the beach again. Cassandra was still standing by herself on the edge of the ocean, her head down.

"We should go see her," I said.

"Cassy?" Alice called out as we approached her. "Is everything okay?"

Cassandra didn't respond. She was twisting the ball of her right foot into the wet sand, lifting it out of the water now and again before digging it back in.

We stopped a few feet away and just watched her for a moment.

"Cassy, I'm sorry," Alice said. "You must think I'm a complete monster. But I only ever did it to…"

"Richard's dead, Mum," Cassandra said, her voice barely audible over the sound of the waves. "They killed him. When we got to the lab, he was…he was…"

I felt Alice's hand go limp.

"No…" she said, her arm falling by her side. "You mean he didn't make it?"

Cassandra didn't reply. She just kept twisting the ball of her foot into the sand in silence, looking down as the waves lapped around her.

Alice shut her eyes.

"This can't be…" she said. "He was supposed to get out of there before we…before…"

But just as Alice was about to finish what she was saying, the space in front of us began to twist and distort, as though someone were rotating a giant lens before our eyes. Out of this distortion, a man suddenly appeared. He looked to be in his late forties. Slightly overweight. Medium height. Narrow shoulders. His short brown hair was groomed neatly into a side parting, his teeth looked almost as white as the sand he was standing on, and his skin had the sort of light tan you might expect from someone who spent most of their time on the golf course. He wore a pair of black-rimmed designer sunglasses, a dark blue suit with a white shirt, and a thin, plain tie.

"Before you faked the accident at your lab to make it look like you'd all been killed in an explosion?" he said, completing Alice's sentence for her.

The man had a strange accent—somewhere in between English and American, with a faint drawl that stretched out his vowels. He spoke quickly, as if there was an underlying impatience in communicating what he had to say.

Alice didn't say anything. She just stood there looking at the man, eyes wide, jaw hanging open. Cassandra leapt to her feet and ran over to me, clutching my arm.

"Don't try to deny it," the man added, walking slowly toward us. "We've already found traces of the explosives you used."

"R-Russell?" Alice stammered. "You...You've been watching us this whole time? How much have you heard?"

The man ran his tongue along the top row of his bright white teeth and smiled.

"Everything," he said.

Twenty-One

"How did you find us?" Alice said. "I thought I'd kept this place a secret…" She spoke quietly, as though the layers of her voice had been stripped away to leave nothing but a skeleton of sound behind.

"Oh, I don't know the details," the man replied, waving a hand in front of him as though the question was a fly buzzing too close to his face. He removed his sunglasses and examined his reflection in the lenses. "Something about a residual coordinate in one of your memory banks. Been accessed more times than any of the others… blaa blaa blaa. You'd have to ask one of the scientists if you want to know more. All I care about is the fact that we found you."

The man angled his face to the left, looked at his reflection a little closer, then flicked his fingers through his hair a couple of times. When he was done, he folded up his glasses, placed them inside his suit jacket pocket, and began to look around.

"So this was your plan, was it?" he said, squinting in the sun as he examined the surroundings. "Make us think you were all dead, then spend the rest of your lives hiding away on a beach?"

"Something like that," Alice replied. Her eyes were fixed squarely on the man, his voice cold and emotionless.

"I like it," he said, loosening his tie a little. "And it is a nice beach, I'll give you that. Romantic. And there's always a bit of civilization on the other continents if you ever get bored. Bit hot for me here though. Anywhere over ninety degrees and I start getting irritable."

I took a deep breath and turned to Alice.

"Who is this guy?" I asked.

"Oh—I'm sorry," the man said, extending a hand for me to shake. "Russell Hardwick. Director of Operations at the Inter-Dimensional Exploration Agency."

"You're Gabriel's boss aren't you?" I said.

"I am indeed," Russell said, still holding his hand out. "And Gabriel's told me all about you—you're Richard Henley, right? I would say the one and only Richard Henley, but that wouldn't exactly be true now, would it?"

I looked down at his hand, although I had no intention of shaking it. A small black mark was just beginning to appear on the back of his thumb. Russell noticed it as well and held it up in the air to examine in the light.

"You know, this is the first time I've ever been to another world," he said, twisting his hand around in the sun to examine. "Never really fancied it before, given the unfortunate side effects." He brought his arm down to his side and turned to face Alice. "But now we know you're the one behind this whole Quantum Displacement thing, I was pretty sure I'd be able to convince you to tell me the cure."

Alice folded her arms.

"By the way—nice job sending so many innocent people into limbo," he added. "I laughed out loud when I heard you reveal that one. Obviously it's horrible and like you said to your daughter, you're a complete monster, but somehow I admire you for it. Never thought you had it in you to make such a ruthless decision in order to do what you thought was right. In fact, in many ways, you and I are more alike than I realized."

"If you're expecting me to tell you anything about how to cure it, you're wasting your time," Alice said.

"Uh-huh…" Russell replied, his eyes looking up at the sky as if he was only half-listening. "That's admirable and everything, but I do think you've failed to take into account the leverage I've got over you at the moment…" He nodded in the direction of Cassandra and smiled. "Know what I mean?"

Cassandra immediately let go of my arm, dropped her leather jacket to the ground and began running back up the beach.

"Oh please…" Russell smirked, cocking his head sideways at Alice. "Can she at least credit me with a little intelligence?"

I looked round at Cassandra. She had only made it a few meters away from us before another spatial distortion appeared in her path, and a tall, broad-shouldered man stepped out. He looked like something in between a security guard and a police officer, wearing a gray padded uniform and a riot helmet on his head, the glass visor pulled down over his face. Cassandra tried to dodge past him, but his sudden appearance made her lose her footing, and she fell over into the sand. She desperately scrambled to get back up again but it was too late—the man tackled her to the ground, pressed her head down, and dug an elbow deep into her right shoulder blade. She struggled to break free for a moment, writhing around on the beach like a fish flapping on the shore, but it was no use.

"Okay, let's wrap this up," Russell said, circling his index finger around in the air. He took a mobile phone out of his pocket and checked it. "I've got lunch with the guys in PR at one o'clock, and I don't want to be late."

At that moment, a number of other spatial distortions began to appear all around us, and a group of men stepped out onto the beach. There must have been at least fifteen to twenty of them, all dressed in the same gray security guard uniforms as the man who had apprehended Cassandra.

Behind us, Cassandra was being pulled up to her feet and pushed toward us. She stumbled and fell against me, holding on to my arm as she reached round to massage her shoulder. I turned her head toward me and brushed away some sand that was stuck to her face.

"You okay?" I said.

Cassandra nodded, picking her trainers and jacket up from the floor and putting them back on.

"I'm fine," she said, barely moving her jaw as she spoke.

Russell strolled up to the nearest security guard and tapped him on the shoulder.

"Is the transport on its way?" he said, looking down at his watch.

"Yes, sir," the guard replied, pointing up at the sky. "Just making its final decent now."

Russell looked up.

"Ah yes—I see it," he said. "You know, I keep forgetting about the altitude difference. How far below ground level would we be in our world again?"

The guard took a small device out of his pocket and tapped a few buttons on it.

"At least two and a half miles, sir," he said.

"Two and a half miles…" Russell laughed. He looked around at us with a big grin on his face, as if we were somehow sharing his amusement. "Crazy, isn't it?"

I tilted my head toward the sky and shielded my eyes. High up in the clouds, I could see a small black dot. As it got larger, a low humming sound began to fill my ears, like a swarm of hornets approaching from the distance. From the way the dot moved, I first thought I was looking at a helicopter, but as it got closer, I could see no rotor blades. No moving parts. It was like nothing I'd ever seen before—a flying craft, able to maneuver in the air without wings. The craft actually looked very similar to a large saloon car—the kind of vehicle you might see at the back of a presidential motorcade. It had shiny black bodywork, an elongated hood, four doors, and darkened windows, but the underside was smooth, like the hull of a space shuttle, with four vents dispensing a bright blue glow where you would normally expect to see wheels.

Russell noticed me staring at the flying craft as it came in to land and walked over.

"Incredible, isn't it?" he called out over the sound of the approaching engines. "Anti-gravitational propulsion. You know, we own the patent on that. Got the designs from some technologically advanced dimension we discovered and then licensed it out to the car manufacturers in our world. Nowadays, it's the only way to travel. Earns us a fortune in royalties."

"Very impressive," I said, watching as the craft hovered a foot or so above the sand. The engine noise lowered to a quiet purr, and the blue vents dimmed in intensity like a gas flame being extinguished.

Russell walked over to the passenger door and opened it. The interior of the craft looked like that of a regular car, with black leather seats, adjustable headrests, and a low ceiling.

"The three of you should be able to fit in there," he said, motioning us over. "Get in."

"Look, Russell," Alice said, walking forward. "You don't need these two. I'll help you, but please—let them go."

Russell smiled.

"That's very honorable," he said, "but there's no way I'm letting any of you out of my sight. Now get in the car."

Three of the guards moved in behind us and pushed us toward the car. Alice got in first, followed by me, then Cassandra. The inside had an overwhelming aroma of leather, and for a moment I was reminded of the restaurant where my ex-wife and I had eaten our final meal together. A man was sitting in the driver seat in front of us, both hands holding the steering wheel, his face obscured by the same visor worn by the guards outside. I cast my eyes over the dashboard—it looked fairly similar to what you would find in a regular car, although there were a few extra levers I didn't recognize and a computer display showing information on altitude, pitch and yaw. Above his head were a few flick switches, like those you would see in the cockpit of an aircraft.

Russell shut the passenger door behind us with a click and walked around the car to the other side. As he lowered himself into the front passenger seat, Alice leaned forward.

"Where are you taking us?" she asked, her hands gripping the headrest tightly in front of her.

"The same place we took you and your pain of a daughter last time," he replied, shutting his door. As he did, the locks in each corner of the car automatically activated. "Only this time, none of you will be leaving ..."

Twenty-Two

The driver flicked a switch above his head, checked a couple of gauges on the dashboard and held on to the steering wheel. A couple of lights began to blink in front of him, the engine got louder, and the whole car started to vibrate.

"Now beginning our ascent," he said, turning to Russell.

"Good," Russell replied, looking out of the window. "Let's get out of here."

We began to ascend, the car vibrating harder as we climbed. The noise of the engines rose to a higher pitch, my ears started to pop, and my stomach felt as though it was folding in on itself. Alice grabbed my hand and squeezed it. Through the windscreen in front of me, I watched as we cleared the tops of the palm trees, and within moments I was looking out across a vibrant rainforest canopy, with trees of all different heights and shapes twisting into the sky like a group of performance artists contorting their bodies into different elaborate poses. In the background, I could see the tall, snowy mountain range I knew so well from Alice's painting, and for a moment I felt as though we were flying over an endless tapestry of different colors and textures—the greens, yellows and browns pulsating as if the whole jungle was slowly breathing in and out.

Russell turned his attention away from the window and took his mobile phone out of his pocket. It was a remarkably thin device: black, no thicker than a credit card. He scrolled through a few different menus, selected a number to dial, and pressed the phone to his ear.

It wasn't long before somebody at the other end must have answered.

"It's Russell," he said, holding up his hand to examine. At first I thought he might be checking to see if his black marks had spread, but it looked as though he was more interested in seeing if there was any dirt under his fingernails. "I need you to put out a press release immediately." He paused. "Yeah, we got them." Another pause. "I don't know—make something up. The papers don't check anything we tell them these days, do they? No. So just put out something like 'IDEA captures terrorist responsible for Quantum Displacement Disorder.' Maybe give them a quick statement from me as well—something short and catchy. Yeah, yeah—that's the idea. But make sure you use the word 'freedom' in it. Oh—and issue that photo we've got of her as well." Another pause, this time longer. "Okay, I'll see you when I get back."

He hung up and slid the phone back inside his jacket.

"Terrorist…" Alice scowled. "Is that what I am now?"

"Oh, I'm sorry," Russell said, throwing a sarcastic glance back at her. "How else should I describe someone responsible for the disappearance of so many people over the years? Someone who has spread so much fear? Someone who has been holding us back for so long?"

"You're the terrorist—not me," Alice said. "The things you've managed to use this technology for, despite the limitations I managed to put in place … well, it makes me shiver."

Russell turned to look out of his window again. We must have been pretty high up by now—the wind outside sounded stronger, a thin crust of frost was beginning to build in the corners of the windows, and we had started to pass through a few layers of cloud cover.

"How much longer?" he said to the driver, checking his watch.

"Almost at the correct altitude, sir," the driver replied, examining some of the instruments on the dashboard. "Just a few more seconds…"

I leaned across Alice's lap and looked down out of the passenger window. Far beneath us, I could just about make out the faint outline of the beach we were standing on a few moments earlier—a long, white arc of sand curving its way around the coastline of whatever country that was below, if indeed the concept of countries even existed here.

"We have reached safe ground clearance altitude," the driver said, pressing a small red button in front of him.

"Uh-huh," Russell said, running his fingers through his hair again.

The car stopped climbing and hovered in midair for a moment.

"Ready for the portal to be activated," the driver said.

"Yeah, yeah—let's go," Russell said.

The space surrounding the car began to blur and distort, as if everything around us were a reel of film going out of focus. Then, almost instantaneously, everything changed. The ground now only appeared to be about fifty meters beneath us, the sole hum of the car's engine was joined by hundreds of other similar noises, and the empty sky faded away into a stunning vista of futuristic architecture.

"Welcome to London," Russell said, looking back at me. "*My* London, that is…"

I leaned forward in my chair and peered through the windscreen. Never before had I seen so many skyscrapers in my life—beautiful, impossibly tall monuments of glass and steel, constructed in all kinds of shapes and sizes, reflecting the blue sky overhead. There was a building that twisted round in the shape of a corkscrew; a sharp, pointed building shaped like the blade of a sword; a bulbous, rounded building shaped like a teardrop—anything you could imagine and beyond. However, these skyscrapers had not replaced the older, more familiar structures beneath them, and in the distance I could still make out the domed roof of St. Paul's Cathedral and the top of Big Ben. The overall effect was a nice visual balance between the old and the new, as if the people in this world had not forgotten the historical roots of their city.

There were so many little details everywhere that my eyes felt as though they were being overloaded. Everything was just so colourful—streets were lit up with bright neon signs, huge television images were being projected onto the sides of buildings, and some of the taller skyscrapers even had giant screens built into the side of them, beaming out everything from soft drink advertisements to news updates from the BBC.

The transport system was also very different to the London I was familiar with. Tube trains, for instance, now appeared to run along an intricate monorail system suspended in the air, snaking its way over the streets and through the maze of buildings like an endless ball of twine that had been draped over the city. I leaned over to the passenger window and looked directly below. Beneath us, the streets themselves were no longer being used by motor vehicles. Instead, the miles of tarmac and pavement had been stripped away and converted into long stretches of parks and grassland, with trees and bushes planted at random intervals to look as though they had grown there naturally. It was an amazing sight, and from up here it made various parts of the town look like quite pretty, with clusters of buildings now surrounded by thick moats of greenery rather than the roads that used to connect them together. Directly beneath us, a few people appeared to be sunbathing in a spot that looked like it was once a busy interchange. Now, it just looked like a peaceful village green.

That wasn't to say that this version of London was free from the bustle of traffic you would normally expect to see; it had just moved from the ground and settled in the sky, hanging over the city like a giant grid-like cobweb of flying cars, busses and trucks, all cruising back and forth in an orderly fashion along straight, preset paths. Russell was right—it did seem as though flying was the only way to travel in this world.

Our car stayed hovering in midair for a moment, as if we were waiting for something.

"What do you think, Mr. Henley?" Russell said, not taking his eyes off of the gleaming skyline. "Beautiful isn't it?"

I had to admit, I had never seen London look so impressive—the futuristic architecture, the beautiful greenery, the amazing technology—it looked like a utopia. A dream world.

"I don't know what to say," I said, rubbing my eyes. "It's…it's…" I stopped trying to speak and shut my mouth—I really was lost for words.

"Let me help you there," Russell said, his lips curling into a thin smile. "This city is perfection. The most technologically advanced, socially balanced, environmentally friendly metropolis there is. It's a marvel of human engineering. It's clean. It's free from crime. It's…a paradise."

"Don't listen to him, Dad," Cassandra said, narrowing her eyes at Russell. "This place isn't a paradise—it's a nightmare. Everything you see has been achieved through a despicable exploitation of other worlds."

"Come now, dear," Russell said, pursing his lips. "We're not that bad really…"

"Not that bad?" Cassandra spluttered. "You steal raw materials from other dimensions so you can build your blasted skyscrapers. Harvest fossil fuels from other realities to power them. Dump your waste elsewhere so you don't have to deal with it. This place isn't a paradise—it is the vilest, most sickening example of overconsumption I've ever seen; a world dripping with greed; a world totally lacking any accountability for what it has become. And while the people here live a life of excess without suffering from any of the consequences, a hundred other dimensions are either being stripped bare or polluted to sustain it."

"Your daughter has quite the way with words, doesn't she?" Russell laughed, running his tongue along his top row of teeth again and smiling at me. It wasn't a very nice habit, and every time he did it I thought of an animal salivating over a piece of meat.

"She does make a good point," I said. "Don't you think?"

"Does she?" Russell said. "Well here's another good point for you: The way I see it, I'm helping this world to grow. To be better than anyone thought possible. I'm improving everyone's way of life. Allowing our cities to develop in a clean and sustainable way. And best of all, with this technology, it's easy. Some of the worlds we take our raw materials from aren't even populated, for goodness sake…"

"It's still wrong!" Cassandra said.

"Is it?" Russell replied. "I would argue that what we're doing is making a difficult choice, but we're doing it for the right reasons. Yes, we're sacrificing the wellbeing of other worlds, but we're improving our own at the same time. Besides—it's no different to what your mother did. She did something that many might say was wrong—sending people into a state of limbo against their will—but she did it for what she thought was right."

Alice leaned forward.

"What I did was send a few people somewhere they couldn't do any harm, to prevent the destruction of billions of other worlds," she said. "What you're doing is exploiting others for your own selfish means! You can certainly question the things I've done in the past, but you have no defense whatsoever!"

Russell shook his finger.

"This is where I think you're making a mistake," he said. "You see right and wrong the same way you see your parallel worlds: two polar opposites, with several layers in between. But it doesn't work like that. Right and wrong can at one moment be at opposite end of a spectrum, yet the next minute they are interacting with each other. They can coexist in the same space or not exist at all. It's more complicated than most people appreciate, so for that reason, I try not to think about them at all. Instead, all I care about are two things—the wellbeing of everyone in *this* world and IDEA's share price. Makes things much simpler, if you ask me."

I tried to think of something to say, but it was difficult—as much as I disagreed with the sentiment of what this man was saying, he put across his argument in a surprisingly elegant way. Even Cassandra appeared to be lost for words.

"And speaking of our share price," Russell continued, "now that we don't have to worry about Quantum Displacement Disorder, IDEA's stock is going to go through the roof. We'll be able to do what we've been doing a hundred times faster than before. Visit even more worlds. Perhaps even colonize a few. And best of all—we'll be able to do it for less money. No compensation payouts for volunteers and all that. It will be the beginning of a historical era—not just for the people of this world but for IDEA as well. And for me."

"Our escort has arrived," the driver said, pointing toward two cars that were breaking away from a stream of traffic flying overhead. The cars were gray and white with orange reflective stripes down both sides, blacked out windows, and blue sirens on the roof. The word "POLICE" was written along the underside of each one in a rounded, capitalized font. The cars glided either side of us, came to a halt, and waited.

The driver pressed a button on the dashboard and checked the display in front of him.

"Entering autopilot mode," he said, letting go of the steering wheel.

Suddenly, the car ascended all by itself and accelerated forward to join the stream of flying cars overhead. The two police cars switched their sirens on and did the same, accompanying us in a precise formation as we slotted neatly into the flow of traffic cruising above us. I leaned over Cassandra's lap and looked out of the window—we were surrounded by all kinds of futuristic-looking vehicles, from huge articulated trucks, to long, single-decker busses, to hovering motorbikes. It was like driving on a motorway, yet we were in midair; the sea of skyscrapers and high-rise apartment blocks passing beneath us as though we speeding over a flooded city in a boat.

We made our way across London quite quickly. Every now and again the car would turn into a different stream of traffic flying above or below us. Not once did the driver seem to touch his steering wheel to accomplish this, and when I looked at other vehicles during our journey, I noticed many people seemed to leave the driving to the "autopilot," paying more attention to the mobile phone in their hands than the road ahead.

After about twenty minutes of flying, the car peeled away from the traffic and began to descend toward the ground, the police escort still accompanying us on either side. As we got lower, the car began to slow down, ducking underneath a particularly high section of the city's monorail and weaving in between one skyscraper after another, like a skier making their way through a slalom course. One of the buildings had a large screen built into its side, probably more than a hundred feet high, displaying the latest news headlines. The screen suddenly flashed up with the words "BREAKING NEWS" before fading into the headline: "IDEA captures terrorist responsible for Quantum Displacement Disorder." Above the text was a photograph of Alice looking straight into the screen.

"Look, you're famous," Russell smiled, pointing toward it.

The picture dissolved into a stock image of Russell on the left, with a statement attributed to him fading in on the right. It read: "Today marks a major victory against those who would deny us the freedom to travel between worlds. From this day forward, IDEA will be able to enhance our way of life like never before."

Russell looked at the image of himself and smiled. The pose looked almost ambassadorial, eyes looking off screen, head tilted up to accentuate his jawline.

"You know, sometimes I think about getting into politics," he said, admiring the towering image of his face as we flew past it. "I mean, don't you think I look quite statesmanlike? Don't you think I'd be a great world leader? I bet people would vote for me…"

"Tell me," Alice said, "how many of those people would vote for you if they knew what you're *really* doing to so many other worlds? About the death and destruction you're responsible for? How many people would vote for you if they knew the *true* cost of their new way of life?"

"They know what they need to know," Russell said, "Besides, I could ask Richard the same thing—how many people in his world know the true cost of those cheap clothes they buy in the supermarket? Or the welfare of the food they eat? Or which country is dumped with the rubbish they want recycling?"

He turned round in his chair and looked Alice straight in the eyes.

"And while we're on the subject of misinformation," he said, "how many times have you lied to Richard today, Alice? And your daughter? How long have you been hiding things from them? And why should I listen to someone responsible for sending so many people into a state of limbo over the years anyway? Before you start accusing someone else of withholding information, you should take a look at yourself…"

"That…that was different," Alice stuttered, squeezing my hand a little tighter. "I did it to keep them safe. I did it…to protect them…"

"Uh-huh—protect them, right. You know, it kind of makes me wonder what else you're not telling them, and in particular, Richard. What was your relationship like with the other Richard, for instance? The one now lying dead in your lab? Were you lovers?"

"No!" Alice replied. "I mean, when I first met him, I thought we might…but…"

"Alice," I interrupted. "You don't have to explain anything. I know what he's trying to do here…"

"But I want to tell you," Alice replied. "Richard and I aren't…I mean we…*weren't* lovers," she said, correcting herself. "When I appeared in that world, I'll admit I looked him up. I wasn't sure he'd even exist, but he did. We became good friends over the years—but I never loved him." She lifted her glasses, pinched the bridge of her nose and sighed. "I can't explain it—he was you, but at the same time he wasn't. I'm not sure I'm making any sense. But you have to believe me."

"I believe you," I said. "But it really wouldn't have mattered. I mean, we've been apart a long time…"

"I know. But this is important to me. I want you to know the truth."

"Don't trust her, Richard," Russell said, raising his well-groomed eyebrows at me. "We may not be able to read her mind properly, but we're pretty sure there's something she's still not telling you."

"Something she's still not telling me?"

"Why would that be, do you think?"

I looked at Alice.

"Is this true?"

She looked back at me saying nothing, but I could tell from her eyes that Russell was right. She *was* hiding something.

"Now arriving at IDEA Headquarters, sir," the driver said, "but there seems to be quite a crowd outside. Do you want me to head for the landing platform on the roof?"

"No way," Russell said. "Have security clear a space for us on the ground. I want to make a real entrance …"

Twenty-Three

The headquarters of the Inter-Dimensional Exploration Agency was an imposing structure, well over a hundred stories high. With two broad sections at both the top and bottom, the building looked a bit like a capital "I", the facia a lattice of cream brickwork and mirrored windows, with at least fifty stone steps leading up to it on all sides. It was as though the architect had mounted his creation on a pedestal to be admired from every direction. At the very top, the IDEA acronym was lit up in bright white letters, shining across London as a beacon for all to see.

As our craft made its final descent, I leaned over Cassandra's lap and peered down. Beneath us, hundreds of people were gathered at the foot of the steps, just as the driver had said. All of them were looking up, holding their phones and cameras in the air, flashing away indiscriminately. As Russell had instructed, the crowd were being marshaled behind a row of gray-uniformed guards who had cleared a small area for us to land. To the left of the clearing, a row of television cameras were lined up, each one pointing toward a different news reporter. The reporters were all wearing brightly colored clothes, clutching oversize microphones, and holding their hair in place from the wind as we came in to land.

I exchanged a quick glance with Cassandra. She said nothing, rolling her head around on her shoulders the way a boxer loosens the muscles in their neck before a fight.

Russell checked his reflection in the rearview mirror and straightened his tie as the craft touched down on the ground, the roar of the engines fading to a quiet hum. All around us, the guards were struggling to keep the crowd at bay, with many bystanders bursting through the cordon every so often and running toward us shouting some sort of inaudible abuse through the window of the car before being carted away by another section of IDEA's security detail.

"Well—it's showtime!" Russell smiled, swinging his door open. The crowd let out a huge cheer. He got out, waved to everyone like a politician who had just been elected into office, and within seconds he was already being interviewed by the nearest three reporters, each one shoving their microphones in his face, probably desperate for a quote or a snappy sound bite.

Three guards approached the car, opening the rear passenger doors and pulling us out one by one. The guard assigned to me grabbed the inside of my elbow and pulled me to my feet with the kind of force that suggested he was used to people putting up a little more resistance, but I didn't resist. I felt submissive, like a puppet allowing its strings to be pulled however they needed to be. I caught my reflection in his glass visor for a moment and sighed. Baggy eyes. Messy hair. Sunken cheeks. I looked like a defeated man.

The crowd started jeering Alice as she was marched around the front of the car and led up the stone steps toward the entrance to the building.

"I hope you're proud of yourself!" someone called out.

"You should be ashamed!" another person cried.

Alice didn't acknowledge the hecklers. Didn't react to the torrent of angry chants being directed at her. She just walked in silence, looking down at the floor as though she were following a trail of breadcrumbs. Cassandra and I were made to follow a few steps behind, arms held behind our backs like criminals being led to the gas chamber. Russell left his interview with the reporters and ran over to join us.

"Russell!" another reporter cried, trotting up the stairs behind us in her high heels, cameraman in tow. She wore a bright pink pencil skirt, a white blouse, and a short pink jacket with gold buttons. Her hair was peroxide blonde, her skin was tanned, and her face was caked in so much makeup it was difficult to determine her age. Looking at her face, my eyes were immediately drawn to her mouth—she had a broad smile, wore deep red lipstick, and her teeth were unnaturally white.

"You've just released a statement telling us how the capture of Alice Everett—the woman who has been terrorizing us from another dimension for all this time—will enable IDEA to enhance people's lives like never before," she said, struggling to keep up with him in her five inch heels. "Can you tell us more about what you meant by that?"

Russell flashed a smile at the reporter and slowed down.

"Certainly, Meredith," he said, smoothing down his hair and adjusting his cufflinks. "What we have achieved today means we can now do whatever we want. Go wherever we please without fearing any consequences. Just think about everything we have accomplished to this date, despite the specter of Quantum Displacement Disorder looming over us. Anti-gravitational transport. Environmental sustainability. Unprecedented urban development. Today's breakthrough will allow IDEA to eclipse all of those things, perhaps even overshadowing our greatest contribution to the modern world so far—the Decision Tree service."

The reporter looked totally amazed at this statement, her mouth hanging open as if she was about to take a bite out of her microphone.

"Well there you have it," she said, turning back to the camera and shaking her head in disbelief as she addressed her viewers. "The end of Quantum Displacement Disorder and a promise from Russell Hardwick of great things to come, maybe even surpassing the Decision Tree service. Will he proven right? Only time will tell..."

Once we had reached the top of the stairs, the three of us were marched through a set of double doors and into a spacious lobby, leaving the noise of the crowd and the glare of television cameras behind. The lobby was one the most ostentatious pieces of open space I had ever set foot in, stretching the entire length of the building and clad from floor to ceiling in a shiny cream marble. To our left, an artificial waterfall cascaded down an uneven section of the wall into a small, semicircular pool, and to our right, a long marble reception desk was manned by a number of men and women, each immaculately dressed in black suits and cream shirts to match the stonework. They reminded me of the concierges you got at posh hotels. Polite. Attentive. The far wall was appointed with eight large elevators, each one waiting with its doors open to receive passengers.

"Welcome to IDEA Headquarters," Russell said, holding his arms out. "The nerve center of our whole operation."

The three of us remained silent.

"Well, what do you think?" Russell said, looking up at the high marble ceiling, his voice echoing all around. "Impressive, right? You know, you can't get marble of this kind from our world. Or at least not enough to build anything like this. But there are mountains of the stuff in other realities, if you know where to look…"

None of us responded. I was too busy thinking about how much my arms hurt, which were being held so firmly behind my back I thought my shoulders might dislocate from their sockets.

"I think you can let them go now," Russell nodded to the guards, leading us across the shiny marble floor toward the elevators. "They can choose to make a run for it if they like, but I think they know that crowd outside won't let them get too far…"

Russell was right—we didn't have much of a choice but to follow him. If we took one step outside, we'd be mobbed.

The guards did as they were told, releasing us from their grip and allowing us to walk freely.

Over by the reception desk, one of the staff—a tall woman with her hair tied back in a neat bun—was holding a phone receiver in her hand and looking toward Russell.

"Sir—I've got the Prime Minister's office on hold," she said. "They're waiting to speak with you,"

"The Prime Minister's office?" Russell sighed.

"What should I tell them?"

"Tell them I'll call back later," he replied, stepping into the nearest open elevator and motioning us to do the same. "I'm a little busy at the moment…"

He reached inside his pocket for a key and inserted it into a panel next to the door. "Come on," he said. "There's room in here for everyone…"

He wasn't kidding—each elevator looked to be about the size of a large double bedroom, with padded, red leather walls, a wood paneled ceiling, and the same marble floor as the lobby. There was easily enough room inside for me, Alice, Cassandra, Russell, and the three nameless guards accompanying us.

"Ready?" Russell said, turning his key.

The doors slid shut in one graceful movement, and the elevator began to ascend. The ride felt smooth, as though we were a pocket of air floating gently to the surface of a lake.

Russell walked over to my side and took his phone out of his pocket.

"Are you familiar with our Decision Tree service?" he asked, typing a four-digit password into the screen. A number of colorful icons flashed up in a smooth animation like a deck of cards being spread out by a croupier.

I shook my head.

"Alice and your daughter have seen this before, but I don't think you have."

I looked across the lift at them. They both looked back, saying nothing.

"Let me show you," he said, placing one arm around my shoulder and holding his phone up for me to see.

"I'm really not interested," I said, looking away.

"I insist," Russell replied, gripping my shoulder a little tighter. "We're quite proud of this little application. You know over a third of our corporate revenue comes from this little baby?"

I sighed and looked back at his phone.

Russell scrolled through a few pages of icons before stopping on one in particular. It looked like the silhouette of a tree on a blue background, except the branches were little straight lines, connecting clusters of small boxes together. He clicked on it and waited for the next screen to load.

"What I'm about to show you," Russell explained, "is arguably the most important technological innovation to come out of our ability to observe other worlds—a computer program that allows people make the right decisions in life."

"What do you mean, the 'right decisions'?" I said.

Russell smiled.

"Let's face it, Richard—people have so many decisions they need to make in life, every day of the week. It never ends. Should I apply for this job or that job? Do I go out tonight or stay in? Shall I watch this show or that one? Shall I turn left or right? It's a minefield. With the Decision Tree application, the user simply speaks into their phone, telling it the choice they need to make. The phone then transmits the question back here, where our computers scan all the multiple dimensions to see what the different outcomes would be. The information is then transmitted back, allowing the user to understand all the various consequences of a choice before they even have to make it."

Russell paused, as if he was waiting for me to respond.

"All for a nominal charge, of course," he added. "In fact, if you subscribe to our premium service, Decision Tree will even send out text alerts, regardless of whether you have asked it a question, telling you when you might want to alter what you are doing to ensure a better outcome to your day. To open up your life to opportunities you might not have known even existed."

The phone flashed up with a question.

"What do you wish to know?" it said.

"Observe," Russell said, releasing his grip on my shoulder and holding the phone up to his mouth. "Which route should I take home this evening?"

The phone displayed a spinning hourglass figure for a few seconds.

"Processing," it said.

Within moments, a flowchart flashed up, with several strands branching out from a box at the bottom of the screen displaying Russell's original question.

"So, let's see," Russell said, following one of the strands with his finger and touching the text box it led to. The box increased in size as he touched it, taking up most of the screen.

"There is a 60% probability that the A12 Flyway eastbound will suffer delays due to an accident," it said. "Recommend avoiding A12 Flyway."

"Okay, let's look at another one…" Russell minimised the box and opened a different one.

"There is a 70% probability that the North Circular Flyway will be closed due to adverse weather conditions," it said. "Recommend avoiding North Circular flyway."

"And one more," Russell said, opening another box.

"There is a 90% probability that the A13 Flyway eastbound will remain clear. Recommend taking A13 Flyway."

"This can't be real," I said. "I mean, scanning multiple dimensions is one thing, but how can you predict the future?"

"Oh I don't know the details," Russell replied, "but apparently timelines aren't necessarily locked in the same point across all dimensions—realities can be minutes, hours, days, even years ahead or behind ours. And because there are virtually an infinite number of worlds out there, we can always find ones relevant to the questions people ask."

I felt the lift gradually come to a halt.

"Well?" Russell said, slipping his phone back in his jacket pocket. "What do you think? Pretty clever, huh?"

The elevator doors opened out onto a long gray corridor with a row of gray, brushed steel doors on one side and a set of windowed laboratories on the other. From where I was standing I could only see inside the first lab, which contained huge racks of computer servers, each one attended by a group of scientists in white coats.

"I think that program of yours is the stupidest thing I've ever seen," I said. "I mean, why would anyone want to know the outcome of making an important choice or want to know when they should change what they are doing? Surely the thing that makes life exciting is the fact that you never know what the future might bring?"

"Richard, Richard, Richard," Russell said, leading us out of the lift and down the corridor. The three security guards followed a few steps behind, each one walking in unison with the other, their faces still hidden behind their visors. For all I knew, they could have been robots. "You have a very closed mind, you know that? Did you ever stop to think about how else this technology might be used?"

"What do you mean?" I said.

"They police it, Richard," Alice said from behind me. "As well as allowing people to see the potential outcomes of a choice, they also use it to make sure people are doing the 'right' thing, as they see it. They use it to control the population."

I looked at Russell.

"Is this true?" I said.

"IDEA's goal is to create the best possible world for everyone," Russell said, looking through a window to our left into the second laboratory, arms folded behind his back like a king inspecting his troops before a battle. Inside the room, another group of scientists were huddled around a large computer screen on the wall, plotting coordinates on a complex line graph. "If a user looks as though they might be doing something that doesn't contribute to that goal, we ... *correct* them."

"What do you mean, you *correct* them?" I said.

Russell smiled.

"We have a small task force that can deployed if need be," he said. "And they are very persuasive ..."

"This is insane," I said, stopping for a moment. "How did people allow this to happen? How did they let this technology become so integrated into their lives to the point where it could be used to control them? Surely they resisted?"

"Oh it was a gradual process," Russell said, stopping by one of the steel doors on our right. "At first, people only downloaded the Decision Tree application out of curiosity. Wanted to run trivial decisions by it for fun. What should they have for dinner that night? What dress should they wear? That sort of nonsense. But over time, people began using it more and more frequently. Became more and more reliant on it. Nowadays, the average person runs nearly every decision they make by it. They trust everything the Decision Tree service tells them, and with that trust, people have opened themselves up to the idea of IDEA policing it. After all, we're only doing it for the safety and security of our world. What is there to complain about?"

"But who are you to decide what's right and wrong?" I said. "What makes IDEA the authority on free choice?"

"Don't lecture me on the moral implications of how we choose to integrate technology into our society," Russell said, reaching for the key in the door's lock and turning it. "After all, I could say a few things about your world. It's riddled with technology that people have come to rely on."

"That's different," I said. "In my world, people can still choose whether they want to use that technology or not. What you're talking about is controlling people's destiny! About taking away their free will!"

Russell twisted the handle and opened the door, the hinges screeching like fingernails on a blackboard. Inside, the room resembled a prison cell. Square. Gray walls. No windows. No adornments on the walls—just a single fluorescent strip glowing on the ceiling. Two metal chairs were bolted to the floor in the middle of the room, with steel restraints on both the arms and the legs.

"You're a fine one to talk about choice," Russell said, walking over to the first chair and unlocking its restraints, "considering you haven't made a single independent decision since your daughter came to see you in your office the other day."

"What are you talking about?" I said. At that moment, the guards behind us closed in, forcing the three of us through the door and into the room. They followed behind, making sure there was no way back out for any of us.

"Think about it," Russell continued. "You lecture me about free will, and yet all this time you haven't made a single choice for yourself, have you? No—you were doing exactly what those notes were telling you to do, or blindly following instructions from your daughter. You allowed yourself to be led down a certain path without ever questioning it. So you tell me—why did you let that happen? Was it because you trusted what you were told? Or is your character so weak you can't decide anything for yourself?"

I opened my mouth to speak but couldn't think of anything to say. In some strange way, he was right. I hadn't made a single decision for myself since Cassandra first came to see me—I had just done exactly what I was told.

"Have a seat," Russell smiled, patting the seat of the first chair.

I walked over to the chair, turned to face Alice and Cassandra, and sat down. As I lowered myself down and placed my arms over the armrests, Russell folded the metal restraints back in place round my wrists and ankles, tightening them until I was unable to move. He then slotted a thin metal bolt along the side, which held them firmly in place. The metal was cold, like someone pressing ice cubes into my skin.

"You next," Russell said, pointing at Cassandra.

"Wait!" Alice said, grabbing Cassandra's wrist. "What are you going to do to them?"

"Well, that all depends on you," Russell replied, unlocking the restraints on the second chair. "We lost Gabriel to Quantum Displacement Disorder not long after he went back to your lab, and to date hundreds of men and women have disappeared, all because of you. Then, of course, there's me." Russell held up his hand and showed Alice the black mark on the back of his thumb, which was still roughly the same size as before. "I'm a victim too now, don't forget. So I tell you what—if you cure me, help me bring back all the IDEA personnel you sent to limbo, and fix it so that no one who travels between worlds ever suffers from this condition again, maybe I'll be nice to them."

"Don't do it, Mum!" Cassandra said, spinning round to look at her mother. "It's not worth it! You know what will happen!"

Alice looked up at the ceiling and sighed.

"And if I refuse to help?" she said, closing her eyes.

Russell ran his tongue along the top row of his teeth and looked at the floor.

"No need to discuss that just yet," he said. "But I think you know what I'm capable of."

"Fine," Alice sighed, letting go of Cassandra's hand. "I'll do it. I'll do whatever you say."

"No!" Cassandra cried. "You can't!"

"Honey," Alice said, cupping her daughter's head in her hands and looking into her eyes, "you need to trust me, okay? Everything will be fine."

"But…"

"Shhh, shhh…" Alice said. "Everything will be fine. You understand?"

Cassandra nodded.

"I understand," she whispered.

"Okay—is everyone happy then?" Russell said, rubbing his hands together. "Excellent." He looked at Cassandra and patted the seat. "Now, if you wouldn't mind…"

"Russell," Alice said, taking half a step forward. "You don't need to do this. I've said that I'll help. Is it really necessary to lock them in those things?"

"Probably not," Russell replied, fastening the restraints back over Cassandra's arms and legs as she sat down. "But I know how resourceful the three of you can be. So if you don't mind, I won't be taking any chances."

"You're a monster," Cassandra spat. "You know that?"

"*I'm* a monster?" Russell replied, locking the final restraint in place over Cassandra's left leg. "If I'm a monster, what does that make your mother? The one who condemned so many innocent people to be stranded in a state of limbo?"

"That's different!" Cassandra stammered, looking at Alice. "I might not agree with what she did, but at least her motivations weren't malicious!"

"But neither are mine," Russell said. "I don't mean anyone any harm. All I want is what's best for the people of this world. I want to explore other worlds, discover things I never thought possible, and most importantly of all—I want to share it with everyone. Don't you see? All I want to do is improve people's quality of life. Does that really make me a monster?"

"The price of it does," Cassandra replied.

"Well, the electricity bill for this kind of operation isn't exactly cheap," Russell said. "At the end of the day, I run a business, not a charity. Somebody has to pay."

"You know what I mean!" Cassandra shouted. "You exploit other worlds for your own benefit! Show no remorse at the loss of life your organization has caused! *That's* the price of all this!"

Russell sighed. "I don't think this is really getting us anywhere, do you?" he said. "But I get the message—we're making some morally ambiguous decisions here, and you're not too happy about it. For the sake of us all being able to get on with our lives, shall we just agree to disagree?"

"Fuck you," Cassandra replied.

"You know, you swear far too much," Russell added. "Strange—I thought with Alice as a parent you would have been brought up to be more articulate."

Alice pushed the bridge of her glasses up her nose and stepped forward. "Come on, Russell—let's get this over with." She looked at us both. "Will you two be okay?"

"Oh, don't worry about us," I said to Alice, resting my head against the back of the chair. "As long as you know what you're doing..."

"I do," she replied. For a split second, it looked as though she had given me a quick wink, but I couldn't be sure.

Russell walked over to the door and held it open for Alice.

"Shall we?" he said, raising his eyebrows.

Alice nodded and left the room in silence, followed by Russell and the three guards. The door closed with a screech, the room echoed with the sound of the lock being turned, and then it was just me and Cassandra, alone, strapped in our cold metal chairs.

"What the hell are we going to do?" Cassandra said, straining her head round to look at me. "We've got to get out of here!"

"I know," I replied, twisting around in my chair. "But I…I can't…move…"

I tried to squeeze my wrists out of the metal restraints, but it was no use. They were holding firm with no sign of any movement whatsoever. I relaxed my body, slumped back in the chair, and sighed, my head hanging down over my chest like a deflated balloon. It was hopeless.

Then, all of a sudden, a note appeared on my knee.

"Russell was right about Alice hiding something from you, back in the car," it said. "She wasn't telling you that I was still alive."

"What?!" I blurted out.

"Quiet," the note said, rewriting itself in my handwriting as it had always done.

"What is it?" Cassandra said.

"You're not going to believe this," I said.

"Come on," the note said. "You know Alice better than anyone. Did you really think she wouldn't have a plan B?"

Twenty-Four

"**R**ichard's alive!" I said to Cassandra.

"W-what?" she said, snapping her head in my direction, her breath catching in her mouth as she spoke. "But… how? We saw his body!"

"What you saw," the note said, "was the body of the Richard Henley who got shot at the docks. Alice and I retrieved it after Gabriel dumped it in the bay…"

"The body belonged to the other Richard Henley," I explained to Cassandra. "The one Gabriel killed…"

My daughter bit her bottom lip and shut her eyes, a single tear running down her cheek like a drop of morning dew trickling down a leaf.

"You mean she faked *both* your deaths?" I said. "Not just hers?"

"That's right," the note replied. "Just before you arrived at the lab, Alice purged the other Richard's body of the black marks, swapped my clothes with his, then staged the explosion to make it look like we'd both been killed. Then, when she transported herself to the world where you appeared on the beach, I fled on foot. You probably know the rest—with everyone apparently dead or missing, we hoped IDEA would stop searching for us, once and for all…"

"What's he saying?" Cassandra asked.

I read the note out loud and continued to do so for my daughter's benefit.

"I don't understand," she said. "Why didn't Mum tell us he was still alive?"

"Because she knew that while there was still a chance of IDEA finding out what she'd done, you couldn't know the truth," the note said.

"You mean she knew this might happen?" Cassandra said. "She planned for all of this?"

"That's right," the note replied. "After Gabriel and his team left the lab, it was agreed that I would go back and make sure everything had been successful. But if something had gone wrong, it would be my job to execute her backup plan. That's why she needed to keep you both in the dark—if you'd known the truth, Russell would have found out while he was observing you or by reading your minds. And if that had happened, I wouldn't be speaking to you now. Most likely, I'd be dead."

"Hang on a minute," I said. "If Alice's lab is now destroyed, how are you talking to us?"

"The damage was only superficial," the note said. "Most of the equipment is still in perfect working order—in particular, the table I've been using to transport these notes to you and our surveillance apparatus…"

My heart began to beat a little faster.

"You mean to tell us you can just transport us out of here?" I asked, leaning forward in my chair as far as I could.

"Unfortunately not," the note said. "That whole building is protected by the same quantum shield they used at the warehouse to stop you from leaving. Thin sheets of paper are the only things small enough to pass through it."

"Great," I said, slumping back down again. "So what do we do?"

"Simple," the note said. "We break you out."

"But how?" I said. "I thought you could only send bits of paper through to us?"

"And believe it or not, bits of paper are all we need," the note replied.

I stared at the words for a moment to make sure I had read them correctly.

"You're joking, right?" I said.

"Not at all. When Alice was last brought here with Cassandra, she made some careful observations of her surroundings. Took note of all the security measures they have in place. Despite all the technology at IDEA's disposal, she believed that if any of you were ever brought back again, she had a way of getting out of there using only a few sheets of paper sent through from our world. Kind of poetic, don't you think?"

"But how on earth could she think of that?"

"Because she's a genius," the note said, "and fortunately, they have detained the two of you exactly as she predicted, restrained in steel chairs in a locked room on the 110th floor of their headquarters."

"That's reassuring," I said. "And you say you can get us out of here using only a few sheets of paper?"

"Let's find out, shall we?" the note replied. "Okay, the first thing we need to do is break you out of those chairs.

"And how exactly are you going to do that?"

"You'll see," the note said. "Now, I'm about to free your right hand. Once you can move it, you should be able to undo the other restraints yourself. I'll then leave it up to you to free Cassandra. Are you ready?"

"I guess," I said.

"Good," the note said. "Here we go."

I looked down at the restraint over my right wrist, curious to see what would happen. All of a sudden, a sheet of tissue paper materialized on top of it, draping itself over the metal. It looked wet.

"You'll need to be careful with this," the note said. "That tissue paper is soaked in a highly corrosive acid. Once the restraint starts to weaken, you should be able to break it open. But try not to get any on your skin…"

"You could have warned me about this!" I said, watching as the metal over my wrist started to hiss and smoke, the surface bubbling up as though it were breaking out in sores.

Within a few seconds, the metal had all but dissolved away, and I was able to break free, the restraint falling to the floor like a crumpled piece of tin foil.

"Okay, you should now be able to remove the other restraints yourself," the note said. "You just need to slide the bolt out on the side and open the latch…"

I did as the note instructed me to, first removing the bolt securing the restraint around my left wrist, then lifting it open. Once that hand was free, I proceeded to release the bolts holding my legs in place. Tossing the bolts to one side, I kicked the restraints open, grabbed the note from my lap and stood up, rubbing my wrists to get some circulation back into my hands.

"Hey—you did it!" Cassandra said, squirming around in her chair. "Now get me out of here, will you?"

I held the note between my teeth and released Cassandra. Once free, she leapt out of her chair, straightened her leather jacket, and tightened the hairband holding her ponytail in place.

"I'm surprised there aren't any security cameras," she said, looking up at each corner of the room to check she wasn't mistaken.

"Maybe they don't exactly want a record of what goes on in these rooms," I replied.

"Now, I'm going to send you a map," the note said. "It's based on Alice's recollection on the floor's layout, so you can assume it's 100% accurate. This should help you find where you need to go."

Sure enough, another sheet of paper materialized out of thin air, floating to the floor like a leaf falling from a tree in autumn. I caught it before it touched the ground and held it out in front of us. Just as the note had said, this second piece of paper was a detailed blueprint of the floor we were standing on. It looked as though there were ten holding cells on the south side of the corridor, with five large laboratories on the north side. At one end of the corridor was a lift—presumably the one we used to get here—and at the other end was a set of stairs leading to the roof.

"You are in the fourth cell from the left," the note said. "And at this moment, Alice is with Russell, two guards, and Dr. Naylor in the last laboratory on the right. Once you get out of this room, you'll need to go to the end of the corridor and get her, then head for the roof. You got that?"

"Yes, but how do we get out of this room?" I said. "The door's locked!"

"Not for long," the note said. "Alice observed that this door has a keyhole on both sides, and that whenever Russell locked the door to the cell, she never heard him remove the key. She also noted that the door had a good centimeter clearance from the floor."

"So?"

"So you have two pieces of paper in your hand. The paper this note is written on is thin enough to be rolled into a tight tube and poked through the keyhole to knock the key out. The map, on the other hand, is large enough to slide under the door and catch the key when it falls… Can you see where I'm going with this?"

"Come on," I said. "That sort of thing only happens in the movies. Surely her plan doesn't rely on this actually working?"

"Don't worry," the note said, "she was just curious to see if it could be done. If for any reason you can't get the key out, I'm supposed to dissolve the lock with more of that tissue paper…"

I looked at Cassandra.

"May as well give it a try," she shrugged, taking the map off of me and sliding it under the door.

"I guess," I said, rolling the note up as tightly as I could and inserting it into the keyhole. Alice was right—Russell had left the key inside the lock on the other side. It only took a few jabs, and I felt the key wiggle out of the door and fall to the floor on the other side.

"Now comes the moment of truth," Cassandra said, pulling the paper back under the door. Amazingly, the key had landed just on the edge, appearing as the very last inch of paper was pulled into the room from the other side.

"Well, what do you know?" Cassandra said, picking up the key and handing it to me. "That actually worked!"

"We were lucky," I said, removing the rolled up note from the lock and inserting the key in its place. "I bet you if we tried that again, it would've bounced over the other side of the corridor or something."

"Perhaps," Cassandra replied. "But it was still cool though …"

I unrolled the note and looked at it again.

"Excellent work," it said. "Now, don't go out into the corridor just yet—three guards are just walking past your cell toward the lift. I'll let you know when they've gone."

I pressed my ear to the door and listened. The notes were right—I could hear their footsteps getting louder as they approached, then softer as they passed by and walked further away.

We waited a little longer before the note rewrote itself.

"Okay," the note said. "They're in the lift now, so you can go. Are you ready?"

Cassandra grabbed the handle.

"Ready," she said.

"Wait a minute," I said, grabbing her arm. "Richard mentioned that Alice wasn't just alone with Russell—she's got two guards *and* that bloody doctor with her. How are we going to get her out of there?"

"I'll explain when you get there," the note said. "But first, you need to sneak in and find somewhere to hide."

"Shall we?" Cassandra said, mimicking the way Russell had spoken to Alice when he had opened the door.

I winced as the hinges creaked, hoping no one could hear.

Cassandra poked her head out of the doorway, scanning both ends of the corridor.

"Looks clear," she said. "Let's go …"

I looked down at the note.

"I'm keeping an eye on security," it said. "Best I can tell, the nearest patrol is nowhere near you at the moment. But you don't have much time, so hurry …"

Cassandra and I ran down the corridor as quietly as we could, passing several windowed laboratories on our way to rescue Alice. The first lab we passed was absolutely huge and had an enormous white machine inside, roughly the same size and shape as the one I had seen billowing smoke at Alice's lab earlier. In fact, the more I looked at it, the more this device looked remarkably similar—it even had the same round glass panel at the front with a red ball of light pulsating inside like a beating heart. Every few seconds, the machine threw out jolts of electricity along some wires hanging from the ceiling, which were collected by four coiled towers stationed in each corner of the room.

"What the hell do they do here?" I whispered.

"Like Russell said," Cassandra replied, "this floor is the nerve center of IDEA's whole operation. Everything the organization does is controlled from these few rooms: from the portals they create, to the computers they use to scan different worlds. It's the crux of all their whole operation."

We passed another lab and looked through the window. Inside, various specimens of tissue, human limbs and organs were being suspended in tanks of blue liquid. Each one looked to be tainted with black marks to a different degree, as though the samples were in different stages of Quantum Displacement Disorder. This must have been where they were studying the disease to see if they could understand it—to see if they could find a cure.

"Let's keep moving," Cassandra said, scuttling down the corridor on her hands and knees.

But just as we were about to reach the laboratory where Alice was begin held, the lift bell sounded out from behind us. The door was about to open.

"Quick, hide!" I said, pulling Cassandra across the corridor and into a room similar to the one we'd just escaped from.

We hastily shut the door behind us and waited, each of us pressing an ear against the cold steel surface for any sign that we'd been spotted.

Nothing. We must have hidden in time.

"Who are you?" a voice said from behind us.

Twenty-Five

The words made my heart stop for a moment.

After all the planning Alice had meticulously put into our escape, we had blown it—we had allowed ourselves to be caught. She was counting on us to escape, perhaps even to free her, and we'd let her down.

But when I looked round at the source of the voice, it wasn't a scientist or a uniformed guard looking back at me, ready to raise the alarm.

It was a young man, maybe in his late twenties, strapped into a tall metal chair much like the ones we had been restrained in.

This was another prisoner.

His face was covered in a thin layer of sweat, his hair look ruffled and greasy, and he had a large cut under his right eye, which was swollen. With dirty skin and dry lips, it looked like he'd been here a while. Couple of days perhaps. He wore a brown suit with a few of the seams popping loose at the shoulders and a cream shirt undone at the collar, stained with a few specks of blood.

"W-who are you?" he repeated. His voice sounded weak. "Because, if you're here to try to intimidate me like the other guys, that ain't gonna work…"

"Whoa," I said, rushing over to him. "What are you talking about?"

"You…work for IDEA?" he said, looking up at me through bloodshot eyes.

"No no no," I said, undoing the restraints over his arms. "We're being held here too! Just escaped from our cell!"

"Wait a minute…" the man said, looking toward Cassandra. "I recognize you…Aren't you the daughter of that woman Russell was after? The scientist?"

"That's right," I said. "But don't worry—we're not terrorists or anything…"

The man smiled.

"I know," he said. "I've learned quite a bit since IDEA made me their guest. I know that whatever your mother did, she did for the right reasons…"

"Well that saves an explanation," I said. "Who are you?"

"Kyle Lewis," he replied, leaning one hand on my shoulder as he eased forward out of the chair and loosened the restraints around his ankles. "I'm a reporter for the BBC…"

Cassandra was still by the door, listening out for anything from the corridor.

"Wait a minute—you're a journalist?" she said, looking round for a moment.

"That's right," he said, sitting down on the floor and rubbing his wrists.

"You okay?" I said, looking at his face in the light. "You look like you've been beaten up pretty bad…"

"Huh…" Kyle laughed, wiping his mouth with his sleeve. "This is nothing like the beating IDEA's gonna get once I get out of here…"

"Is the coast clear yet?" I said, turning to Cassandra.

"I don't think so," Cassandra replied. "I can hear some talking from the other end of the corridor."

"I don't understand," I said, sitting down next to Kyle. "What's a journalist doing being held up here? What happened to you?"

"It's a long story," Kyle replied.

"Well, until those guards leave the corridor, we're not going anywhere," I replied.

Kyle looked at me for a moment, crooking his neck to one side until it clicked.

"It all started a few weeks ago," he said, pressing the palm of his hand against his swollen eye for a moment before lowering it again. "I'd been doing some background research on the science behind Decision Tree for a silly feature I'd been asked to do. It was a slow news week, and my editor wanted something light that everyone would be able to relate to. So I thought a few minutes about the app people rely on to make choices for them would be a good idea. Problem was, when you start looking deep enough, you begin to realize there is *no* science behind it. Once you start to understand the nature of how parallel worlds work, you soon realize that the premise of Decision Tree is total nonsense. Scanning multiple worlds for the outcomes of different choices? Predicting the future? It cannot happen. Someone has made it up and tricked the general public into paying for bogus advice on how to live their lives."

"But Russell Hardwick showed us a demonstration earlier," I said. "It told him which route to take home later tonight. Sounded pretty convincing to me…"

"It's a con. A fraud. If Decision Tree says something is going to happen, it's either because it's something easy to predict like the weather or a wider thing that's going to be orchestrated by IDEA themselves to authenticate the information they are giving people. And it's all done in probabilities anyway, so if it's wrong, no one can question it."

"Very clever," Cassandra said.

"So you see, suddenly I was sitting on the biggest news story of my career," Kyle continued. "The biggest deception ever carried out against the general public, by the world's largest technology company. It was then that I began to look at the implications of what I'd discovered. If IDEA were using Decision Tree to tell people what to do, what was their agenda? Why were they doing it?"

Kyle stopped for a moment to catch his breath. After a few seconds, he looked up at the ceiling and continued.

"The answer was power. When IDEA was first set up, the senior board members like Russell Hardwick began to realize the enormous potential it had to control everything from populations to politicians. After all, many of its employees were the scientists responsible for having just saved the world, so it had the highest public mandate imaginable. People were happy to support the company no matter what it chose to do, and once IDEA started a new technological revolution with sustainable power, anti-gravitational transport and hyperconnectivity, that support only got stronger."

"So in the eyes of the people, IDEA could do no wrong…" I said.

"That's right. In fact, it got to the stage where they were becoming hugely influential in matters beyond their remit. One bad word from IDEA about this politician or that politician could topple a government. Any suggestions about changes to the law or legislation carried a huge amount of weight. Of course, this began to cause a problem for those in power, and conversations soon began to take place around the world about curbing IDEA's influence. Scaling down the company. Bringing it back under the control of the world governments. Of course, Russell Hardwick and his peers didn't want this to happen—a government buyout would not only devalue their stock, it would strip them of all the power they had grown accustomed to."

"So what happened?"

"IDEA realized that if they wanted to keep their dominance in society and still remain an independent company, being influential wasn't enough anymore—they needed to be able to control people directly, tell them what to think. If they could get inside the heads of everyone from the regular man on the street to President of the United States; if they could literally tell everyone what to do, they wouldn't have to answer to anyone. That's when the Decision Tree application was conceived."

"My God," Cassandra said. "Do these people have no shame?"

"To be fair to IDEA," Kyle said, "the intention at first was to have a genuine application that could be tweaked to suit the company's agenda. Only problem was, the science didn't stack up. So they took a shortcut, releasing the program anyway to the world and lying about the accuracy of the advice it gave. Fortunately for IDEA, public trust in the organization was so high, nobody questioned them, and within a year, everybody was using Decision Tree to tell them what to do."

"So how did you end up here?" I said. "How did you end up becoming their prisoner?"

"Well, like any good journalist, once I had my story, I wanted to confront IDEA. Give them a right to reply. When I called up, Russell offered me an interview, and I accepted. Only problem was, he wasn't waiting for me in his office when I was shown in. His guards were."

"I see…"

"Hey—I hate to interrupt while we're in the middle of this story," Cassandra said, opening the door a couple of inches, "but I think the coast is clear…"

"I can't believe they got away with this," I said, getting to my feet. "I mean, surely Decision Tree has been wrong so many times, people have begun to question it?" I helped Kyle to his feet and walked toward Cassandra.

"You say that," Kyle replied, following me closely behind, "but people rarely find out whether it's right or not, since they usually ask it what they should do rather than asking them what will happen if they do it. And besides, there is *some* technology at work in how it makes its predictions—sweeps of other worlds to assess outcomes—but in general it relies on two things: people's trust and the fact that it offers only probabilities as an answer."

"Well, I predict a 100% probability that we're gonna find Mum and get the hell out of here," Cassandra said, stepping out into the corridor.

The three of us exited the cell where Kyle had been held and ran over to the entrance of the last laboratory. This lab looked far more cluttered that the other ones we had passed, with stacks of charts littered over desks, thick textbooks piled everywhere, and tall filing cabinets overflowing with paperwork. I could see Alice on the far side of the room, facing away from us, typing a number of commands into a computer terminal. Russell was leaning over her shoulder, watching closely. To their left, Dr. Naylor was looking up at a large display, which showed a number of equations and scrolling numbers, and just behind him, two guards were standing at ease. Like all the other guards we had seen today, they were dressed in gray padded uniforms, complete with helmets and glass visors over their faces. None of them appeared to have seen us.

"Kyle," Cassandra said, "we need to get my mum—head for the roof and wait for us there, okay?"

Kyle nodded and ran along the corridor, disappearing through the door at the end.

"Now's our chance," Cassandra whispered to me, easing the door open and crawling inside. She ducked behind a short steel bookcase, crammed with dossiers and lever arch files, and motioned me to follow.

"Come on!" she whispered.

I scampered across the floor and crouched down next to her, looking over the files toward the other side of the lab. The room smelled like plastic, the lighting a strange off-white that made everything look as though it was shrouded in a thin fog.

"There," I overheard Alice say, watching as she lifted her glasses up and rubbed her eyes. "Once you activate this resonance cycle, the quantum filter I placed between worlds will purge itself. I've also provided instructions on how to cure Quantum Displacement Disorder and given you everything you need to retrieve your people from limbo…"

"You mean we'll be able to bring back everyone you took from us?"

"Everyone," Alice said.

"Even Gabriel?"

Alice shut her eyes. "Even Gabriel."

"Hmm…" Russell muttered under his breath, turning to Dr. Naylor. He didn't sound entirely convinced. "What do we think?"

"Amazing," Dr. Naylor replied, looking up at the screen. His condition had got marginally worse since I'd last seen him, the black marks just beginning to claw their way over his face, but he looked nowhere near as bad as Gabriel had done earlier. "This is quite an accomplished piece of quantum manipulation, Miss Everett," he said. "Very impressive indeed …"

"Has she given us everything we need or not?" Russell said, checking his watch.

"I think so …" Dr. Naylor said, not taking his eyes off of the screen. "Yes … yes, I see what she's done. This is perfect."

Alice stood up and faced Russell.

"Okay," she said, placing her hands on her hips. "I've done everything you've asked. Now let me and my family go."

Russell waggled a finger in Alice's face and smiled.

"I'm not so sure I want to do that," he said, placing a hand on her shoulder. "I mean, how can I ever be sure that you won't interfere with our plans again?"

"But … you promised!" Alice cried.

"No I didn't," Russell frowned. "In fact, I believe my exact words were: 'Maybe I'll be nice to them.' You forget, my dear—I'm a businessman. Noncommittal language is my speciality …"

Dr. Naylor and the two guards laughed.

I ducked back down behind the bookcase and looked at Cassandra.

"I really hate that guy," I said.

"Yeah," Cassandra agreed. "I'm not his biggest fan either."

"So how the hell do we get her out of here?" I said, looking over my shoulder at the group. "I mean, look at those two guards— they're massive! How do we deal with them?"

"Wait," Cassandra said. "Didn't the other Richard say he was going to help?"

"You're right," I said, opening the note and holding it out in front of us so Cassandra could read it as well.

"Okay," the note said. "Here's what we're going to do. In a moment, I will incapacitate the two guards. However—what I'm going to do won't last very long. When I say 'go', I need you to both come out shouting. When Russell turns around to see what's going on, Alice is going to push him as hard as she can and make a run for it. Once you're out of the lab, the three of you need to turn left and sprint for the roof. And I mean *sprint*. You think you can do that?"

"No problem," Cassandra whispered, looking at me. "Right?"

"Let's do this," I said.

"Good," the note said. "Are we ready?"

I took a deep breath and nodded.

"Ready," I said.

"Okay," the note said. "Three, two, one…GO!"

As instructed, Cassandra and I leapt out from behind the bookcase and ran toward Alice, screaming at the top of our lungs. As Russell looked round to see what was going on, Alice bolted toward us, shoving both hands into his back and sending him flying over the top of an office chair into the side of a desk. I looked up at the two guards as I reached for Alice's hand—just as the note had promised, both of them had been momentarily incapacitated, the inside of their visors plastered with black paper, rendering them completely blind. The two men desperately tried to undo the catches on their helmets, but the sudden disorientation caused them to bump into each other, their large frames crashing to the floor as they struggled to remove their headgear.

In all the commotion, Doctor Naylor barely had time to react, and by the time he seemed to realize what was going on, Cassandra and I had already grabbed Alice and started to head for the door.

"GET THEM!" Russell screamed, his legs flailing about on the floor as he struggled to get to his feet.

The three of us ran out of the laboratory and turned left, bursting through the set of double doors at the end of the corridor and sprinting up the stairs. We only had to climb one flight before reaching another set of doors, which opened out onto the roof of the building.

We ran out into the fresh air and looked around what appeared to some sort of landing platform for several flying cars, with all sorts of vehicles parked in different bays around the edge of the roof. All the models looked quite sporty, and at a quick glance I realized that I recognized a few of the manufacturers—Porsches, Ferraris, Lamborghinis—the people who worked for this company couldn't have been short of money. Kyle was waiting for us right next to the door.

"You guys okay?!" he said, looking down the stairwell we had just emerged from. "What happened?"

Alice looked at me for a second in confusion.

"No time to explain—he's with us!" I said.

"Well, we all need to get to Russell's car!" Alice said, pointing toward a convertible red Ferrari with its roof down, parked over in the far corner. "With any luck, he'll have left his keys in the ignition, as he always does!"

"Let's go!" I huffed, tucking Richards's note inside my trouser pocket as the four of us ran toward the middle of the roof. Behind us, the sun was beginning to set over London, the sky casting a warm red glow over the sea of glass towers and sprawling architecture beneath us. For a split second I wondered how this could be, since it had only just turned to morning a few hours ago. But then I remembered that that was in a different world. Anything was possible, I guessed. Here, the sun was setting, and in front of us, the giant letters of the IDEA logo must have been casting an enormous shadow down on the city, but from where we were standing, we couldn't see it.

Behind us, the doors from the stairwell burst open, and an army of guards ran out, closely followed by Russell and Dr. Naylor.

"They're over there!" Russell shouted, pointing toward us. "And they've got that fucking journalist with them too! Don't let them get away!"

Cassandra sprinted over to Russell's Ferrari and leapt over the door, landing smoothly in the driver seat and grabbing the wheel. Kyle took the front passenger seat.

"Come on!" he screamed. "Let's get out of here!"

"Wait a minute," I said, rushing over to the side of the car and jumping in the backseat next to Alice as our daughter started the engine. "Does she know how to fly this thing!?"

TWENTY-SIX

"Are you sure you know what you're doing?!" I cried, my hands clutching on to the side of the car as the engine roared to life.

"Not entirely!" Cassandra said, looking back at me over her shoulder as she quickly jabbed a few buttons on the dashboard. "It's been a while since I've flown!"

"Come on, come on—you can do it!" Alice said, leaning over the front seat. "Get us out of here!"

"I'm trying, Mum!"

I looked back. The guards had already made their way halfway across the roof, running toward us like a herd of stampeding wildebeest. Behind them, Russell was pointing toward us and barking instructions at his men, though I couldn't hear his voice over the noise of the engine.

"Here we go!" Cassandra shouted, jabbing her foot down on one of the pedals. "Hold on to something!"

The car began to ascend, jerking upwards and away from the roof erratically like a startled pigeon, the engines rising in pitch like a jumbo jet about to enter takeoff. Cassandra didn't look like she was in full control of the vehicle, desperately holding on to the wheel with one hand whilst manically flicking a few switches with the other.

And then, just when it looked like we were going to clear the roof and make our escape, the car began to splutter and drop in altitude again.

"We need to be going up!" Kyle said.

"Shit!" Cassandra said, pumping her foot on a different pedal. "Give me a second!"

"We don't have a second!" Alice screamed.

"I know, I know!" Cassandra said, flicking another switch to the side of steering wheel.

Suddenly, the car lurched into reverse, knocking the two closest guards over like skittles before scraping along the passenger side of a black Porsche parked on the opposite end of the roof. Russell stopped shouting at the guards for a moment and brought a hand up to his mouth.

"I think I've got it!" Cassandra said, straightening the nose of the car up and ramming her foot on the pedal again. This time, the car began to ascend more smoothly than before, but it was too late—one guard managed to leap toward us from a few feet away and grabbed onto the rear spoiler, locking his arm around it so as not to fall off.

"Richard!" Alice cried, ducking down into her seat as the guard made a swipe for her with his free hand. "Help me!"

"No you don't!" I shouted, standing up in my chair and wrestling the man away from her, throwing my arms around his neck. "You…leave…her…alone!"

The man pulled himself up onto the back of the car and punched me in the face, his fist hitting me straight in the jaw. I fell back in my seat, my left arm hanging over the side of the door. I looked down for a second—we were now at least fifty feet above the roof. Down below, Russell and his men were running back inside.

"Seatbelts!" Cassandra said, strapping herself in. "Put them on, now!"

Alice, Kyle and I reached for ours quickly, stretching the two straps over our shoulders and clicking them into place as the man on the back of the car climbed closer toward me.

"Okay, here we go!" Cassandra said, spinning the steering wheel around full circle. The car responded by turning completely upside down, like a canoe stuck in the middle of an Eskimo roll. As we turned, the guard lost his footing and slipped, his hands holding onto the rear spoiler as the rest of his body dangled from the car like an overripe fruit about to fall from a tree. I hung in my seat, suspended by nothing but my seatbelt. The feeling of blood rushing to my head felt extremely uncomfortable, but at least I was secure.

"Agghh!" the man screamed, kicking his legs about desperately as he tried to get a better grip on the car. "Don't let me fall!" he begged. "Turn over again! Turn over again!"

"I'm going to take us back down to the roof so he can let go!" Cassandra said, pushing the steering wheel forward.

Still facing upside down, the car banked around in the air and headed back down to the roof of the IDEA building. A few guards still remained on the landing platform, looking up at us. Once we were only a couple of meters above the building, Cassandra kept the car hovering in midair and looked back at the man. His fingers looked like they were beginning to slip.

"Time to get off!" Cassandra said, nudging the steering wheel to the left.

The car rocked slightly, and the man lost hold of the rear spoiler, falling down onto the roof but landing safely on his feet.

"Everyone okay?" Cassandra asked, spinning the car back the right way up and pushing the steering wheel forward.

Alice and I nodded. Kyle was grinning.

"That was good," he said.

"Right," she said, pressing her foot down on the accelerator. "Let's get the hell out of here…"

We began to move forward, with Cassandra dipping the Ferrari over the edge of the IDEA building and flying toward the ground at high speed before pulling up and accelerating through the city, the tall glass skyscrapers of futuristic London whizzing past us on either side.

"Woo hoo!" Cassandra yelled, punching the air. "I think I'm getting the hang of this again!"

I leaned over toward Alice, who was trying to keep her hair under control in the oncoming wind.

"When did she learn to fly?" I asked, trying to raise my voice over the sound of the air stream.

"A couple of years ago," Alice replied, tying her hair up tightly in a bun and pulling her shawl around her neck. "She and I have visited quite a number of different worlds over the years, and when we discovered some realities had flying cars, I didn't hear the end of it: She just *had* to learn to fly one. She's a real petrolhead, our daughter…"

"Tell me about it," I said. "You should have seen what she did to my car earlier…"

Alice laughed.

"Yes, I was watching," she smirked. "Sorry about that…"

"So where are we going?" I asked.

"As far away from IDEA Headquarters as possible," Alice replied. "We need to get to a distance where the other Richard can activate a portal and get us out of here…"

"And you can drop me off anywhere," Kyle said. "All I need to do is get to a phone, and this is all over for IDEA."

I leaned over the edge of the car and looked down. We were flying high enough to clear some of the shorter tower blocks and older buildings, but most of the newer buildings towered high above us as though we were cruising through a thick forest of curved mirrors and angular steel, the ergonomic structures rising up like pillars of glass holding up the sunset-red sky. In front of us, streams of airborne traffic were flowing at high speed in all different directions, headlights darting across the sky like shooting stars streaking through the atmosphere. Tube trains were winding their way around the sprawling monorail like snakes slithering through a maze. And as the sun began to set, the bright neon lights and huge television screens of the city began to cast everything in a thousand different colors, the reds, yellows, blues and greens bouncing off of each other and glittering like a beautiful constellation of electricity.

As we weaved our way past a particularly tall skyscraper to our right, a huge television image was projected onto its side. "BREAKING NEWS," the image said, before fading into the headline: "Terrorists escape from IDEA building. Russell Hardwick issues nationwide alert, appealing for the capture of Alice Everett and her accomplices." Next to the text, an image of Alice, Cassandra and me flashed up, our faces cold and emotionless like police mug shots.

"No, no no…" Kyle said to himself. "If only they knew…"

"This is bad," Alice said, looking up at the image as we flew past, her face illuminated in its bright glow. Across the city, the picture began popping up all over the place, as though the three of us were looking out across the city from every viewpoint.

"We've got company!" Cassandra said, looking in the rearview mirror. "Behind us!"

Alice and I swiveled round in our seats. Not far behind, five or six police cars were in pursuit, their sirens flashing angrily in a fit of blues and reds.

"Take us higher!" Kyle said. "Try and lose them in one of the Flyways!"

Cassandra nodded and pulled up, my stomach turning inside out as the Ferrari fired its rear engines and propelled us into the sky like a rocket. Our trajectory took us right alongside the edge of the nearest skyscraper, the car vertically hugging the mirrored slope of the building as if it were a road of glass. I turned around in my seat and looked down—directly beneath us, the police were still following close behind.

"There!" Kyle said, leaning forward in his seat and pointing toward a thick stream of traffic flowing high up in the sky. "That one looks busy—aim for that one!"

"Okay!" Cassandra replied, banking the Ferrari around to the right and maintaining our ascent. "Hold on!"

We climbed higher and higher until the flow of traffic was directly above us, screaming over our heads in a blur of metal and light like a swarm of fish caught in a strong current. Cassandra accelerated harder, matching the speed of the traffic before slotting us into the lane above. Behind us, several cars had to swerve out of the way to avoid hitting us, blaring their horns and flashing their lights in horror.

Then a moment of calm, Cassandra steered the craft deeper into the lanes of traffic, matched the speed of the vehicles around us, and waited. And for a few seconds, I felt safe again, as though we had wrapped ourselves in a blanket of humming engine noise and warm jet air.

"Did we lose them?" I said, looking behind us for the flash of sirens. "Are they gone?"

Alice, Cassandra and Kyle said nothing, their eyes drifting slowly from left to right, scanning the space all around.

Alice looked as though she was about to reply when suddenly, and for no particular reason, the adjacent car veered straight into the side of us, the bodywork scraping the front wing of the Ferrari in a screech of sparks.

"Shit!" Cassandra cried, looking round at the other car and wrestling with the steering wheel to compensate. "What the fuck is he doing?"

I looked back at the car myself. Inside, the driver looked equally surprised, waving apologetically and shrugging his shoulders. As I looked closer, I noticed his hands weren't even on the wheel.

"That shouldn't have happened…" Kyle said, narrowing his eyes. "He's on autopilot…"

"Autopilot?" Cassandra said. "Then how could he possibly…?"

"Oh my God!" Alice cried, jerking forward in her seat. "Cassandra—we have to get out of here! Right now!"

"Why?" Cassandra replied. "What's the matter?"

"Wasn't it IDEA who introduced anti-gravitational propulsion to this world?" Alice said. "Aren't they the ones who own the technology? Who's to say they can't flick a switch and control *all* of this if they want to?"

"She's right!" Kyle said.

"Holy shit!" Cassandra said, looking around at the cars flying above, below and either side of us. "But we're completely surrounded!"

"Exactly!" Alice said, digging her hands into the seat. "That's why we need to get out of here! Now!"

Cassandra nodded and grabbed the wheel, but just as she began to steer out of the traffic, another car began to drop onto us from above.

"Duck!" I said, throwing myself toward Alice and pulling her to the floor of the car. Cassandra let go of the wheel and slid down in her seat, just managing to avoid being crushed as the underside of the vehicle above crashed into us, flattening the windshield and shattering glass everywhere. To our left, another car careered into the side of the Ferrari, the front bumper grazing along the top of the passenger door, buckling the metal frame inwards as though the car were being squeezed inside a trash compactor.

"Get us out of here!" Alice screamed.

Cassandra's foot must have found the accelerator because I felt the Ferrari jolt forward, flying out from under the car above and bashing into the rear end of a bus in front. All around us, horns started beeping like a thousand alarms going off at the same time. I sat up and looked around—the car that had crashed down on us from above dropped back, clipping the rear spoiler and descending to the same altitude as us. It then accelerated forward, its hood pressing against us like a locomotive pushing a train car. Through the windscreen, I was shocked to see a regular family sitting inside—mum and dad in the front, desperately jabbing the controls on the dashboard; kids in the back, screaming. They clearly had no idea what was going on or why their car was doing this all by itself, charging into us as though it had a mind of its own. At the same time, the bus in front of us slowed down, its brake lights flooding us in a bright red glow. Through the back window, a group of teenagers were looking down at us in bewilderment, unsure as to what was happening. Suddenly I noticed a shadow being cast over us, and as I looked up, I saw another car descending on us from above. IDEA were trying to box us in.

"I've had about enough of this!" Cassandra fumed, straightening herself up in her seat and wiping a gritty film of exhaust from her forehead. "Hang on!"

She spun the wheel around 180 degrees, tilting the car on its right hand side like a racing yacht sailing perpendicular to the water. Then, with the push of a button, the engines on the underside of the car roared to life, and we were thrust sideways out of the traffic, emerging into the open air like a bullet from a gun.

"Jesus!" I said, rocking back in my chair as Cassandra steered the craft the right way up again. We were still high above the city with only the tips of the very tallest skyscrapers matching us in height. "We could have been killed!"

"We're not out of this yet!" Cassandra replied, turning around in her seat, her eyes focussed on something in the distance.

I looked back. The six police cars that had been following us earlier were circling around in the air, flying toward us in a pincer formation, their sirens still flashing.

"Great," I said, my body lurching back into my seat as Cassandra hit the accelerator. As we sped forward, the crumpled windshield began to rattle and loosen in front of us before eventually flying off over our heads.

"Take us lower!" Kyle said.

"All right…" Cassandra replied, pushing the steering wheel forward and entering a dive. "Let's just hope IDEA can't remotely control *this* car…"

"No…" Kyle said, his voice wavering in the force of our descent. "If they could, they would have done that by now. This car must be different."

"Looks like Russell likes to be the controller, not the controlled…" I said.

Once we had descended a few hundred feet toward the ground, Cassandra pulled the car out of its dive and headed west. In front of us, the sun had now almost set, the night sky lit up by hundreds of different lines of traffic, heading off in all directions like a network of interwoven threads stretching as far as the eye could see.

"Right," Alice said. "Let's steer clear of Flyways from now on, agreed?"

"Agreed," Cassandra and Kyle replied in unison.

But at that moment, the patterns of headlights in front of us began to change, the previously straight lines of vehicles now oscillating like erratic radio waves.

"What's going on?" I said, leaning forward in my seat.

"You've got to be kidding!" Cassandra yelled, watching as the nearest Flyway suddenly changed trajectory, the traffic dipping down from above and swinging toward us like a rollercoaster gone out of control. "It's one thing steering clear of these things, but I don't think they're gonna steer clear of us!!"

"Go go go go go!" Alice shouted, the oncoming traffic reflected in her glasses, lighting up her wide eyes.

Cassandra pulled down on the steering wheel and accelerated, the car narrowly flying over the approaching vehicles and dropping lower again as though we were surfing over a tidal wave. I could hear people screaming inside their vehicles as they shot by, passengers shrieking in terror as their lives were put in jeopardy, their cars suddenly taking them along a dangerous path: a path they hadn't chosen. And no sooner had we cleared one stream of traffic when another began heading our way, this time even faster. Cassandra immediately plunged the car into freefall, the Flyway again just missing us like a serpent pouncing moments too late to catch it's prey.

"We can't stay in the air!" Kyle screamed.

"He's right," Alice shouted, scrambling forward in her chair and grabbing Cassandra's shoulder as a passing taxi cab clipped the back of the car. "Take us down! Take us down!"

"I'm trying!" Cassandra replied, pulling the nose of the car up again, then back down to avoid another stream of traffic moving in to cut us off. "Hold on!"

I gripped onto my seatbelt as Cassandra veered one way then the other on our vertical descent, dodging the endless onslaught of traffic coming at us from all directions. If we didn't land soon, we would be pulverized.

"I'm going to drop us down in that park!" she said, pointing toward a small patch of grassland in the middle of a cluster of tall office buildings. From up here, it looked as though the area actually used to be a large roundabout before the introduction of anti-gravitational propulsion allowed all roads and junctions to be converted back to vegetation.

As we reached street level, the Flyways stopped trying to intercept us, the flow of traffic reverting back to its normal state. At first I wasn't sure why this would be, but I soon realized that the buildings nearer ground level looked close enough together to act as a shield, protecting us from the barrage of vehicles under IDEA's control. I looked up at the sky—amazingly, all routes had returned to normal, the rows of busses, trucks and cars flowing as they always had done, in a uniform network of straight, interwoven threads. It was as though nothing had ever happened.

My hands were shaking, my skin coated in a layer of cold sweat.

Cassandra touched the battered Ferrari down in the middle of the park, killed the engines, and jumped out onto the grass. Kyle leapt out over his door, and I did the same, lending Alice a hand as she climbed out behind me.

"That does it," I said, slamming my fist against the car. "I'm sick of running. I'm sick of everyone coming after us. I'm just…sick of it."

"Well, at least we appear to have lost the police," Cassandra said, scanning the night sky for any sign of their sirens.

"So what now?" I said, running a hand over my head and looking around. On one side of the park, I saw a row of bars and Italian restaurants with people standing outside in groups, laughing and drinking together, or sitting down to enjoy an evening of alfresco dining. On the other side, the park appeared to be host to a number of designer outlets; the windows lit up with displays of flowing ball gowns, expensive shoes, and lady's accessories. A few bystanders had begun to notice our arrival, staring at us from all directions as though we were a group of mysterious aliens visiting them from another planet.

"Guys—I'm really sorry to leave you, but I've got to find a phone right away!" Kyle said, running toward the nearest shop. "I need to get this story to someone before it's too late!"

Alice tapped my arm.

"Give me the note," she said. "If the other Richard is still watching, he might be able to guide us somewhere he can open a portal…"

I took the paper out of my trouser pocket and handed it to her, all the time looking up at the tall office blocks surrounding us. One of them had a large television screen built into it, displaying the headline: "Autopilot malfunction causes chaos over London."

"Autopilot malfunction my arse," I said to Cassandra, pointing up at the screen. "Can you believe that?"

"No, but these people will," Cassandra replied. "They'll believe anything they're told."

"Hey!" a man called out, standing up from his table outside one of the restaurants. He was pointing straight at us. "It's them! It's the terrorists!"

A number of people around him were looking down at their phones, then toward us, then back down to their phones again. Their faces were glowing a pale blue, their eyes lit up by the screens in their hands.

"He's right!" another voice said. It belonged to a woman standing outside one of the bars on our right, a glass of wine in her hand. "Those are the people who escaped from IDEA!"

"Decision Tree is telling me we should stop them!" another man called out, looking up from his phone.

"It's telling me that too!" came another voice from behind.

All around, people began to make their way toward us, leaving their meals and drinks behind, the crowd quickly growing in numbers as men, women, and children of all ages looked up from their phones and headed our way. They moved apprehensively, but I sensed an underlying aura of anticipation, as though somebody was going to try to do something at any moment.

"We need to get out of here," Alice said, grabbing my sleeve.

"No," I whispered, tugging my arm back.

"What?" Alice gasped, watching as the crowd edged closer. "Richard—we can't stay here! And besides—the note says we only need to go two blocks further west before we're clear of IDEA's quantum shield! You know what that means? The other Richard will be able to open up a portal! We'll be able to get out of here!"

"I don't care what the notes are telling me to do," I said. "You go. Take Cassandra and get her out of here; go somewhere safe."

"But…what about you?"

"I'm staying right here," I replied. "Someone needs to show these people how they are allowing themselves to be manipulated. How they are relying too much on technology. How they are letting something else make their decisions for them."

I held Alice's head in my hands and kissed her forehead.

"Someone needs to tell them the truth," I whispered in her ear.

Alice looked up at me with teary eyes.

"No!" Alice said. "I won't allow it!"

"This is my choice, Alice," I said. "Go."

"I can't lose you again, Richard," she said, sniffing, her arms wrapped tightly around me. "I can't leave you here…"

"Please," I said, wiping a tear from her cheek. "Please, Alice—I have to do this."

Alice nodded quietly to herself, looking down at the ground.

"I love you," she said, backing away. She took hold of Cassandra's hand and made a run for it, ducking down the nearest alleyway. A few members of the crowd watched them for a moment, but all eyes were soon trained back on me—the man who refused to move.

As I stood still, watching more and more people huddle toward me, an image of my father flashed in my mind: the man whose choices in life had been made for him, the man who was forced to sacrifice his future when his father had had a stroke, caring for his family from the age of fifteen. He had had no control over his destiny, and it had ended up killing him.

I knew I was outnumbered, that I would most likely be taken back to IDEA headquarters to endure an insufferable punishment. Maybe this decision would even end up killing me.

But I didn't care.

This was my choice, not anyone else's.

For the first time in years, I was the master of my fate.

I was the captain of my soul.

TWENTY-SEVEN

"**D**o you think he's dangerous?" a young lady near the front of the crowd said. She was dressed in a long fur coat and white dress, as though she had been making her way toward one of the designer shops when we'd landed. Her hair so immaculately styled it could have been mistaken for a designer hat.

"I don't know," someone else replied. Cyclist. Luminous vest. Crash helmet under his arm.

These were all normal people.

"Why isn't he moving?" another voice said. "Why isn't he afraid?"

I kept a careful eye on the increasing number of people as they approached. Once they were close enough, I climbed on to the hood of the Ferrari and stood tall, ready to address them.

"Listen to me!" I called out, holding my hands up to my mouth to amplify my voice. "My name is Richard Henley. I am not your enemy! I mean you no harm!"

The crowd slowed down for a moment, looking up at me in silence.

"Please," I shouted, my voice reverberating off of the surrounding buildings as though I was standing in an amphitheater. A few people began emerging from inside the bars and restaurants, looking my way. "You have to listen to me!"

"Why should we?" someone called out. "That woman you were with is the one IDEA's been after all this time! She's the one responsible for Quantum Displacement Disorder!"

"You're right," I replied. "You're right. Alice created Quantum Displacement Disorder. But did you ever stop to think *why* she did it?"

The crowd went quiet again.

"She did it to protect other worlds from being put in danger, from being exploited. She did it to stop the technology from being abused. I know it must be hard to understand, but it was her only line of defense against IDEA, an organization that indiscriminately ruins other worlds, just to make a profit…"

"What are you saying?" a man shouted. "Are you saying our world is causing damage elsewhere?"

"Like you wouldn't believe," I replied. "Only earlier today, I was standing amongst the ruins of a world destroyed by IDEA. The world you sent that asteroid to, twenty years ago."

"But that planet was uninhabited," a middle-aged woman near the front of the crowd replied. "Everyone knows that."

"No it wasn't," I said. "People lived there. People like you."

"That's ridiculous," the woman said. "If that were the case, why weren't we told about it?"

"Because it was easier for IDEA to lie to you," I replied. "And that's what they've been doing to you ever since. Everything you see and hear around you is a fabrication. The news is lying to you. Russell Hardwick is lying to you, and worst of all, that 'Decision Tree' service of yours is lying to you."

"Rubbish!" a man called out from the back of the crowd. "I don't believe it. The Decision Tree service *never* lies! It's impossible!"

"Don't you see?" I said. "You're being manipulated! IDEA are using the Decision Tree service to control you; they're using it to make you serve their agenda!"

I noticed a few people were beginning to take pictures of me on their phones as the crowd grew in numbers, while others were typing some sort of messages into various handheld devices. For all his deceptions, Russell certainly wasn't lying when he said this world was hyperconnected: on the huge screen beaming down on us from the building in front of me, the news was already breaking a story on what I was doing, running with the headline: "BBC receives text reports of terrorist addressing crowd in south London."

"Well my decision tree says we should take him down now!" a businessman near the front yelled out, holding his phone up to the crowd for them to see. "Who's with me?!"

"Wait!" I said, climbing down from the Ferrari to get closer to the crowd. I hoped this gesture would make them understand that I was just like them, that I had no reason to keep my distance. A few people in front of me weren't so sure, backing off slightly as though they feared I was going to attack them.

"Let me ask you a question," I shouted out. "How does the Decision Tree service actually work?"

"Everybody knows how it works," a middle-aged lady replied to my left. "IDEA analyze all the possible outcomes of a situation, then tell us the best choice to make."

"And what is it telling you to do now?" I asked.

"Right now," the lady said, looking down at her phone for a second, "it's telling us all to bring you in!"

The crowd began nodding and murmuring in agreement, walking a little closer again.

"Exactly," I smiled, looking as many people as I could straight in the eyes.

Everybody frowned to themselves and stopped walking, as though my reaction wasn't what they were expecting.

"IDEA analyze all the possible outcomes of a situation, right?" I said. "They look at every other dimension where a different outcome occurred and tell you what your options are, correct?""

"That's right," a few people agreed.

"Really?" I said, looking up into the night. "Is that *really* how it works?" As I spoke, a number of news vans were descending from the sky and landing on the ground near the edges of the square, with cameramen flinging their side doors open and dashing toward me with their equipment. Within a few seconds, my face was already being broadcast live on the television in front of me, like a giant mirror looming down from overhead.

"Of course that's how it works!" a man called out. "How else would it be able to tell us what to do?"

"How else indeed?" I said, looking from one person to the other. "Okay, so answer me this: How many other dimensions do you think this exact situation is occurring in?"

"What do you mean?" somebody called out.

"Think about it," I said. "Right now, you are talking to a man who has traveled to your world from another dimension. On top of that, the people I came here with are from yet another dimension. That's a pretty unique set of circumstances, wouldn't you say? How many other realities do you think this could possibly be happening in right now?"

The crowd looked at me in silence, a few people exchanging awkward glances. I sensed the penny was beginning to drop.

"I'll tell you how many," I said. "Zero. There is no way this exact situation can be happening in any world other than this one, let alone happening enough times to produce several different outcomes. It's impossible. It cannot be happening. The odds are astronomical. And if that's the case, there are no alternative scenarios for IDEA to analyze, right?"

"But aren't there an infinite number of alternate dimensions out there?" a man called out to my left. "And if that's the case, isn't anything possible?"

"Yeah!" A few people called out in support.

"No," I said. "There aren't an infinite number of realities. I'll admit I'm no expert on this, but apparently there is a limit to how many worlds are out there."

"He's right," a voice called out from behind me. I looked round—Kyle Lewis was emerging from a crowd of people that had gathered behind me. "In fact, if you look at the science behind how Decision Tree supposedly works," he continued, "it's all a load of nonsense…"

"You're back?" I said. "Did you get through to the people you needed to speak to?"

"Yeah," Kyle said, looking up at the screens around us. "In fact, the news should be updating itself any moment now…"

"Who are you?" someone called out from the crowd.

"My name is Kyle Lewis," Kyle replied. "And I'm a BBC journalist. You all need to listen to me and listen to this man. The Decision Tree is a fraud. A con. It is lying to you to control you, and it always has been…"

"Prove it!" a woman shouted out.

"Look at me," Kyle said, pointing to the wounds on his face. "You know who did this to me? IDEA. They did this to me because I found out too much. I found out the true purpose of the Decision Tree service…"

"Why should we believe you?" the woman called out.

Suddenly the TV screens began to change around us. A picture of Kyle flashed up with the headline: "BBC Journalist held hostage by IDEA. Accuracy of Decision Tree service called into question."

The crowd looked up at the screens, their mouths wide open.

"You see?" I said. "If this scenario isn't happening in any other world, there is no basis for the options given to you by the Decision Tree, right?" If it supposedly bases its recommendation on the best possible outcome, how is it telling you to apprehend me?"

"The truth is," Kyle said, "the Decision Tree service was introduced to control you. To manipulate you to serve a different purpose if needed. If they don't want you to vote a particular government in, they'll use the Decision Tree service to influence you. If they object to a politician putting forward a particular policy, the Decision Tree service eliminates the problem. And that's exactly what they're trying to do now—they are trying to eliminate a problem. The choices you can see in front of you aren't choices—they are lies: a series of fabrications designed to make you fall in line. But you do have a choice: a *real* choice. You can choose to rise up against IDEA. Tell them you won't be controlled anymore. Tell them that you want to have the freedom to make your own choices again."

A moment of silence fell over the crowd. Some people looked as though they were giving Kyle's words some very careful consideration. As we waited, an elderly gentleman at the front crowd broke free and walked toward me. He looked about eighty, with a thick white beard; his eyes nestled away behind a pair of bushy white eyebrows. He stood next to me, placed a hand flat against my back, then turned to address the people in front of us.

"You should all listen to this man," the gentleman said, his voice well-spoken, almost operatic. "I too believe IDEA are trying to control us. Trying to get us to accept their technology into our lives and do as it tells us to do. And they are succeeding. Ask yourself how many decisions you made today of your own free will. Two? Three maybe?"

I looked up at the big screen, which was still showing a live broadcast of everything that was being said. I hoped this message was reaching as many people as possible.

The man let out a deep cough before continuing. He didn't sound well.

"A few months ago," he said, "I tried to stop using the Decision Tree service. Fancied stepping into the unknown for a change. I hadn't thought for myself for so long, and I wanted to go back to the old ways. For a while, I was really enjoying myself, not knowing what each day might bring. But after the first week, some men from IDEA showed up on my doorstep. Said they had been monitoring the fact I wasn't using the service and wanted to know if there was a problem. When I explained I didn't want to be told what to do anymore, they got aggressive. Told me it wasn't wise to stop using Decision Tree. They even said that if I wasn't careful, something bad might happen to me. They made it sound as though they were referring to the risk of me making a bad choice, but if you read between the lines, it was clear what they were really saying: start using the service again, or suffer the consequences. Since then, I've been too scared not to use it and too scared to mention what happened to me. But enough is enough. I want to be free again."

Just as the crowd looked as though their opinion was on the verge of tipping in my favor, a number of black saloon cars began to descend toward us, the vehicles landing on the opposite side of the square to the news vans. As they touched the ground, the doors opened, and a number of IDEA guards jumped out, dressed in the same gray uniforms and riot helmets as before.

The officer at the front of the pack held a megaphone up to his mouth and began to speak.

"Thank you, everyone," he said to the crowd, clearing a path toward me with a wave of his hand. "We will take it from here. Please return to your homes. The situation is now under control…"

"Wait a minute!" a younger man in the crowd said, refusing to move out of the way of the guard. He looked in his early twenties, with a short, spiky haircut and several piercings in his ears. "I've got some questions for you! About the Decision Tree service! About IDEA! Have you really been manipulating us? Lying to us about the effect we are having on other worlds? Tell us the truth!"

"Please move to one side," the guard said, his voice still amplified through the megaphone.

"No." the man said. "I refuse."

"Sir," the guard said, "what does your decision tree tell you?"

I looked up at the screen—this was all still being televised.

The man looked down at his phone and smiled.

"It tells me to get out of your way," he replied. "And that's my problem." He turned around and pointed toward me. "This guy is right—how can it possibly be telling me to do that? Someone at IDEA is trying to tell us what to do! And they could have been doing this for years, for all I know! How do I know some of the choices I've made in the past were the right ones? I've always trusted the Decision Tree in the past, but now I'm not so sure!"

"Sir, this is your last warning," the guard said, taking a step closer to the man, his chest thrust out. "Please get out of the way."

The man folded his arms.

"Make me."

What happened next was like watching something unfold in slow motion, like when Cassandra and I were being chased through the oncoming traffic back in my world. The guard threw a punch at the man, who took it squarely in the stomach and fell to his knees. Behind him, a number of onlookers gasped, shocked to see a member of IDEA behave in such a way. Then things began to get violent. People started throwing things at the other guards. Tackling them to the ground. Stripping their helmets from the heads and tossing them to one side. Beating them in the head. It was as though my speech had done just enough to generate an inner animosity toward IDEA and bring a feeling inside so close to the surface that all it took was the slightest provocation to unleash it.

"Do you see?" I shouted out to the crowd. "Do you see the true face of IDEA? This is who you have handed over control of your lives to. Not a benevolent organization with your interests at heart but a selfish, violent group of thugs who have turned your world into a paradise at the cost of so many others. Lied to you about so many things, not least the say you have over your own destiny. Now it is time to open your eyes. To see what your world has become. To choose to do things differently."

In front of me, a few people were looking down at their phones, switching them off, and putting them in their pockets. Some even dropped them to the floor and just walked away.

I took a deep breath and looked up at the huge television image in front of me: For the first time since I had been in this world, the headline I saw was true:

"IDEA in conspiracy to control the population," it said. "Russell Hardwick wanted for police questioning."

The news then went on to show a wave of outrage spreading across London, fueled by the up-to-the minute television reports, feeds on the Internet, and social networking. Apparently, some people were so furious with what had been exposed, they were trying to storm the IDEA building for answers.

I turned to Kyle and shook his hand.

"Thank you," I said. "I'm not sure that would have worked had you not been here with me."

"No, thank you," he replied. "If it wasn't for you, I'd still be locked in a cell back at IDEA."

"Richard!" a voice called out.

I looked round. Alice was standing a few meters away with Cassandra, right next to the alleyway I had seen them disappear down. I smiled, my heart beating a little faster at the sight of my family, the hairs on my arms standing on end. But then my smile faded, and my body felt numb. My mind was picking up a strange signal from them, as if something wasn't quite right.

They were trembling.

"Is…everything okay?" I asked, taking a few steps closer to them. "Is something wrong?"

"Oh nothing's wrong." A velvety voice purred.

My mouth fell open. Out of the shadows, Gabriel emerged from behind Alice, the barrel of his gun stuck in her back. "Nothing's wrong at all."

For a moment I couldn't breathe. How was Gabriel here? When I had last seen him, he was covered in black marks—a shadow of his former self. In fact, if I wasn't mistaken, Russell had even said they'd lost him to Quantum Displacement Disorder. Yet now, the marks were completely gone. His skin had returned to normal, his blue eyes were lit up with the same intensity as when I had first encountered him at the docks, and he looked invigorated, like a new man. He wore a clean suit. White shirt open at the collar. Shiny shoes.

"Lucky for me, Russell was able to bring me back to this world quite quickly," he said, pushing Alice forward. She winced, staggering toward me as though she was being made to walk across a bed of nails. Cassandra was at her side, walking at the same pace. We all knew not to make any sudden moves. Gabriel would kill Alice in an instant if we tried anything funny.

"Hey!" Kyle said, walking toward Gabriel. "What are you doing?"

"No!" I said, grabbing him by the arm. "Keep back—this man is extremely dangerous…"

"You should listen to him," Gabriel said, nodding toward me. "He knows what I'm capable of…"

"Well I don't," Kyle said, shrugging his arm free from my grip. "And I say to you…"

But Gabriel didn't give him a chance to say anything. He took out another gun from inside his jacket and shot Kyle straight in the head.

The square echoed with the shocked gasps of several onlookers before falling completely silent.

Kyle fell on his knees, balancing on the ground for a moment with a hole through his temple, before falling face-first onto the grass.

"Does that clarify the situation?" Gabriel said. "Or would you like me to repeat it?"

They immediately backed off, their hands in the air, disappearing into the crowd.

"NO!" I cried, looking down at Kyle's lifeless body. "What have you done? What have you done?!"

"Sorry," Gabriel said. "But he caught me in a particularly bad mood."

"What do you want?" I said, my voice trembling as I watched him march Alice and Cassandra closer toward me.

"I just want my wife back," Gabriel said. "That's all I've ever wanted … to see her again …"

"Gabriel," Alice said, looking round, "for what it's worth, I'm sorry what I did to you. If there was another way …"

"Shut up!" he said, pointing his gun at Alice. "Just shut up!! You took her from me! You made her disappear!"

"Please, Gabriel," I said, holding out my hands. "I know what Alice did was wrong, but I'm begging you—don't kill her …"

Gabriel lowered his gun and sighed. "As much as it goes against everything my mind is screaming at me to do, I'm not going to kill any of you," he said, motioning me to turn around and walk ahead of him.

"You're not?"

"No. Russell wants to see the three of you."

"But why?" I said. "Surely it's over? Surely IDEA are finished?" He appeared to be walking us toward the Ferrari, which was still parked in the middle of the square.

"Don't be so sure of that," Gabriel replied, stopping by the car and yanking open the crumpled passenger door. "Now, get in …"

TWENTY-EIGHT

Gabriel made Cassandra fly us back to the IDEA building, with him sitting in the front passenger seat and with Alice and me in the rear. For the whole journey, he stayed in the exact same position, leaning over the back of his seat, his gun pointing directly toward us. If we tried anything stupid, he'd told us, he would shoot.

After what we saw him do to poor Kyle, none of us doubted him for a second.

"By the way," Gabriel said, looking at Alice down the sights of his gun as we made our way across the city, "I didn't thank you for sending me into that limbo state, once that little disease of yours finally got hold of me."

Alice said nothing.

"Aren't you going to ask me how it was?"

"How … was it?" Alice asked hesitantly.

"I don't remember." Gabriel replied, tapping a finger against his forehead. "I don't remember … anything."

"That's what I thought," Alice said. "Once you're outside of existence, it's not possible for you to understand where you are. It's just a dream you never wake up from."

"And that's okay to you is it?" Gabriel said. "I might as well have been dead!"

"You know," Alice said, "I had thought about sending everyone to some other dimension when the disease consumed them, instead of suspending them in limbo. Some primitive world where they couldn't do any harm."

"Why didn't you?" Gabriel said. "At least then we would have still been alive!"

"Because I thought it would have been worse knowing your predicament," Alice replied. "Isn't it better to be blissfully unaware of your situation instead of being conscious that you're stranded in another world?"

"It's a difficult choice," Gabriel said. "But then, from what I understand, you're good at making those for other people … Like my wife, for instance. I still don't know if I'm ever going to see her again."

He turned to Cassandra, who was flying us steadily back to the IDEA building, both hands on the wheel.

"How are we doing?" he said, bringing his free hand up to his face and smoothing the edges of his dark beard.

"We're making good time," she replied, her voice flat, eyes looking straight ahead. "For some reason, the sky is remarkably clear."

I leaned forward and scanned the area ahead of us. She was right—I couldn't see a single flying vehicle in the air, couldn't hear the noise of another engine with the exception of ours. The night was quiet, the sky empty. Earlier this evening, the airways had been teaming with traffic—streams of cars, taxis, trucks and buses flying off in all directions, with huge trails of vehicles stretching as far as the eye could see in a blur of light and metal. Now, the only lights in the sky were the stars, shining down on us from far, far, away.

"What happened?" I said, turning around in my chair to look for the signs of any other vehicle. Nothing. "Where's all the traffic?"

Gabriel wrinkled his mouth.

"Now that word has got out about what we've been doing," he said, "Russell has decided to disable all forms of transport."

"He's what?" I said.

"You've seen the news reports," Gabriel continued. "People are angry. They're trying to storm the building for answers. And whilst we can try to keep them from breaking through the front door, we can't have anyone trying to land on the roof now, can we?"

"Nice," I said, continuing to scan the sky around us. Without any traffic flying around them, the tall skyscrapers and gleaming glass towers of London looked a little lonely. "You mean to tell me he just switched all the traffic off? Can he even do that?"

Gabriel smiled.

"Why don't you take a look down?" he said. "Slowly…"

I leaned over the side of the car and looked directly beneath us. Down below, the city was littered with thousands of vehicles, all of them lying lifelessly in the same pattern I had seen in the sky earlier. Huge stretches of cars were draped across buildings and streets in straight lines, as though someone had cut the supporting strands of a spider's web and let it fall to the ground. I could see coaches stranded on top of office blocks, the passengers standing on the roof, looking over the edge for a way down. Motorcyclists stuck in trees. Taxi cabs bobbing in the River Thames. What I saw before me was total chaos, but to my relief, it didn't look as though anyone was hurt. The traffic didn't look like it had dropped out of the sky like a stone—Russell must have let it down gradually. People were huddled around their vehicles, some looking under the hood, trying to figure out what had happened. Others were gathering their belongings and beginning to walk to their destination.

As we flew through a dense cluster of skyscrapers, a screen on the side of one of them flashed up with the headline: "City in chaos: IDEA grounds all anti-gravitational craft." Another one said: "IDEA stock falls in value by 98% in five minutes."

"My God," Cassandra said, looking up from the steering wheel. We weren't far from the IDEA building now, the "I"-shaped structure coming into view as we weaved between two massive glass towers either side of us. At the very top of the building, the four letters of the IDEA logo were still proudly lit up on the roof, beaming into the night like a lighthouse guiding us into shore

"What is it?" I asked, lifting myself up in my seat.

"People look like they're going crazy outside!" she said. "Check it out!"

I looked down toward the base of the building. It was completely surrounded, with people swarming over the stone steps like ants on an anthill. They were throwing bricks through windows, ramming the front doors, lighting fires, chanting—this was a massive protest; something on an unprecedented scale; something that few people must have anticipated.

"Bring us down on the roof," Gabriel said.

I watched as we approached the landing platform at the top of the building. It was completely deserted, save for a lone figure standing right on the edge of the roof in between the base of the "D" and the "E" letters of the IDEA logo. The figure was looking down at the crowds gathering below, and as I looked a little closer, I realized the figure was Russell Hardwick. His hands were behind his back, his legs were straight, and he held his head high.

Once we were directly over the roof, Cassandra flicked a switch on the dashboard, causing the engines to quieten down and the craft to descend. No one said anything as the car got lower and lower, and within a few seconds, we had touched down on the landing platform, right back in Russell's parking bay.

Gabriel kicked his door open with his foot and stepped out.

"Okay," he said, still pointing his gun at Alice. "Everybody out."

We did exactly as we were told, climbing slowly out of the car and standing next to each other in the adjacent parking bay, with Alice in the middle. It was cold on the roof, the wind just beginning to pick up and give a bit of bite to the air. Alice pulled her shawl closer round her neck and looked at me, her shoulders slouched. It was strange to think, but she was still wearing the same outfit as she had worn on the beach—the long summer dress printed with blue flowers and the open toed sandals. Her glasses were sliding down her nose, but she wasn't making any effort to push them back up again. She looked defeated.

"Good," Gabriel said, nodding at us. Behind him, Russell was still standing on the edge of the roof, looking down at the mayhem ensuing below.

"Any news?" Gabriel said, looking around at Russell. "About my wife?"

"We're still looking," Russell replied, leaning further over the edge.

"Go on, jump!" Cassandra shouted out, folding the collar of her leather jacket around her neck to protect it from the cold. "We won't stop you!"

Russell didn't react—he just kept surveying the crowd from above, like a zookeeper looking down on an animal enclosure.

"Ungrateful bastards," he finally said, not looking at us. "Don't these people understand what I was trying to do? Don't they realize I was trying to help them?"

"All these people understand," I said, "is that you're a kidnapper and a control freak, a man obsessed with telling people what to do. They just woke up to the fact that you were forcing them down a path you had chosen for them."

"But… everything I did was in their own best interests!" Russell insisted. "Can you imagine if IDEA went back under government control? If we had to answer to those bureaucrats? It would have set us back decades!"

"That may be so, but the cost for most people was just too high," Alice said. "And let's not forget—this was for your own best interests as well. Maybe they thought that was wrong…"

"Ha!" Russell laughed. "Wrong? Wrong?! This coming from the woman who willingly sent hundreds of innocent people into a state of limbo because she decided it was for the greater good? I gave the people of this world the power to fly; gave them the ability to connect with each other like never before; allowed them build them a cities on a scale never thought possible; improved their quality of life like nothing they would have believed. What have you done for your world? Nothing! The choices you made for people just ended up wiping them from existence! Innocent people, like Gabriel's poor wife! So don't talk to me about deciding what's best for others! At least I can say some good came from the things I've done!"

"This isn't about the choices you and Alice made," I said. "This is about being honest. People don't like being lied to."

"What the hell are you talking about?" he replied, turning round. "When was I ever *dis*honest? I mean, why has this come as such a surprise to everyone? I made no secret of the level of control people were handing over to us. What the implications were." He paused for moment and turned round. "I thought everyone understood it was necessary. Didn't people realize we could do all this if we wanted?"

"Why would anyone suspect that?" Alice said. She had tried to tuck her arms under her shawl as best she could, but she was still shivering. "Why would anyone imagine you were capable of this? These people thought IDEA was about making things better for them, not about bringing them under your control!"

Russell walked toward us, laughing.

"Then these people are idiots," he said. "And ungrateful ones at that."

"Laugh all you like," Alice said. "It's true that perhaps these people didn't stop to think about what they were surrendering when they started using your cars, and your phones, and all the other things you've introduced over the years, but at the same time, the very technology you've been using to control them was the exact same thing that freed them. Without it, word of what you were really up to would never have spread so fast."

Russell walked right up to Alice and held his face a few inches away from hers.

"These people aren't free just yet," he breathed. "We may not be able to control their minds anymore, but we do control everything else. Everything they need to survive. We control the way they travel. We source the food they eat. We give them their power. They may not like it, but they need us. Without IDEA, and without me, they are doomed."

They stared at each other in silence for a moment, their faces only inches apart.

"Why did you bring us here?" Alice said eventually.

"I'm glad you asked," Russell said, taking a couple of steps back. Behind him, the tall towers of the London skyline glimmered on the horizon, like shards of light breaking through the dark. "Truth is—I have a small favor to ask of you…"

Alice almost choked.

"You must be joking," she said. "You expect *me* to do you a favor?"

"You still haven't got your head around this whole 'leverage' thing, have you?" he said, pointing toward Cassandra and me with both hands.

Alice looked down at her feet and held a hand out for each of us to hold. I held it immediately, feeling her cold fingers loosely wrap around my own.

"What do you want me to do?" she sighed.

"The way I see it," Russell said, looking out across the city, "recent events have put me in a difficult position. You see, you may think I'm evil. A megalomaniac even. A control freak. But I still believe in what I am doing. I still believe in my mission. I care for this world and want to continue to see it grow. To see it benefit from all the treasures yet to be discovered in other worlds. I don't want to give up being the overseer of that, but there's no way I can do it from here anymore. Despite everything I've done for these people, they will never understand. I'd be a prisoner in this building or at the very least, reviled wherever I go. That's no way to live. So I've come up with a plan. A compromise. A way in which I can still help the people of this world but without suffering any of the trappings that come with it."

"Which is…?" Alice said, tilting her head.

"Simple. I'll do it all from another reality. Perhaps even turn my attention to a few other worlds worthy of civilizing. Make them like this one. That is the favor I have to ask of you: I need you to get me out of here; I need you to send me through to another world, a world where I can set up a base of operations and expand my reach to other dimensions…"

"I don't understand," Alice frowned. "Dr. Naylor is as familiar with multidimensional physics as I am—can't he do that for you?"

"Dr. Naylor didn't make it to the upper floors in time before we secured the building," Russell replied, waving his hand dismissively. "We're not sure if he's even still alive. And besides, what I'm asking is a little more complicated that just opening up a portal for me to escape. In order for me to keep control of this world, I need all of this to come through with me."

"All of what?" Alice said.

"All of this," Russell said, gesturing to his surroundings. "The labs. The equipment. The computers. Everything I need to keep control of other realities and travel between worlds is contained within the top floor of this building. That is why I want you to recreate what happened to you all those years ago, when your entire lab was sent through to another world; I want you to create a portal large enough to send me, and the entire top floor of this building, through to another dimension."

Alice thought about this for a moment. She seemed intrigued.

"Where would you go?" Alice said, pushing the bridge of her glasses up her nose. She seemed to be standing a little straighter, her grip on my hand tightening.

"I don't know," Russell said. "But somewhere nice, obviously. Maybe that world you went to—you know, the one with the beach. That looked perfectly bearable…"

Alice's grip tightened even more, to the point where I could feel her pulse beating through her fingers. What was she thinking?

"I thought you said that world was a bit hot for your taste?" she said.

"I'll get used to it," Russell said. "And if I don't like it, I'll just go somewhere else. After all, I'll have everything I need with me to come and go between worlds as I please…"

"W-what about my wife?" Gabriel said.

"We'll keep looking for her, Gabriel," Russell replied. "You have my word on that."

"I have to hand it to you Russell," Alice said. "You've really thought this through, right down to the last detail."

"I'm not finished," Russell said. "Obviously, there is one small problem."

Alice seemed to slouch again, her hand going limp again inside mine.

"Problem?" she said.

"Yes. Obviously, I can't operate the equipment by myself. I'm a businessman, not a physicist—I wouldn't know where to start with half the stuff we've got down there. That's why I'd need you to come with me. I'd need you to be my operator."

"Of course," Alice smiled, tightening her grip around my hand again. "I didn't think of that. And what exactly makes you think I'll go along with this?"

"Again, leverage," Russell said. "Richard and Cassandra would need to come through with us as well, and Gabriel would be there to … how should I put it … 'watch over them' just in case you ever thought of doing something out of line … He'd want to be there, anyway, once you help us get his wife back."

Gabriel smiled, shifting his weight from one leg to the other.

Alice looked at me, then at Cassandra.

"Well?" Russell asked. "Will you help me, or do I get Gabriel to kill the three of you right here?"

Alice let go of my and Cassandra's hands and stepped forward.

"I'll help you," Alice said. "But on one condition—Richard can come with us, but you let Cassandra go, right now. Let her take that car of yours and fly far away from here."

"No Mum!" Cassandra cried, running toward her mother. "You can't do this!"

"No deal," Russell replied, shaking his head. "With your daughter freed, who's to say you won't start misbehaving once we get there?"

"You'll still have Richard," she said. "And you know how I feel about him. I won't do anything stupid, I promise. I'll do whatever you tell me to."

"I don't like this," Gabriel whispered to Russell. "Cassandra is the better hostage, not Richard."

"Those are my terms," Alice said, folding her arms. "I will not help you unless you let Cassandra go. And if you don't accept them, fine. Kill us all right now."

"With pleasure," Gabriel said, aiming his gun toward me.

"Wait!" Russell said, pushing the barrel of the gun to one side. "Wait. Okay, you've got a deal. Cassandra goes free."

Gabriel huffed and slumped his shoulders, like a child being told he wasn't allowed to go out to play.

"We do not have a deal!" Cassandra shouted, stamping her feet. "I can't let them take you away from me! I won't…"

"Cassy!" Alice said quietly, pulling her daughter's body in toward her and stroking her head. "You need to trust me, okay?"

"But…"

"Trust me," Alice repeated, running a hand along her cheek. "Everything will be fine." She then pulled her daughter's ear close to her mouth and whispered something. It only took a second, and whatever words were being spoken came so quickly from Alice's mouth, I don't think Russell or Gabriel even noticed it. From where they were standing, it just looked as though they were having a hug.

Once Alice was finished, Cassandra looked into her mother's eyes and nodded. They appeared to have an understanding.

"Okay, are we all done?" Russell said, turning toward the stairwell on the other side of the roof. "Are we ready to go?"

Alice gave her daughter another hug.

"We're ready," she said.

Cassandra ran over to me and wrapped her arms around my waist. "Look after Mum, okay?" she said, her eyes welling up. "Never let go of her."

"I won't," I replied.

"I mean that," Cassandra said, moving her head close to mine. "*Never* let go."

Russell began marching across the landing platform impatiently.

"Come on, people," he said, waving to us over his shoulder. "We don't have all day!"

"Move," Gabriel said, motioning us to follow his boss.

Alice and I did as we were told, walking a few steps behind Russell. Gabriel followed not far behind, his gun trained on both of us. Over the edge of the roof, I could hear the commotion of people protesting down below. They didn't sound very happy.

Just as we reached the entrance to the stairwell, I took one final look back at Cassandra. She was sitting in the driver's seat of Russell's Ferrari, staring vacantly ahead.

The engine was running, but she didn't seem to want to go anywhere.

She was just sitting there, tapping her hands nervously in the steering wheel.

What was she waiting for?

Twenty-Nine

It wasn't long before we found ourselves inside one of the labs Cassandra and I had passed the last time we were here—the one with the enormous white machine inside, the machine with a red ball of light pulsating in its center like a beating heart. I'd only had a second to look at this room before, but now I was standing here, I had a chance to take in a few more details. Just as I'd remembered, four coiled towers stood in the far corners of the room, each one capturing intermittent jolts of electricity that shot along conductive wires hanging from the ceiling. But there was more: the walls were covered in huge white panels that had a strange texture to them, the floor was semi-reflective, and the far wall had a huge panoramic window looking out across London.

The machine in the middle of the room was a strange thing: rectangular, about the size of the trailer on an articulated truck, with rounded edges and a matte finish to the sides. Other than a circular glass panel on the front which showed the red ball of light inside, the machine had no distinguishing marks at all. No buttons. No screens. Just a white surface, completely unblemished all the way round.

Gabriel stood in the corner of the room, leaning against the wall and watching us like an assessor for a group exercise.

"Have a seat," Russell said, pressing a square red button on the wall next to him.

All of a sudden, a cluster of several small white columns rose from the floor next to the machine in silence, each one stopping at a different height to form a perfectly symmetrical, ergonomic chair.

Alice sat down in front of the machine, facing one of the featureless, white surfaces.

"Well?" Russell said. "Don't try to pretend you're unfamiliar with this device! The one you've got in your lab is practically the same. Let's get on with it shall we?"

"As you wish," Alice said, pressing her palm against the machine.

As her skin made contact with the white surface, the corners began to light up with several pinpricks of blue light, blinking in a rhythmic sequence. The next thing I knew, a panel unfolded in front of her to reveal a silver keyboard and a large blue screen. It was amazing—the edges of the panel had been so flush with the rest of the machine, you would never have known it was there.

Alice started typing a few of commands into the keyboard, her fingers moving at such a fluent pace across the keys you could have been watching a pianist hammer out the third movement of Beethoven's "Moonlight Sonata."

"How long is this going to take?" Russell asked, looking at his watch.

"Oh, not long," Alice replied, deleting a few lines of existing text from the screen and replacing it with her own code. "Five minutes, maybe?"

"Good," Russell said, pacing up and down the room. "Well then, don't let me distract you."

Alice nodded and continued to type.

Russell stopped pacing for a moment as if he'd just remembered something and looked directly at me.

"By the way, Mr. Henley," he said. "I never did thank you for fucking all of this up for me. Congratulations."

"My pleasure," I smiled back at him.

We both turned back to Alice's screen, watching as it filled up with all sorts of letters and symbols. To me the text looked completely random, but I knew what I was seeing before me was some of the most complex equations known to quantum physics and beyond.

After a short amount of time, her typing slowed down until eventually she was just scrolling backward and forward though the code to check what she had written, adding the odd symbol here and there. Eventually, a command flashed up at the bottom of the screen. It read: "EXECUTE: Y/N"

"Are we ready?" Russell said, leaning over the screen.

"We're ready," Alice said, standing up from the chair and walking toward me. "If my calculations are correct, that code should spread out the diameter of the portal enough to send the whole of the top floor through to that other world."

"Fantastic," Russell said, rubbing his hands. "You mean all I have to do is hit 'enter', and we're done?"

"That's right", Alice said, grabbing hold of my hand. I looked round at her in surprise—her grip was incredibly tight.

"Great," Russell replied, pushing his finger down on the keyboard. At first, nothing seemed to happen, but then the machine began to make a high-pitched noise, and the light in the middle changed from red to blue.

Suddenly, the machine got much louder, and the ball of light began to sparkle. I wasn't sure if I was seeing things, but in the very center of the room, it looked as though space was beginning to warp. Russell walked around the spatial distortion and smiled.

Alice began to laugh.

Russell looked at her and frowned.

"What's so funny?" he said.

"I can't believe it!" Alice shouted over the increasing noise of the machine. "I can't believe you forgot the first rule of inter-dimensional travel!"

"What the hell are you talking about?" Russell replied. "What rule?"

"Portals take you to exactly the same place in another world!" she shouted. "That means the same longitude, the same latitude…and the same altitude!"

Russell's eyes widened, his jaw falling open as he realized the implication of what Alice was saying.

"Make it stop!" he said, running over to the computer terminal and desperately hitting the keyboard with his fist. "Make it stop!"

"Too late!" Alice said, shutting her eyes as the whole room flashed white.

The next moment, the entire top floor of the IDEA building emerged in the other world, and it was daylight again. Time must have worked differently here after all.

For a split second, everyone stood there in silence.

Through the window, we could all see the blue sky, the sun shining up above, and the peaceful ocean stretching into the distance—a full two and a half miles beneath us.

THIRTY

As the top story of the IDEA building entered freefall, my body experienced a brief feeling of weightlessness. For a moment, everything and everyone around me began to float in mid air as though the gravity had been switched off. It wasn't long however, before the building began to plummet toward the vast expanse of ocean below with greater speed, and we soon found ourselves being thrust into the ceiling as the true force of the fall began to make itself felt. For a second I couldn't comprehend what was happening—the wind was roaring in my ears, my mind was disorientated, and I couldn't breathe. My internal organs felt as though they were being pushed out to the extremities of my body.

All around us, the laboratory started to break apart as it fell. The tiles on the floor began to crack, the white panels on the walls started to peel away, and the huge panoramic window at the back of the room immediately shattered into a million pieces as the structure of the building was subjected to extreme physical stress. The large machine in the middle of the room broke free from whatever had tethered it to the floor, and crashed into the ceiling, its smooth white surfaces buckling as it slammed into the upper corner of the room.

"We need to get out of here!" Alice screamed, locking her arm with mine and holding us steady against the ceiling as the whole room began to list to one side. Her white shawl was still wrapped around her neck, and as the material blew in the wind, it almost looked like a cape flowing behind her. "The window!" she said. "Aim for the window!"

We began pulling ourselves across the ceiling as the room continued to fall, narrowly avoiding the debris of metal coils and conductive wires crashing all around us. A few feet ahead, Gabriel was also trying to make his escape through the broken window, but just as he was about to reach it, one of the metal coils ricocheted off of the wall to his right and struck him in the back, pinning him against the far corner. He was trapped.

I looked around for any sign of Russell. He was behind us, clambering along the back wall of the room like a spider trying to scuttle away from being sucked down a plughole.

As Alice and I continued to make our way along the ceiling, the room began to tilt completely on its side so that the broken window was now positioned directly above us. The sudden rotation of our surroundings forced the two of us up along the ceiling and against one of the walls, our backs pressed against the white panels like astronauts in a g-force simulator. I could feel the skin across my face rippling as my body was buffeted by streams of air blasting their way through the room.

"What are we going to do?" I called out, my voice barley audible over the blistering wind. My eyes were watering like nothing I'd ever known.

Alice looked up though the shattered window and pointed to a red speck high in the sky above us.

I wiped the tears from my eyes as best I could and looked closely at the red speck. It was getting bigger, and if I wasn't mistaken, it was Russell's Ferrari, speeding down toward us through the air as fast as it could.

"Is that…Cassandra?" I screamed.

Alice nodded. "I made that portal big enough to bring her through as well!" she shouted, holding her hair back. "Now it's her job to catch us before we hit the ocean!"

"A-and h-how long do we have b-before that happens?" I said, struggling to speak.

"Not long!" Alice replied.

I watched as Cassandra raced toward us, the Ferrari descending through the sky like an eagle going into a nose dive to chase its prey. She must have been flying at a phenomenal speed, the car constantly banking left and right to avoid various pieces of debris that had broken away from the building.

"Come on!" Alice shouted, using her hands to drag us along the wall toward the window. "She won't be able to get us if we're still in this room!"

I tried to move as best I could, pressing my hand against the wall and using it to pull us toward the window. It was a good technique, but our progress was suddenly helped all the more as the room began to tilt again, throwing us directly toward the side of the room we needed to be, face-first against the wall next to the broken window.

We twisted our bodies around so our backs were pressed against the wall and began to climb through the shattered window, our arms still firmly locked together. But then, just as I had one leg in the open air and one still in the lab, I felt Alice being pulled away from me. I looked back—out of nowhere, Russell had managed to catch up with us, grabbing the back of Alice's shawl and pulling the material tightly round her neck. He had an insane grin on his face, his teeth gritted like a vice.

"Go!" Alice said, letting go of my arm as Russell hauled her back inside the falling room.

"No!!!" I screamed.

I desperately tried to grab hold of her again, but the force of the fall was too great, and I soon found myself being blown free from the building, my body falling helplessly through the open air.

We were still incredibly high up, and now that I was free from the building, I could see miles of ocean stretching off into the horizon to my left, the calm waves reflecting back the pale blue sky. To my right I could make out the sandy coastline curving its way across my view, and as I continued to fall, I could just about make out the tall, snowcapped mountains Alice had painted for me in the distance. This was the view that had always helped me relax, but looking at it now wasn't providing me with much comfort.

My ears felt like they were exploding as the wind roared through them, but it wasn't long before I heard a different sound. A mechanical sound. The sound of an engine getting louder and louder. Then all of a sudden, Cassandra appeared to the side of me in the Ferrari, changing speed to match the velocity of my descent.

"Grab hold of me!" she screamed, throwing her left arm in the air.

I stretched my hand toward my daughter, wrapping my fingers around her wrist and pulling myself toward the car. As I did, she banked the craft underneath me and positioned it so that I was directly above the front passenger seat.

"Hold on!" she cried, slowing down the descent of the car so that I fell into the seat head first. Once inside, I quickly sat the right way up and fastened my seatbelt.

"Are you in?" she said, flashing me a glance.

"I'm in!" I said, tugging on the straps over my shoulders to make sure they were secure. "Go go go go go!"

Cassandra nodded and pushed the steering wheel forward, plunging the car into a vertical dive again. From up here, I could now appreciate the size of the portal Alice must have created— it wasn't just the entire top floor of the building that she'd sent through to this world, it was the whole of the roof as well, complete with the four tall letters of the IDEA logo.

As we screamed toward the falling building, I noticed the structure was beginning to break apart quite badly, with huge sections of the external cladding breaking off and flying toward us, the letters on the roof detaching themselves and spinning uncontrollably like unwanted cargo being jettisoned from a plane.

"Hang on!" Cassandra shouted, dodging the Ferrari past several sections of brickwork falling through the sky and weaving us between huge sections of stonework and structural girders that had broken free. The remainder of building wasn't far ahead of us now, but then again—neither was the sea.

"There she is!" I cried, pointing toward the lab. I could see Alice was trying to climb sideways out of the broken window again, but Russell was still pulling back on her shawl, determined not to let her escape.

"Get closer!" I screamed. "Closer!"

"I'm trying!" Cassandra replied, pushing on the steering wheel as hard as she could.

The Ferrari accelerated forward on a vertical path so that the car was now falling parallel to the building, and as I watched Alice still struggling to break free of Russell's grip, Cassandra flicked a switch on the dashboard. Suddenly, the craft propelled itself horizontally toward the window so that Alice was no more than a meter away from the top of my head.

This was my chance to save her.

"Grab hold of me!" I shouted, stretching both arms out toward her.

"I…can't…reach!" Alice replied, straining against the shawl being pulled around her neck.

I undid the strap over my left shoulder and lifted myself out of my seat as far as I could, my fingertips stretching toward Alice's extended hand as we continued to fall. Behind her, Russell was still grinning, his eyes filled with rage. It was as though he had accepted his own fate, but even on the verge of death, he wanted to have control over someone else's.

"Come on!" I shouted, trying to get as close as I could without falling out of the car. "You can do it!"

"I can't!" Alice spluttered, reaching toward me with one hand and trying to loosing the shawl around her neck with the other.

Russell began laughing

"That's right!" he said, pulling the material tighter around her neck. "You're coming with me!"

Then all of a sudden, the shawl vanished into thin air, and Russell dropped back into the depths of the lab, screaming. At the same time, Alice lunged forward, falling free from the building and into my arms.

"I've got her!" I cried, watching in horror as we still continued to plummet toward the surface of the ocean. "Pull up! Pull up! Pull up!"

Cassandra slammed her foot on the brakes and pulled down on the steering wheel, my stomach dropping down to my feet as the car entered a steep climb. As we ascended back into the air, I looked round to see the remainder of the building slamming into the ocean behind us, the structure crushing in on itself upon impact in a huge cloud of dust. Then a flash. Something in the rubble started glowing violently, and the next thing I knew, the sky was lit up by a huge explosion, which sent massive tidal waves rippling out in all directions from the epicenter of the blast.

After a few seconds, Cassandra leveled out the car and slowed to a cruising speed, the sky around us warm and blue under the bright glow of the sun. Alice lay peacefully in my lap, her arms limp, head resting against my shoulder.

"Are you okay?" I said, pulling her hair back to examine the red marks around her neck from where Russell had been strangling her.

"You saved me, Richard," she whispered. "You saved me …"

"It was nothing," I replied.

Alice smiled. "I was talking to the other Richard."

"Oh …"

"I'm kidding," she said, holding a hand up to my face. "All of us had a part to play in this. We all saved each other."

"Particularly me," Cassandra smiled. "I mean, did you see how awesome I was at flying this thing?"

"Yes, you were magnificent," a voice said from behind us all. "Very well flown indeed …"

The three of us spun around to see Gabriel lying along the backseat, his gun pointing straight toward us. His other hand was clutching his right leg, which looked as though it had been badly cut. Somehow, he must have freed himself from the corner of the room and jumped into the car while we concentrating on saving Alice.

"Gabriel?!" Alice said, jerking upright. "How did you …?"

"Enough talk!" he said, sitting up in his seat. "You three are dead!" He pointed his gun toward me and smiled. "Starting with you, Mr. Henley…"

And with that, Gabriel pulled the trigger, the shot ringing through my ears as a bullet exited the barrel of the gun and headed toward me at six hundred miles an hour.

THIRTY-ONE

But the bullet never reached its target. As the gun fired, I raised my hands instinctively in front of my face but felt no impact. No searing pain shooting through my veins. Instead, I felt nothing, as if Gabriel had fired a blank.

I lowered my arms to see Gabriel desperately examining his gun, probably wondering why it hadn't succeeded in turning me into a corpse. I was wondering exactly the same thing.

The next thing I knew, Gabriel pointed his gun at me again and fired another shot. And again, although the gun sounded as though it had fired a bullet, no bullet made contact with me.

In many ways, it was as though they were vanishing into thin air.

Then I realized that was exactly what must have been happening—Richard must have opened a portal up between Gabriel and me, sending the bullets through to another dimension as they were being fired.

It was the only logical explanation.

Gabriel fired his gun again, and again, and again and again until it was empty, but not one bullet made contact with me. Even after all his shots had been fired, he just kept pressing the trigger, the hammer of the gun clicking uselessly against the empty chamber.

"Agghh!!!" he screamed, throwing his gun to one side and leaping toward me, his arms outstretched ready to break my neck. But just as he was about to wrap his fingers around my throat, his body completely disappeared, presumably through the same portal Richard had used to dispose of the bullets.

Then silence.

The three of us looked at each other and sighed, slumping back in our chairs as though we'd just finished a strenuous workout. At long last, we were safe.

"That was too fucking close," Cassandra said.

I looked round at Alice.

"You know, for all of Russell's faults, he was right about one thing," I said.

"What's that?"

"Our daughter swears too much."

THIRTY-TWO

Cassandra took us up to a high enough altitude so we could emerge back in Russell's world without materializing underground. It was a little difficult to breathe at such a height, the air much cooler than down below.

"Are we sure we want to go back there?" she said, looking round at her mother, who was now sitting in the rear passenger seat. "I mean, I know we managed to expose IDEA for what they really were, but do you really think people will be okay with the fact that we've completely destroyed them? Now that they won't be able to move between parallel worlds, this is going to have huge implications for them..."

"Not to mention the fact that we're still accountable for so many people still being stuck in limbo..."

"It's true that none of us have come out of this whiter than white," Alice said, holding her hair back to stop it blowing in her face, "but that's the way the world works. Everyone has had to make sacrifices. I don't know how they're going to react to us, but we've got to go back and make sure everyone's okay."

"So how do we get there?" I asked.

"Oh don't worry about that," Alice replied. "Now that IDEA has been destroyed, everything they've been using to restrict our ability to open portals has been destroyed with them. That means the other Richard should have no problem using the equipment in my lab to move us back and forth between worlds however we please, a bit like how he just did with those bullets..."

She paused for second.

"Isn't that right, Richard?" she called out into thin air.

Her answer came in the form of a portal, which wrapped itself around the car in a bubble, distorting the space around us briefly. Just like before, the empty sky quickly disappeared, and we were soon surrounded by the familiar sight of several tall skyscrapers, with the sprawling city of London stretching out before us in a tapestry of diverse architecture. It was nighttime again, and in the sky, I noticed all the flying vehicles were operational once more, with lanes of cars, taxis, buses and trucks heading off in all different directions again, the blur of headlights streaking across my view like little scratches running through a film stock.

We had materialized only a few hundred meters away from the IDEA building, which was now missing the whole of its top section, thanks largely to Alice's portal. As Cassandra steered us toward it, I looked down at the exposed structure, and for a moment I felt as though I was looking at a monarch that had been decapitated for abusing their power.

At the very bottom, hundreds of people were gathered round the steps, looking up at the ruined edifice.

Cassandra brought the car in to land at the top of the steps, hovering a few meters above the ground before killing the engines and touching down gently outside the front doors to the building.

A number of people ran up to the side of the car and helped us out.

"Hey, you're the guy who was on TV!" a man said, holding the passenger door of the car open for me to get out and shaking my hand. "You're the man who told us what these guys were really up to!"

"Well, it's over now," I said. "IDEA has been shut down."

"Excuse me!" a loud female voice shouted. "Out of the way please!"

The people around us looked back and made way for a female news reporter, who was running up the steps with her cameraman in tow. If I wasn't mistaken, it was the same lady who had interviewed Russell earlier today.

"Hi there," she huffed, holding her microphone up to her mouth. "Meredith Allen, BBC news. Do you mind if ask you a couple of questions?"

"Erm…I guess so," I said.

"Great," she replied, signaling her cameraman to start rolling.

"Can you tell us what happened here tonight?" she asked, holding her microphone toward me.

"I'm not sure," I replied, taking a deep breath. I felt exhausted. "All I know is that the days of IDEA being able to control you are over. Russell Hardwick is dead, and his empire has been destroyed."

"Did you kill him?" the reporter asked.

"No," I answered, picturing the last look on Russell's face as he fell back into the lab. "He was responsible for his own death."

"So with IDEA gone, what will happen to us now?"

Behind her, a circle of people had gathered closely together, all ready to listen to what I had to say. My hands were shaking, but I knew what I wanted to tell them. It was something I had only just realized myself over the last couple of days, something as true for my world as was for any other.

"It's simple really," I said. "For the first time in many years, you people have a choice to make. A real choice."

"What sort of choice?"

"If you want, you can continue to live as you have always done. Keep building your huge cities and steeping yourselves in more and more technology. But you won't be able to sustain it. With no alternate worlds at your disposal, sooner or later your planet will collapse. But there is another way. You can start to try to live within your means; start to think about the effect you have on the environment and those around you. I guess what I'm saying is—you are now the masters of your fate. You can make this world whatever you want it to be."

"Thank you," the reporter said, lowering her microphone.

"I also have something to say," Alice said, stepping forward.

"Yes?" the reporter said, turning to face her.

Alice looked directly into the camera behind the reporter and spoke.

"I know a lot has happened here today, and many of you will be relieved to be free from IDEA's rule. But at the same time, some of you may be scared, nervous, and unsure at what comes next. Well I'm here to say you have nothing to fear—for the first time in years, your fate is in your hands, so embrace it."

She paused for a moment.

"However, there will be others out there who are angry—not only at IDEA, and Russell Harwick, but at me as well for what I did to all those innocent people lost to Quantum Displacement Disorder."

"And what do you say to those people?" the reporter asked.

Alice smiled.

"You know, for all of Russell Hardwick's faults," she said, "he was right about me—I'm a lot like him, making choices on behalf of others. Many years ago, I was faced with a difficult choice to make: the protection of billions of people at the expense of a few. It's a decision I will take to my grave. Because of me, hundreds, if not thousands of people from this world were trapped in a limbo state between worlds, unable to return. And I'm sorry. Just as you have all been manipulated by Russell and his Decision Tree application, in the same way this was not my choice to make for those lost in limbo. But I'm going to make it right. We're going back to my world now, and when I get there, I'll start work on returning everyone to their loved ones. Everyone I took away from you. I'll bring them all back, and then that will be the last you will hear from me. I promise."

"Thank you," the reporter said, turning back to the camera.

"We should leave," Alice smiled, touching me on the shoulder. "I don't think there's anything left for us to do here."

THIRTY-THREE

And so one minute we were standing on the steps to the dilapidated IDEA building, overlooking a dense city of towering skyscrapers, tall office blocks and glass structures of all shapes and sizes; the next we were standing on top of a small grass mound, overlooking a thick forest of oak trees. In an instant, the other Richard had brought us back to his world, and it was strangely appropriate to see the city before us regress back to a more natural state—a place more in balance with the environment, more in keeping with nature. This is what the people of that other world would have to address, if they wanted to survive.

The three of us began the long walk back to Alice's lab, which took us down a few winding country lanes, over a couple of wheat fields, and alongside a number of pretty streams. I knew we were getting close when I saw the sign for the River Fleet, and as we approached the small concrete entrance to Alice's lab, nestled in the middle of its overgrown field, I could see someone waiting outside, waving toward us.

It was me.

It was Richard Henley.

The man's dark hair was a little shorter than mine, but otherwise he looked exactly the same, except he was wearing what looked to be a slightly damp, dark suit, his shirt stained with blood. For a moment I thought this was a little odd, until I remembered he'd swapped clothes with the Richard Henley who'd had picked me up in my car the other day—the one who had been shot and dumped in the bay.

"Richard!" Alice cried, running toward him.

The man opened his arms to receive Alice and gave her a big hug, kissing her on the cheek.

"You did it!" he said, looking up at Cassandra and me as we approached. "You actually did it!"

"Richard, this is Richard," Cassandra said, raising an eyebrow.

"So we finally meet," Richard said, extending a hand for me to shake.

"We do indeed," I said, returning the gesture. "Thanks for everything, by the way—particularly that little trick with the bullets in the car. Pretty ingenious, I thought."

"Thanks," the other Richard replied. "I thought that was pretty quick thinking myself…"

"Where did you send Gabriel, by the way?" I asked.

"I sent him to the most utopian world we know of," Richard replied. "The one you visited earlier, where the taxi driver refused to take your money."

"You did what?" I said. "Why on earth did you send him there?"

"Don't worry," Richard said. "Due to the altitude difference between the two worlds, when he arrived there, he was about half a mile underground."

"Good grief," I said. "That's horrible."

"I know. But the way I look at it, if he'd stayed in the back of the car and surrendered, he would still be alive. It was only because he tried to kill you that he ended up burying himself alive. He chose his own fate."

A shiver ran down my spine as I thought about what it must have been like to materialize somewhere like that. But then again, my other self was right—he'd brought it upon himself.

"Oh, I've got something for you," Richard said, turning to Alice. "Here."

He pulled out her shawl and wrapped it around her shoulders.

"Thanks," she said. "Though it would have been nice if you could have removed it a little quicker—do you know how close I was to getting killed?"

"Hey, it's not easy plucking things out of thin air across dimensions when you're falling at over a hundred miles an hour! Took me twenty attempts to get that bloody thing off you!"

"Well, thanks anyway," she said. "You saved my life."

"No, *both* of us did," Richard corrected her, nodding toward me.

"So what do we do now?" Cassandra asked.

"Well, I don't know about you," I said. "But I need to go home ..."

"Home?" Alice said, raising her eyebrows.

"Yeah," I replied. "I mean, it's all very well putting an end to a dictatorial organization and saving hundreds, if not thousands of different worlds from ruin, but at the same time, my cat hasn't been fed in at least two days. Poor thing's probably trying to eat the curtains by now."

Alice laughed.

"And what do you want to do after that?" she said.

"I don't know," I said, walking over to her and placing my hands on her shoulders. "All I care about is spending time with you again."

"Well then, why don't you stay here with us?" Alice said.

"Yes!" Cassandra said. "Stay here!"

"Here?" I said, thinking about everything I would be leaving behind in my world. Apart from the cat—which I could bring back with me—I had nothing. No ties.

"I'd love that," I said, but then I looked at Richard. "Would that be okay with you?"

"Hey, don't look at me," he said. "I don't care what you do. Alice told you—there's nothing going on between us."

"But how can that be?" I said. "Aren't we more or less the same person?"

"Ha!" my other self laughed. "We may look similar, but believe me, the similarities end there. We have different upbringings, different values, different senses of humor—everything about us is just ... different."

"Besides," Alice said. "When I found him, he was already engaged to be married ..."

"He was?"

"That's right," Richard said, holding up his hand to show me his wedding ring. "Got engaged to my high school sweetheart when I was twenty and never looked back. In fact, my wife just gave birth to our third kid last month..."

"Well then, it's settled," I said. "If he's not interested in you, I certainly am..."

"There is one thing you must promise me though," Alice said.

"Name it," I replied.

"I love this world, Richard. I love the simplicity of it. The peacefulness. The birdsong that fills the air. The calm. I don't want it to change. I want to make sure that it never falls victim to the things that have spoiled so many other worlds. If people here start to make choices that send them down the wrong path, I'll want to step in and stop them. Can I count on you to be by my side if that happens?"

I looked Alice in the eyes and smiled, but for a moment, I felt conflicted. If I did what she was asking, wouldn't we be as guilty as Russell was? Wouldn't we be imposing our own view on others?

"I...don't know how I feel about that," I said, looking at the ground, my smile faltering.

"I haven't finished," Alice said, holding her hand up. "I want you to be by my side...to stop me."

"What?" I said, looking up again.

"Everything we've been through today has shown me how important it is for people to control their own fate," she continued. "To decide what they want to do for themselves. Right from the start, I thought I had this situation under control. The notes, the backup plans—I thought I'd covered every angle, even if it meant making some difficult choices along the way. But it was only when you acted against my wishes and stayed behind to talk to those people that things started to change. And it was at that moment that I appreciated the importance of letting go. Of trusting others to do the right thing. That things can turn out okay by themselves."

"So what do you want me to do?" I asked.

"I want you to promise me that if I ever start to forget these values, you'll remind me of them again. You'll remind me how we were able to free those people—not by telling them what to do but by handing the power of choice back to them. Can you remember that for me?"

"Sure," I said, tapping a finger to my temple. "Note to self."

THE END

About the Author

Peter Ward was born in 1980 and studied English Literature at the University of Southampton. He is also the author of *Time Rep* and its sequels *Time Rep: Continuum* and *Time Rep: Pandemonium*. He lives in London with his wife Lucy.

Website: Peterwardauthor.com

Blog: https://peterwardauthor.com/blog/

Email: peterwardauthor@hotmail.co.uk

About the Publisher

This book is published on behalf of the author by the Ethan Ellenberg Literary Agency.
https://ethanellenberg.com
Email: agent@ethanellenberg.com